SUDDEN TRANSITION

A violet ring slipped free of the alien spaceship.

It spun on its axis twice, like a coin on a tabletop. Then it rushed toward them.

Tsoong Delilah slapped quick fingers on the board, and their rocket bucked and tried to turn away. Thrust forward, she reached out despairingly toward the weaponry board, but there was no time to solve the riddles of the arming and aiming and launching of the missiles, either.

The ring was on them.

The ring swallowed them. It slipped past the plunging stern quarter of their ship like a hoop over a stake. For the tenth part of a second something in Delilah's stomach lunged toward her throat.

Then it was over.

The ring sailed away from them. They were floating in space.

The star-sprinkled black of the sky was all around them.

But the stars were different stars.

Frederik Pohl

BLACK STAR RISING

A Del Rey Book

BALLANTINE BOOKS • NEW YORK

CASTOR

was halfway across the paddy, part of the long line of farm workers, when he stepped on the dead man's head. He was not thinking about dead men. He wasn't really thinking about poking the rice seedlings into the muck, either, or about the warm rain dripping on his bent shoulders or about the ache in his back; he was thinking about Maria and her problem and about going for a swim and about whether it was possible that the people at the observatory would let him apply for a job there and mostly about what he and Maria would do in bed that night, and then all of a sudden there it was. He didn't know it was a dead man's head at first. He couldn't see it, though the water was only centimeters

1

deep, because the sowers had stirred up the bottom mud. His foot told him it was solid, and heavy, and didn't belong there. "Tourists," he muttered to old Sarah, next to him in line. "They throw their garbage anywhere they like!"

He reached down into the muck. Tiny tilapia slipped between his fingers, angry as poked wasps at the disturbance. Castor felt that the thing was round and soggy, and then as he lifted it up he saw what it was. His scared, furious bellow brought the whole production team splashing and *squash*ing over to him. Fat Rhoda came up scowling, because she'd had enough of Castor's foolishness, and old Franky was giggling and calling out jokey questions—"What is it then, Castor, you found another baby in the bullrushes?"—and almost all of them smiling, because nobody but Rhoda minded an excuse to pause for a moment from the endless stoop labor of transplanting the seedlings.

Then they saw what Castor was holding, and all smiles froze. They stood staring, sweating through the rain-glistened skin, while the tilapia played about their toes and no one knew what to do. "It's a murder!" quavered old Franky, leaning on his stick. "Don't say that!" ordered Fat Rhoda, but her voice was a lot more frightened than commanding. Then she reached for the talkie that hung around her neck and said, "Commune, this is Production Team Three. We've just discovered a dead body. Part of a dead body, a head." She licked her lips and added, "Call the cops, and tell them it isn't one of us. It looks like a Han Chinese."

Although the Heavenly Grain Collective Farm was more than a hundred kilometers from Biloxi, the police helicopter was there in half an hour. It was a long half hour. The production team was ordered to do nothing but stay right where they were. Stay they did, all fourteen of them sitting on the dike, looking at the place where Castor in horror had dropped the head back out of sight and old Franky had jammed in his hobbling stick for a marker. "They'll drain the paddy," Franky predicted gloomily, "and everything to do all over again!"

Little Nan cried out with shock, "We'll lose the fish. Rhoda! Sixty kilos of tilapia fry, we just put them in!"

"I know," Rhoda said crossly, frowning. The ecology of rice farming was not just rice. First you prepared the paddy, then you flooded the paddy, then you seeded brine shrimp, then you seeded tilapia. The shrimp fed on bits of anything and on insect larvae. The tilapia fed on the insect larvae and on the shrimp; then, when they had grown, people fed on the meal made from the adult tilapia; it was the commune's best and cheapest protein. Since both shrimp and tilapia were resolutely carnivorous, insect pests were destroyed and the rice seedlings were spared.

"Get traps," Franky suggested. "Maybe we can save the tilapia."

"I'm just *going* to get traps," Rhoda fretted and talked to the commune again on the little radio that hung around her neck; though what good the traps would do no one was sure, for the baby tilapia were so tiny that many of them might slip right through the mesh and be lost.

At least the rain had stopped, though the burning sun was no easier to take. The excitement had attracted a tour bus away from the village's souvenir shops. Forty Mainland tourists were snatching pictures of the paddy, the grumpy production team, and each other. Already two schoolgirls from the village had hurried out with bikeloads of sweet persimmons and golden limes from the

3

private plots. The tourists bought eagerly. The production team looked wistfully at the fruit but didn't buy—not at tourist prices—not, especially, when the tourist renmin-dollars were pouring into the village's economy so easily. One tourist persimmon was worth more than a kilo of state-bought rice, and no taxes to pay.

The production team heard the sudden buzz of tourist cameras before they heard the flutter of the approaching choppers. They all stood up as three police helicopters settled on the truck hardstand. Three! What were they expecting, an armed gang of murderers waiting to shoot it out with the cops? But the six police from the first craft wore the green shoulder boards of traffic control and ex-peditiously shepherded the grumbling tourists back to their bus and away. The second chopper carried real police, armed and helmeted, along with a couple of unarmed, older police carrying cameras and black attaché cases. The third seemed to hold only one person, a woman wear-ing the collar insignia of an inspector.

She stepped down and paused. She gazed at the rice paddy, at the departing tourist bus, at the clouds building again out over the Gulf of Mexico; and then she turned to the production team. In excellent English she asked, "Which one found the body?"

Grateful hands pushed Castor forward. "It wasn't a body, only a head," he said to set the record straight.

She confronted him staring up into his face. She was less than shoulder-high to him, but she did not seem to notice the difference in their heights. "Oh, only a head, then? I see. But that makes quite a difference, if it is only a head rather than a whole body! Still, in my experience I have learned that if a dead head turns up, then some-where there is a dead body it has belonged to."

Castor's annoyance at her sarcasm exceeded his worry

at being involved with the Renmin Police. In faultless Mandarin he answered her. "A high police officer will understand these things better than a peasant, I know."

"Ah!" she exclaimed. "I am in the presence of a scholar! But please, permit me to speak in your language, since some of your colleagues may not understand the high tongue. Tell me, then, scholar, how did you find this thing, whether it be body or merely inexplicably separate head?"

So Castor told her, and all the other members of the production team told her, and the police began their work. Some did indeed stamp and scuffle around the paddy, ordering the water level be lowered a little at a time. Others conducted separate interrogations of all fourteen witnesses; others still took pictures and bottled little samples of water and mud and other things. There was a flurry when the interrogating police found that some of the production team did not have their passport cards on their persons. Castor was one. He thought angrily of the criticism that would follow, perhaps even punishment duty. But the inspector would have none of that. "Forget that!" she ordered. "Of course these people don't carry cards on their own farm, that is foolishness. You can perfectly well verify their identities in the village." And she was equally short at Fat Rhoda's request to be allowed to trap as many of the tilapia as possible as the water was drained away. "No one wishes to waste valuable food! Certainly, catch your fish." And so half the production team was set to placing the traps and bailing out their squirming contents to be put in transport tanks, while the other half was put to walking the paddy with nets to capture as many as possible of those flapping away in the mud. That was Castor's job—the job of a ten-year-old, really! It was an indignity. He was always suffering indignities. Even being assigned to planting rice was an indignity. Stoop-labor

gangs were picked from the shortest members of the commune—they didn't have so far to stoop—and Castor was
nearly two meters tall. He felt the amused eyes of the
People's Police inspector on him from time to time as he
tripped or fell in the pursuit of the glittery, flopping little
creatures; and all in all it was a bad day.

The good part of the bad day was that it was saved
from getting worse. The People's Police didn't let Production Team Three go until it was nearly dark—questions and requisitions, much time spent merely waiting
while the water level in the paddy was lowered stage by
stage and the police technicians sifted the mud and strained
the water for clues. There were none. No weapon. No
other part of the body. No convenient passport card carelessly dropped by the murderer—nothing. But the good
result was that they were so late getting back that the
evening educational meeting was canceled and the subject
that Castor didn't want to discuss was postponed.

What there was instead was a quick meeting in the
assistant director's office, all fourteen of the production
team squeezed in anyhow and made to stand so as not to
soil his good furniture with their muddy bodies. It was
not a criticism meeting. It was only the assistant director's
desire to hear for himself just what had happened; so all
fourteen had to tell their stories one time more. It took
time the production team would have been glad to use to
clean up for the evening meal. Although it was not a
criticism meeting, Castor found himself being scolded
anyway. "Cousin Castor," said the assistant director
coldly—they were both Pettymans, though that didn't
make them close, since only seven families made up more
than half the commune—"Cousin Castor, watch your
tongue! Why were you impudent to the Renmin inspector?"

6

"I wasn't. She was making fun of us."

"Of us! Of you, you mean, and rightly so. You are a vain young man, Cousin Castor. A potentially troublesome element. I am really very dissatisfied, and not only with you. How are you going to make up this lost time, Cousin Rhoda?" And so the meeting ended only in the usual exhortations to meet production norms and take more seriously the education meetings, and Castor was allowed to escape to the showers.

Somewhat cleaner, he met his wife, Maria, in the dining hall. She was late, too. Her job was in the handicraft store, and they had been able to close the doors just minutes before. In fact, a couple of tourists were still standing around, photographing the villagers at the business of their daily lives, tossing the village's handmade Frisbees back and forth, greatly enjoying their day among the quaint peasants of the Bama Autonomous Republic. They kissed—he with pleasure tempered by concern, she with reluctance modified by duty. He was bursting to tell her how rotten his day had been, but she did not look as though she wanted to hear.

Maria was tall and fair—almost as tall as Castor, and far paler than anyone else in the village. Her parents had come to the B.A.R. as glum volunteers twenty years earlier. They had not lasted long. The mother was dead in a tractor accident a year after Maria's birth. The father was once again a "volunteer," but this time he actually did volunteer, all of his own volition. He went off to the calamitous deserts of western Iowa and never was heard from again. The infant was left behind. The village didn't protest greatly; the pressure to hold down the birthrate was not yet strong.

But of course that had not been forgotten, either. "Do you want to eat at home?" Castor asked. Maria shook

7

her head, though it was often their custom for one of them to go to the hall with their own pots, fill them up, and bring the meal back to their own apartment to dine in privacy.

"We don't want to look as though we're hiding," she said. "Anyway, I'm not very hungry." She hesitated. "I'm going for my tests tomorrow."

"Oh," said Castor, there being not much more to say. But then he cheered up, because as they approached the counter, he saw that the meal was one of his favorites, a curry with plenty of meat and plenty of their own good rice.

Maria only picked at the food. Castor braced himself for jokes from the other people at their table about Maria's lack of appetite, because the gossip had got around, but they were few. The hall was buzzing with excited talk about the other topic; the unscheduled pregnancy of one villager could not compete in interest with the discovery of the dead man's head. A dozen times Castor had to retell the story of finding it, for the people at the table, for table hoppers, for those next to him as he lined up for the curry, for the fruit, to refill his cup from the tea urns. News and rumors flew about the room—it was hard to tell which was which. The Renmin Police were scouring the neighborhood for the murderer. The People's Police had caught the murderer in the Biloxi airport. The Renmin Police suspected the murderer was one of the villagers— no, they suspected no one. The head had fallen from the sky as the result of a stratosphere jet explosion. But all the rumors were only rumors. At least the news-video panel at the back of the room had nothing informative to say about them. There was a shot of the paddy, and even one quick glimpse of Castor looking sullen as he pointed to the spot where he had stepped on the head, but the whole item came and went in twenty seconds. The only other thing of interest was a reminder that *High Noon* was going to be shown that evening. "Want to watch it?" Maria asked.

"I saw it when I was ten years old."

"No, no, this is a new production. They say it's really good."

So Castor said yes, and then he was reminded he was on cleanup duty that night, supervising the schoolchildren as they moved the chairs and tables and wiped up the dinner mess. He had counted on a little private time with Maria to make up for the day's aggravations, but he never got out of the dining hall. Which was also the senate hall for village meetings and the community theater and gymnasium and, once a month, dance floor. It was big enough for all, twenty meters across under a shallow dome of black plastic. Even before Castor had made the last teenager push a broom one more time over a sloppy corner of the floor, the villagers were coming back for the evening's entertainment.

The village had its own video dish, of course. From the geosynchronous satellite hanging over the trackless jungles of Bolivia twenty channels of television rained down on the Bama Autonomous Republic. Six of them were in English. As a formality the old director dragged herself to the front of the room for a vote, but there was no question about it; the villagers wanted to be entertained. Actually, the show sounded good to Castor, too, but he had an idea on how to make it better. When Maria came back to the hall, he was waiting for her. "Here or there?" he whispered, nuzzling the back of her neck. Since they had been together only six months and were still so actively in love, they usually took their entertainment as they did their meals, in the privacy of their apartment.

9

Their flat screen was tiny compared to the huge holo in the common hall; they offset that debit against the great gain of being able to watch in each other's arms—or to stop watching for other entertainment when they chose. But Maria pushed him away—gently, to be sure. "Here," she said firmly. "Let's not make it worse." And for the same reason, insisted on sitting apart from him when the show began.

Castor was neither a mean-hearted young man nor a stupid one, but he was a young one. He had not yet discovered that the world had its own interests and spent little time looking after his—not the whole world, not the village that was most of the world to him, not even his wife. So his mood was sulky. But it improved, as he got caught up in the grand old story of the Renmin marshal of a century earlier, fresh from Home, threatened by a gang of anti-Party elements. The marshal, whose part was sung by the famous Feng Wonfred, was all alone against six armed enemies, but aided by the schoolteacher and other cadres, he struggled against the anti-Party rightists and forced them to criticize themselves. It was a marvelous production, beautifully sung, stirring and tender in turns; the sets beautifully showed the America of the late twentieth century with its endless empty stretches of burned-out land and the few brave pioneers trying to make it liveable. Castor lost himself in the story.

At the end of the opera, the anti-Party gang handed over their weapons and boarded the bus that would take them to Pennsylvania for reeducation, while the Renmin marshal and the schoolteacher led the cadres in a victorious procession across the sagebrush landscape, banners flying. The audience applauded in delight, Castor included. As the images faded from the holo area and the hall lights went up he looked for Maria to share his pleasure, but she had gone.

Castor found his wife in the screen room, rapt before one of the consoles. She was listening to the audio portion through earplugs and did not hear him enter; when she caught sight of him, she clicked the screen off. By the time he could see it, the screen was only winking in orange letters *Waiting . . . Waiting . . . Waiting . . .* in both Chinese and English.

There were twenty screens in the room, each with its own seat. Castor knew every one of them. This was where he had got most of his education after schooling stopped for him because his university application was turned down. His teacher had fought for him—and failed. Had coached him in the high tongue until he was almost accent-free—to no purpose. Had begged him to continue on his own with the teaching machines, because his mind was too good to waste on plowing rice paddies. And indeed he had done so, every chance he got, doggedly pursuing one course after another out of the limitless catalogue, until Maria had made him aware there were other things to do with his spare time than study.

She was still watching him politely, waiting for the interruption to be explained. He said awkwardly, "You're not finished yet, then?"

"Not really."

He nodded, looking around at the empty machines. "Well," he said, surrendering to the impulse, "listen, take your time. I'd like to, ah, check out a few things, too." And it was true. He had always liked that, every time he got a chance at the screens. He liked it now. So much so

11

that as he punched in his codes and instructions, his wife's peculiar behavior slipped out of his mind.

What Castor had mostly studied was space. Everything about space, theory and practice. It was his dream. Because it was only a dream, it was also his curse. He had discovered bitterly early that only an ethnic Han Chinese had any real prospect of receiving space-going training. For that matter, there was hardly any space program to be trained for. The Chinese had a few Comsats, of course, and some meteorological and resource-spotting satellites. That was all—even for China. For America, of course, there was nothing at all.

No human being had gone into space, from any country, for nearly one hundred years. Oh, there were human beings up there even now, to be sure. Dead ones. Astronauts and cosmonauts caught in orbit by the outbreak of the war, unable ever to get back. In the data stores of the screens, there were fifty or sixty "identity uncertains" stored—some of them actual sightings, some only recorded trajectories.

What fascinated Castor was that there was a new one in the stores. "Identity uncertain" barely described this one. It was on the far side of the Sun, well over an A.U. away, far too small for any detail to be seen. So it could be anything, and Castor's imagination was unchecked. Spacelab gone adrift? One of those old Russian Soyuz things? A lost shuttle, an Ariane—anything!

He gazed longingly at the smudged dot that was all telescopy had been able to retrieve of the object. It was there all right, though what "it" was he could not say. Still, the orbital elements were clear enough. In a few months it would be close to Earth—then there would be plenty to see! Of course, it almost certainly was one of the sixty other "identity uncertains" perturbed, perhaps, by passing too close to the Sun...

But what if it were not?

Castor was smiling as he pulled the earphones off and turned to his wife. Surprisingly, she did not seem quite finished with what she was doing—whatever she was doing. She glanced up at him politely, still awaiting the explanatory key, her great blue eyes cool and hooded. He hesitated, trying to think of a conversational gambit that would turn this polite and distant woman back into his wife. He pulled out a packet of honey-dried fruit sticks and offered her one. She shook her head. He said, "But you didn't eat much dinner, either."

"I wasn't hungry," she explained.

Castor nodded as though that clarified the subject completely, chewing the edible paper off his own stick. He bit into the rich, delicious pear flavor. There was no use asking Maria any question she didn't want to answer, and no use asking questions at all when she'd been given every chance to volunteer. Still, he was curious. "What were you looking up?" he asked with a generous, wise, I-know-you've-got-some-little-secret grin.

"Oh, just some things," she said vaguely, and that settled that.

Castor shrugged. "I'm about ready to go to bed," he said, all subtlety put aside.

The blue eyes gazed at him coolly, then turned to the machine. She paused, then made a decision. Briskly she clicked the screen off and clicked off the cool, distant Maria at the same time. "So am I," she said, standing up and untangling the earplugs. When she put out her hand to his arm her touch was warm and intimate, and so was her voice. "*Real* ready," she added. "After all, what harm can it do now?"

13

II

If anyone had asked Castor if he loved his wife his
answer would have been instant and loud. Of course he
did! Even when she was withdrawn. Even when she insisted on taking chances with getting pregnant. He certainly did not blame her, he would have said at that point
in any conversation (or perhaps was rehearsing in advance
of the conversations that he knew were bound to come),
for the problem they now confronted. She was very dear
to him—

But strange, all the same, for after a night just like old
times, in the morning she was cool and withdrawn again.
She slipped away to catch her bus for Biloxi before breakfast was over. She didn't have to. She needn't have left
till almost noon. She certainly needn't have left it to him
to explain to the exercise leaders why she had skipped
the group aerobic dance and tai chi. So Castor's day began
sulkily again, and when Fat Rhoda called on all of Production Team Three to put in a voluntary day's work, in
spite of the fact that this was officially a rest day for them,
to make up for the time lost yesterday, Castor set his chin
and refused. And, as he didn't want to hang idly around
the village after that, he took out an electrobike and went
to the beach. He stripped quickly on the sand, sniffed for
methane—but the air was clean today—and slipped on

14

backpack and face mask as he was already wading into the salt, warm waves.

As soon as he was underwater, safe in the amniotic sea, Castor felt soothed, alive, almost joyous again. It had been much too long since he had swum there last!

It had been since his marriage, in fact, for Maria was terrified of sharks. Castor decided he would have to teach her better or even go without her, because this pleasure was too great to give up. Ever since he was ten, barely old enough to be allowed to swim by himself, he had biked or trudged the long, quiet roads to the coast, between the cane fields or the marshes, skirting the edge of the giant radio-telescope installation, heading for the sea. And it never changed.

He had an hour's air in each tank, and so he let himself follow the gentle fall of the sea bottom, out half a kilometer and more. He knew where to find the trail buoys, but allowed himself to be diverted from the straight swim to poke into interesting-looking hummocks or bits of debris, chasing the fish—and sometimes being chased by them, too, because although he had no fear of the occasional stupid shark, he went away from its annoying presence. It was always cool under the water and so much cleaner than the land; the currents that fed the Gulf brought no muck, no industrial wastes, no city sewage—no reminders of the terrible wiped-out world of a century ago. Or not very many, anyway. There was always the deathglass. It was far out, but the closer patches of it not yet very deep; sometimes on a dark night you could see the pale blue fire in the water, even from the beach. The children were warned against them. Of course, that kept no child away.

It didn't keep grown-up Castor away, either, because he was convinced from his courses that the most dangerous radiation had had plenty of time to fade away. Besides, the deathglass was beautiful. Castor swam down through the fish and the kelps, circling and admiring the blobby glass objects that shimmered like jellies in the underwater light. There were tall, angled ones like prisms, bent-over ones that seemed to have been partly melted in the middle, and many, many that had softened themselves down into random roundnesses before they had hardened again. Castor knew that, really, they were garbage. They were vitrified radioactive wastes, hurriedly barged out to a disposal area in the middle of the Gulf in those frantic days of the war when everything went crazy at once. You could not blame the bargemen for strewing them over a hundred square kilometers in their haste. But he could not think of them as garbage, because they were too beautiful. He followed their trail to the sixty-meter depth and then, reluctantly, turned around and swam steadily back to the beach, still underwater. One tank was gone already; it was time to come out. He paid little attention to the fish or the sea on the homeward trip. He was thinking about the deathglass and how it had come to be there. He wondered what the world had been like, in those days just before the old United States and the old Soviet Union had thought about the unthinkable and reached the wrong conclusions. Suppose they hadn't? Suppose they had sometime said to each other, "Look here, there's no sense in stinging each other to death like scorpions in a bottle, let's toss these things away and think of something else to do with our hostilities." What would the world be like if the war had not happened and if the Han Chinese had not come? Would he have been allowed, then, to go to the university? To take some other job than working on the rice plantation? Would he have been spared such annoyances as that infuriatingly superior Renmin Police inspector, with her sarcasm and her authority?

He was still asking himself these questions when he emerged from the water and saw the inspector standing on the beach waiting for him.

The woman was standing with her back to him, smoking a little lacquered pipe and frowning at the distant lip of the radio-telescope. Castor was wearing no more than the face mask and the tanks—what was the use of swimming trunks when no one was there to see? He paused, uselessly knee-deep in the gentle waves, wondering whether to be embarrassed.

The policewoman had no such problem. When she turned, the frown gave way to a pleased grin. "Well, Pettyman Castor! You're looking very well today!"

He stood belligerently straight. "It's nice to see you again, Inspector Tsoong Delilah."

She laughed. "How did you know my name? No, never mind—the same way I knew yours, I suppose—by asking." She was walking toward the water and stopped with her glassy-bright boots in the wavelets, not a meter away. She bent to feel the temperature of the sea and rose slowly, her eyes studying every part of him on the way. "I almost think I ought to get out of my clothes and join you for a swim," she observed thoughtfully.

He pointed out, "I only have one set of gear."

She studied his expression, and this time her laugh was slightly soured. "Well, Scholar, you can get dressed then," she said, turning her back and marching to the bluff. She sat down, silhouetted against the huge arc of the telescope, refilling her pipe as she watched him pull up his shorts. "Have you ever been over there?" she asked suddenly, pointing at the radio-telescope. He shook his head. "Not even to visit?"

"No. They're almost all Han Chinese, and they come and go in their own aircraft. We never see them at the village, although—"

She filled in for him. "Although you would like to be assigned to work there, I understand?"

He was angry, but said nothing—if she had taken the trouble to study his records, of course she would know that.

She persisted. "But how can you hope to work in such a place without a degree?"

"It isn't my fault I don't have a degree! I was rejected. They said I was more useful growing rice."

"Quite right! Food is the foundation of socialism," she quoted approvingly. He didn't answer, not even a shrug, just stood swinging his scuba gear by the straps as he waited for her to get to whatever point had brought her here. She nodded as though satisfied, puffing on her pipe. The smoke was like heavy perfume. "We found your missing body, Scholar Pettyman Castor," she said suddenly. "At least, we found the bones. They were crushed along with hog bones at the slaughterhouse in the cattle collective, but not so crushed they couldn't be identified." She watched his face with sardonic amusement as she added, "We could not find any flesh, however. Apparently each part had been put through the mechanical deboner and all the meat taken off . . . tell me, did you enjoy your dinner last night?"

This time Tsoong Delilah's laugh was full-throated as Castor dropped his face mask in the sand and his mouth spasmed. "No, no, don't puke!" she chuckled. "I was only joking. This meat was fed to pigs, not people, we are quite sure."

18

"Thank you for telling me that," Castor said angrily, resolving not to eat pork for some time.

"Oh, you are quite welcome." She glanced again at the radio-telescope, then became businesslike. "I have enjoyed this conversation with you, Scholar, but my duties require attention elsewhere. This is for you."

"This" was a summons, red-sealed and Renmin-coded with magnetic inks. Castor took it dumbly in his hand. "It means you must come to testify at the inquest on this unfortunate person, young Pettyman Castor, since you made the mistake of finding the only part of the cadaver we can identify. You will be notified as to the time; meanwhile, you must not leave your village."

"Where would I go?" Castor growled.

She took no offense at either words or tone, but said cheerfully, "When you get to New Orleans you will report direct to me. Who knows? Perhaps I will then get diving gear for two and we can enjoy a nice, private swim."

Biking back, Castor went slowly to let the dust of the policewoman's car settle. But as he drove along the chain link fence that enclosed the area of the radio-telescope, two guards appeared and shouted at him for dawdling, so he speeded up again. That was curious; no one had ever been visible there before. When he had gone there himself to ask humbly if there was any chance of being taken on in some capacity, sweeper, student, anything at all, it had taken twenty minutes before anyone responded to the gate bell. And then he had only told Castor to go away and, all right, if he chose, submit a written application through channels. Out of sight he could hear the buzzing of several helicopters in the private landing field; if important officials were visiting, that might explain it, but what would explain what important officials were doing bothering with this out-of-the-way place?

By the time he was back in the village square his mind was full, mostly, of wanting to tell Maria about his curious conversation with the Renmin policewoman—to be sure, in a somewhat censored version. She would be interested, he was sure...

He was wrong. She was not interested at all. What she herself had to tell was far more important in her mind. When he found her in their apartment her expression told him what the words only confirmed: "Yes, Castor, it's definite. The ovum is lodged and dividing; I'm pregnant."

"Oh—" he began, but "hell" was the next word, and he changed it. "Oh, that's it, then." He took her hand tenderly, ready to be her sword and shield in this catastrophe; but the look on her face was confusing. Her eyes were not cool, not loving, either; they were serene. Then he thought. "Oh! Tonight's meeting! It's going to be pretty awful, unless—Well, maybe they won't have your records yet—"

"Don't be so silly," she flared, "of course they'll have the records. The diagnosis was ready this morning."

"I see." He thought that over until, looking around the room, he realized why he didn't see. "But it looks as though you just came in."

"I did. I was in the screen room," she said. "And other places. Come on, it's time for dinner."

The dinner might have been an ordeal, but there was a distraction. The director tottered up to the front of the room to announce that, obedient to a Renmin "request"—that was the word she used, "request," though there was no history anywhere of the village ever refusing one—all electrical machinery would be off for seventy-five minutes, reason not given. So the last half hour of the dinner was eaten by candlelight, and by candlelight the cleanup crews whisked away the scraps and lugged the tables and chairs to make the hall ready for the evening meeting. With the light poor there was plenty of opportunity for the idle and heedless to chatter, wasting time, so the work went slowly. The chatter was about the murder, about the thrilling discovery of most of the body in another commune (removing the worry, leaving the excitement of the crime), most of all about the terrible annoyance of having the power off. It was a rare event, and there were many guesses about the reason for the order; but as no one, really, had any facts to go on, they were quite wild.

What there was no gossip about at all was the impending problem of Castor and Maria, and that, thought Castor gloomily after the lights were on again and the meeting had come to order, was a very bad sign. They were saving themselves for the meeting.

For movies, the little stage at the end of the room held the holo projectors and mirrors. For meals, the projectors sank into their safe, covered wells, and buffet tables were lined up to serve the diners. For criticism the platform held a single chair, with all the others arranged in arcs before it and below.

Castor looked at the hot seat as a condemned felon might view the electric chair of old. To sit there was not an honor. To sit there was to be hopelessly and painfully alone. The man or woman sweating in the hot seat matched three hundred pairs of accusing eyes with his own abashed ones, heard three hundred condemning voices with his solitary pair of shamed ears, spoke in self-criticism or (foolishly, vainly) in defense in his own single, stammering voice—and then heard it roar back at him over the heads of the three hundred from the row of speaker-buttons along the walls. It was not a prominence anyone sought.

Since there was no point in trying to avert the storm anymore, Castor led his wife to the very first row and sat proudly, holding her hand. She did not resist. She was relaxed and calm, and for all one could tell from her face she might have thought this evening would pass without ever hearing her own name.

Indeed, at first she did not, for the first person in the hot seat at criticism meetings was almost always a team head. Production was what the village was all about, after all. Tonight it was Fat Rhoda, summoned by name by the wrathful voice of the assistant director from his desk at the side of the room. "You, Pettyman Rhoda!" he thundered. "You are two hectares behind plan. How is this possible, in view of the fact that food is the foundation of socialism?"

But he had no scared novice victim in Fat Rhoda. Wise in the skills of the hot seat, she hurried forward to the seat, beginning to criticize herself on the way. "I have been too lenient with the team," she confessed. "I have failed to give proper leadership in volunteer work to achieve the plan. I have allowed Pettyman Castor to withdraw from today's extraduty work without clarifying for him the importance of political understanding—" She didn't stop there, but she might as well have as far as Castor was concerned. He was furious. Just like her, to start blaming him when she knew, must know, what was coming next!

So did everyone else, and the criticism of Rhoda was no more than perfunctory. When she had finished abasing herself she was let go with no more than a promise to work and study diligently.

Then the assistant director waved a hand, and a second chair was brought to the stage, and it began.

* * *

Ten minutes was the usual length of time in the hot seat. The vilest of criminals sometimes were there an hour—the hard cases whose deeds could be expiated only by expulsion from the village. Or worse. Yet an hour later Castor and Maria were still there and the crowd just seemingly getting warmed up. Every last member seemed to want to be heard—not just about the pregnancy, but about every misdeed anyone could remember—

"Why did you study Chinese and astrophysics instead of something useful to the village, like soil chemistry or accounting?"

"You showed vanity, Castor, and pride! You should learn your place!"

"You spoke impudently to a high state official, Castor. Why are you so arrogant?"

"Did you not think, Castor, of what may happen to the village if we exceed birth limits? Do you want us sprayed like the Africans?"

"If you were loyal to the village, why did you ask for a transfer?"

"Vanity, Castor! Pride, arrogance, vanity! You should be more humble."

—and always it was Castor this and Castor that, but what about Maria, who had got them into this trouble in the first place? Oh, not without complicity, Castor admitted to himself, his jaw grim and eyes fierce as he stared back at the accusing villagers. But it was Maria who had decided that if a child was to happen then it should happen, and he had merely agreed—who could blame him for that, six months married and still hungry every night? Should he answer back? Denounce her? Criticize them both and get off as Fat Rhoda had done? But he couldn't do that; pride—yes, he had pride; maybe arrogance, too, but whatever the reason he sat mute and glowering and let them say what they liked. He wished the two chairs were closer. He would have liked to reach out and hold Maria's hand to comfort her—or to comfort himself, more likely. But actually she seemed to have no need of comforting. She was sitting quietly with her hands folded calmly in her lap and that serene and untroubled gaze in her eyes.

At last the assistant director clapped his hands for the microphone, and as the automatic sound-seekers turned toward him he said, "Speak, Castor! Answer the people's just anger!"

Castor ground his teeth. Angrily he said, "I was wrong. I did not fulfill my obligations to the people."

"And?" demanded the assistant director. Castor did not speak; he could not make himself. "And what else?" the man went on remorselessly. "What of this pregnancy you have caused? What steps are you willing to take?"

Castor, raging, opened his mouth to answer, he had no idea what. But it never came out. Maria clapped for the mikes and said clearly,

"Castor has nothing to say about it."

The assistant director's mouth opened. It hung that way until he recovered enough to croak, "What? What did you say?"

"I said it is not Castor's decision. I am divorcing him. I have applied for divorce through the screens, and it will be granted in twenty-four hours unless he protests."

"But I protest!" Castor croaked, managing at last to speak.

"No," she said, turning toward him calmly, "you will not, because I will not abort my child. I have done one other thing. I have volunteered for service in a prairie

24

grain commune, where there are no birth limits, and I have been accepted."

She smiled at Castor and then at the villagers in the suddenly soundless hall. "So you see," she finished, "there is nothing more to say on this subject."

And indeed there was not.

There was not, at least, until the next morning, when Castor finished the sleepless night's packing and weeping and arguing and pleading and put his wife on the bus for, ultimately, Saskatchewan. Maria had been sleepless, too, and Maria had done her own share of weeping at the last, but by the time the bus rumbled up she was smiling. "I am still very fond of you, Castor," she announced, "and I will send you pictures of our child."

"Oh, Maria!" he groaned. Then, suddenly despairing, "Wait, don't go today, wait until tomorrow. I'll go with you!"

She shook her head. "You can't," she pointed out. "You aren't allowed to leave the village while you're needed to testify." And then, standing on the step of the bus, bending down to kiss him good-bye, "You don't really want to, anyway, do you?"

III

It was six days before the court summons came. In that time Castor had made his mind up about Maria a hundred times—a hundred different ways. The result was he did nothing. He had lost Maria. He was terribly, terribly hurt, a broken man. But on the other hand, he thought, if she could leave him so easily over so small a thing as an unborn child, why, then, why not?

He was not much use to the village in those six days. The assistant director did not fail to tell him so—then, adding in more human tones, "Be careful of your money, Cousin Castor, don't stay too long, and oh yes, please, if you have a chance, do pick up for me some of those chocolate mints—what's the matter?"

"These," grumbled Castor, waving his tickets. Han Chinese, high officials, and persons on government business were authorized air transport, as everyone knew, but the assistant director only laughed at Castor's pretensions.

"Government business! You are a witness, not a high cadre! You'll go to New Orleans, you'll tell what you saw, you'll come home—with the mints, please. No. Your government business is here, Cousin Castor, and how am I to make up the work you will miss? You'll take the bus." So Castor's long trip, the first time in all his life he had been outside the Bama Autonomous Republic, crawled

26

along the coastal roads, across rice paddies and mud flats and stock-grazing land, up the delta to the big city. For the first five hours of the trip, Castor saw nothing he had not seen before, or something just like. That was bad. That gave him time to think. The same subjects kept coming up in his mind. They were subjects he was tired of and had no joy in pursuing. Castor knew very well why volunteers for Saskatchewan did not have to worry about the birthrate. It was because of the death rate—from the terrible winters, from the scant harvests, from the lingering pockets of radiation—from being there, on the frontier of a continent that had almost annihilated itself and still had not completely healed. He should have kept her from going. He could not do that, but should have gone with her. He couldn't do that, either, not until the inquest was over, but certainly he could go after her, next week, or next month . . . And that was where the thinking reached dead end. That he could do.

But she had been right in what she said to him as she left: He didn't really want to, after all.

Then the bus entered the outskirts of New Orleans. Maria disappeared from his mind.

They were still in the newer eastern fringes of the old city, but it was wonderland. Electric trolleybuses whizzed along the streets, people in bright clothes meandered from shop to shop, gazing at the displays in the windows and pausing to buy stick ices, cones of sherbet and cream, paper cups of drinks. The buildings towered over the sidewalks, three stories high, five, sometimes ten or more— later, as they approached the muddy trickle that was still called the Mississippi River, incredible skyscrapers of forty stories and more. Castor's mouth hung open. He was an abandoned husband, very nearly a father, a full-fledged working member of his commune, with grave matters on

27

his mind. But he was also twenty-two years old. He dissolved in wonder and joy as he beheld the marvels all around. It wasn't until they had crossed the river and entered a huge, noisy terminal that he began to worry. He shouldered his backpack, checked his money to see it was still safe, exited through great, treacherous revolving doors that nipped at his heels for being slow, and stood on the curb, wondering what to do next. His orders were to report to the Criminal Courts Building; very well. Of course. But how, exactly, did one do that?

A green-shouldered traffic policeman defended an island in the middle of the road. Ask him? Again—of course, but how? To gawk at the traffic from the safe shelter of the bus was one thing. To be so dangerously in the middle of it was quite another. The number of vehicles was frightening—trucks, trolleybuses, private cars, vans, taxis darting in and out—surely every human being in North America was in New Orleans that day, and every one driving madly past the bus terminal. He watched from the curb for a long time, trying to solve the riddle of the traffic lights. Then, at a break, he dodged bravely in front of a slow-moving farm truck to the island. The policeman gazed at him sternly. "The Criminal Courts Building," Castor gasped, "where is it?"

He got the information, along with the news that he had foolishly gone more than two kilometers past his destination and a free lecture on the obligations good citizenship imposed on those who would cross a busy street. He was glad to get away from there. But, once he gained skill enough to be relieved of the fear of imminent death by being run over, his spirits rose again.

It turned out to be a very long walk. Castor did not mind, for there was so much to see! Even better than from the bus window, for you could smell and feel and jostle as well; Biloxi was nothing like this! There were excursion buses full of Home-Han tourists—it was not only the farm communes they found quaint enough to photograph. There were sidewalk vendors with tomatoes and grapes and pale, long lettuce stalks from their private plots, in town for the day to sell their produce and see the sights. Artisans lined up or filled the alcoves with the tools of their trade, to repair a shoe or cut a head of hair. Nearly all the sidewalk merchants were Yankees. Nearly all the strolling pedestrians were Han Chinese, but no one seemed to notice Castor among them.

He discovered he was hungry and paused to study the mob in front of a frozen-sherbet stand. When he had absorbed the technique of sliding to the counter, he unbuttoned his money pocket and slipped a note off his small wad of bills. The vendor regarded the red-rimmed Bama money suspiciously when Castor at last got his attention, but shrugged and accepted it—without, however, returning any change. As Castor turned away, irritable because he had been cheated and hadn't protested, a grinning Han Chinese youth slapped him on the shoulder. In nearly incomprehensible English he demanded jovially, "You just up from downcountry, brother? Never fear! Catch on quick-quick, you see!"

Castor winced at the English but was grateful for the good will. He asked in the high tongue, "Am I going the right way for the Criminal Courts Building?" Yes, he was; but it took minutes for the new friend to decide that that was so and then to explain to Castor which turnings he must make and how he must cross on the pedestrian bridges at certain intersections—all of it accompanied by many pats on the shoulder and slaps on the back and friendly nudges. Castor was surprised that a Han Chinese, of a people who traditionally avoided touching another person as much as possible, should show so much physical intimacy, but he remained grateful. For nearly an hour.

Then Castor took thought. Not the least of the attractions of New Orleans were the shops, the department stores, the clothing establishments, the hardware emporia; it was not only the assistant director who yearned for the goodies of the big city, and Castor made up his mind to carry back as many luxury items as he could afford. When he thought to count his money to see just what he could manage to buy, he discovered he had none. The pocket was unbuttoned and empty.

Castor stopped feeling grateful to the jolly young Han.

When he got to the Criminal Courts Building they told him that he had been given peremptory orders to check in with Inspector Tsoong Delilah; when he had finished hoofing the extra kilometer to the police headquarters, she wasn't there; when at last her secretary reached her for instructions the word was for Castor to report to a transient hotel and show up in court in the morning—a kilometer and a half, that time, and the sun already down. The desk clerk told him the good news and the bad news when he checked in. The bad news was that the hour for serving dinner was over. The good news was that that didn't matter, because there were plenty of fast-food restaurants within a block's walk...

But, of course, only if you had the money.

Pettyman Castor's testimony amounted only to answering three questions, with none of the answers above one word, but it took some time to do it in spite of the fact that he was the first witness called. First there was a lot of whispered wrangling among the five judges and various functionaries, while Castor and everyone else sat restless (and, in Castor's case, gnawed by hunger) and waited for the show to get on the road.

Hunger was less important, though, than excitement. Castor used the time profitably to rubberneck. The courtroom was divided into three concentric quarter-circle shells like the floor plan of a concert hall. At the front, which was the "stage," were the benches for the judges, the people's law advisors, and the clerks. One remove away, the seats for the witnesses and specialists, where Castor sat—and where, ahead of him in the front row, he spotted the black-bobbed hair of Renmin Police Inspector Tsoong Delilah. Behind Castor was a transparent screen, to cut off the spectators' gallery and their noise from the court itself. There were seats for several hundred gawkers, but only sparsely occupied—mostly by the idle and the curious, he supposed. There did seem to be a number of Yankees watching the proceedings, and one or two of them looked vaguely familiar to Castor. Were they members of the cattle collective? That made sense, for certainly that village had an interest in the matter—but so did Castor's own, and none of his people had come to watch his performance. Some of the other spectators were more interesting, though. There was a busload of the omnipresent tourists from the Mainland and even a smaller party of Indians, saris and turbans and cameras. Some of the spectators seemed quite queer. There was a man with a very large head—or a very large hat, almost like a football helmet five sizes too big for his skull; Castor could not decide which. He was Han Chinese, but his face seemed to change at every look, and his behavior was odder than his face. He could not seem to make up his mind what he wanted to do. Stand up, start to leave— then clamber back along the seats to his place; stand up again for an instant; sit down with a crash of folding seat.

Castor was surprised the attendants didn't throw him out, but evidently the attendants considered him privileged.

Then, when the judges finally came out of their huddle and the proceedings began, there was a second delay.

The stern-faced clerk who approached Castor, squirming before all those eyes on the witness stand, addressed him in the high tongue: "Do you understand the penalties for perjury, and will you undertake to speak only truth and all truth here?" And when he started to answer, she looked shocked, made him wait while another clerk translated the question into English before she would let him reply. Castor resentfully understood that he was not considered capable of comprehending the high tongue. He allowed the charade to proceed, but it rankled. He glared back at the staring eyes, not least the queer old big-headed man in the visitors' gallery and most of all Inspector Tsoong herself. The sardonic half smile played about her lips as she studied him. At last came the three questions:

"Are you Pettyman Castor, citizen of the Bama Autonomous Republic, member of Production Team Three of the Heavenly Grain Village Collective?"

Pause for translation, then Castor was allowed to answer: "Yes."

"*Hsieh-hsieh*," reported the translator, and the attorney asked the next question.

"Did you one week ago, while engaged in your duties in the transplanting of rice seedlings, discover a human head?"

"Yes."

"*Hsieh-hsieh*."

And then the final question:

"Is this the head?"

And that question would have needed no translation for even the most exclusively Anglophone witness, because the woman thrust before him a picframe, life-size, of the head itself in all its ruin. The tilapia had eaten the soft parts out. The face was awful. Worse than the sight was the knowledge that he had *touched* that terrible thing. "Y—yes," he croaked, trying not to retch, and was dismissed.

The image of that once-human horror followed him back to his seat, and it was some minutes before he was able to take interest in the proceedings again.

But, really, it was interesting. It was almost like a detective opera. Methodically the state paraded its evidence, and how this piece fit in with that was an absorbing puzzle to work at. The second witness was a young boy from the River of Pearl Cattle Collective, where the corpse's bones had been ground to powder. The youth was frightened but enjoying his prominence as he said that yes, he and some other boys had sneaked away from tai chi to play baseball and yes, they had found part of a human arm. As the cattle-herding dogs had found it before they did, it was well chewed. Castor was glad he didn't have to look at that pic close up, but it didn't seem to bother the boy.

Then there was an elderly man, also from the cattle collective. He was obviously even more scared than the boy. He took it out in belligerence, delivering his answers as though spitting them in the face of the translator. Yes, he was in charge of the packinghouse. Yes, he was responsible for the use of it. Yes, he always kept it locked when not in use—children might hurt themselves there. No, he had no idea how anyone could have gained admittance to it to debone the parts of the corpse and grind its skeleton for spreading on the fields. When he was excused he tottered off to the end of the back row and sat with his head down, paying no attention to the next witness. That was a forensic surgeon, reporting that the fragments found in the bonemeal were human. Then it was Tsoong Delilah, who came back to sit down next to Castor when she had finished testifying how she had supervised the team that had interrogated the witnesses from the B.A.R. and located the various fragments of the deceased. "Scholar," she whispered in his ear, "you spoke very well." But as Castor could not tell how much of what she said was mockery he didn't reply.

To his surprise, there was only one more witness that morning—another police official, to add a few details to Tsoong's evidence—and then the judges conferred and announced that there would be a two-hour recess for lunch. After only an hour and a half or less! Oh, yes, these Han Chinese did themselves well. Fat Rhoda would have allowed no such slackness on her production team. As Tsoong Delilah started to get up she saw Castor still rooted to his seat and paused. "What's the matter, Scholar? Aren't you hungry?" she asked.

"I am nearly starved," Castor said bitterly, explaining how his pocket had been picked and how he had been wakened too late for breakfast in the transient hotel.

"What a fool you are!" the policewoman scolded. "Don't you know that witnesses are entitled to payment and reimbursement for expenses? Go downstairs to the accounts room. Simply identify yourself and draw your pay—or, no, better, come with me. We'll eat across the street, where the food is good, and I will find out just how naive you are, Scholar!"

An incident occurred before they reached the crowded street and the dazzling sun. As they left the courtroom, just at the crystal barrier, they saw a commotion in the spectators' gallery. The queer old man who didn't seem to know what he wanted to do had found a new way of making a disturbance. He was sprawled across two seats, while white-jacketed Health Service emergency corpsmen were administering oxygen to him. He waved his arms and tried to talk, his eyes glowering at Castor through the glass, but the oxygen mask made him mute. Castor laughed out loud. "What a nut," he remarked, and the policewoman frowned.

"You are speaking of Fung Bohsien," she reproved him, "a famous scientist and high party member! You must show more respect." Then, relenting, "But it's true, Manyface should stay in his laboratories. Every time he leaves there is trouble."

"What kind of trouble?" Castor began to ask, interestedly, but they were out of the building by then and had the street to cross. If anything it was worse than any before in his experience, because it was the height of the working day and all the vehicles were desperate to get where they were going before any other. What Castor wanted to do was hold the inspector's hand as they crossed. Pride did not allow that—even if she would have—and his heart was pounding by the time they reached the opposite curb.

The restaurant, however, soothed all hurts. The smells were marvelous! They found two seats at a great round table in a corner of the room, overlooking the busy street. All the other seats were occupied, but each party confined its attention to itself as waiters and waitresses brought steaming tureens and plates of sizzling-hot fried fish and crisp green vegetables and tall half-liter bottles of beer and orange soda. Tsoong Delilah, seeing that Castor was indeed starving, allowed him to feed his young metabolism without talking while she picked at her food. Finally, after his second helping of crisp chicken wings and third bowl of rice, he asked, "Who is this 'Manyface'?"

"You are not to call him that," she commanded. "To you he is Professor Fung Bohsien, as well as a number of other names—etcetera, as you would say in English."

"'Et cetera' isn't English," he pointed out, with his mouth full.

"Oh, what a scholar it is! In any case, Manyface is no concern of yours." Castor shrugged, eyeing the platters of fresh fruit that the waiters were just depositing on the revolving lazy Susan in the center of the table. To make conversation while he was helping himself to the dessert, he asked, "How did you know to go to the cattle collective?"

"Simply good police work," said Tsoong Delilah sternly, "and you must not discuss the case until the inquest is complete." Then she thought for a moment and added, "However, perhaps you can be of some help."

"It is a citizen's duty to assist the police in their work, Inspector," he said formally.

"Oh, Scholar! How sarcastic you are! Have you been treated so badly, then?"

"I was not admitted to the university," he said, as though that answered everything.

"Yes, I am aware of that. But I am aware, too, that you did in fact then proceed to educate yourself through the teaching machines, and in such curious subjects! Astronomy. Mathematics. History—and, of course, your admirable command of the high tongue; is being an autodidact so much worse than a college degree?"

He shrugged, impressed not only by her use of words like "autodidact"—he had never heard it spoken in a conversation before, though perhaps that was not surprising on a rice farm—but by her detailed knowledge of his studies. "I suppose," he conceded, "that I lost very little, really."

"And have you been mistreated here? Made to sleep with pigs?"

There was enough country bumpkin left in Castor to make his eyes sparkle. "I guess not," he admitted and, with a rush, "Actually, the hotel is *grand*! If only they'd fed me—But I have in my room my own toilet and shower! And a screen that gets fifty-one channels, including the Indian programs!"

"Han is not good enough for you?" she joked. Then, coming to the point, "So it is fair for me to ask you for your special knowledge, then. Tell me, have you had much contact with the cattle collective?"

"Not really. Oh, we see them, now and then. At dances and rallies, mostly, and my cousin Patrick's son married a girl from there—but I don't really know her, because they volunteered for reassignment in Texas. She didn't like our village, I guess."

"Tell me what you do know, at least," Tsoong Delilah commanded, and obediently Castor searched his memory while they dawdled over their tea. The River of Pearl Cattle Collective got its name from its origins. The first group of settlers had once been tourists, caught browsing the shops of Hong Kong when the war broke out. When it was over they had a real problem. They couldn't stay in China, because there was no way for China to feed even its own people, much less bourgeois jet-setters who had no real right to be there in the first place. The tourists couldn't go home, because most of them didn't have any homes left to go to. For three or four months they were tossed around from camp to camp, always hungry, as psychically shaken by the war as any and even more despairing than most. When at last they were offered

37

transportation back to America on condition that they
start a livestock farm in the least ruined parts of what had
once been Alabama, they jumped at the chance. Not with
pleasure; simply because all the alternatives were worse.
As, mostly, retired English teachers and vacationing
mutual-fund salesmen, they were not very good at slop-
ping hogs and birthing calves. It didn't matter. Most of
them did not survive the cruelly hard conditions very long,
anyway. It was the handful of younger American tourists
who had survived to build the collective, supplemented
as the years went by with drafts of undesirables from the
cities. Many of the new recruits were Overseas Chinese—
third- and fourth-generation Chinese-Americans, who
found the Han colonists who arrived to repopulate the
devastated continent even harder to take than did their
Anglo compatriots. So River of Pearl had more than its
share of malcontents. Their neighbors had built up a tra-
dition of leaving them alone.

When he saw the policewoman consulting her watch
Castor realized he had told her as much as she wanted to
know about the River of Pearl Collective. "What should
I do now?" he asked. "Am I supposed to go back to the
village?"

She looked astonished. "Now? Before the inquest is
over? Certainly not. Any witness may be recalled; you'll
be told when you may leave. And anyway," she said,
grinning, as she waved to a waiter for the check, "this
afternoon will be especially interesting for you, I think!"

There had been time to draw his witness fees and
expenses after all. Castor turned the green-edged Renmin
currency over in his fingers curiously as he waited for the
afternoon session to begin. The spectators' gallery was

fuller than before, though the queer old man called Manyface was not among them as far as Castor could see. Inspector Tsoong Delilah had not rejoined him. She was seated once more in the front row, along with three other police. All four of them seemed intently poised for something special.

The first witness had barely begun to testify when Castor lost interest in the other spectators and jammed his money back into his pocket. The witness was a police technician, a white-haired man whose ease and control suggested many hours in court. The questions and answers were quick and direct:

"Were you assigned the task of identifying the deceased?"

"I was. Through cell typing and analysis of the hair patterns at the base of the skull, the deceased was identified as Feng Avery, seventeen years old, citizen of the Bama Autonomous Republic, apprentice slaughterer at the River of Pearl Livestock Collective. Apprentice Feng was an Overseas Chinese, of pure strain for six generations."

"Have you examined the dossier of Apprentice Feng Avery?"

"I have. He was arrested twice while a university student. Both arrests were for counterrevolutionary activities. The first was for participating in a rightist meeting. The second was for defacing the people's property by spray-painting graffiti. He painted such slogans as 'America for Americans' and 'Chinese Go Home' on the walls of his dormitory. Apprentice Feng was expelled from the university after the second arrest and has since been the subject of observation."

By then Castor was riveted to his seat. He was almost afraid to look around for fear of drawing attention to himself. This was dangerous territory! It was not just a simple murder. It entailed a state crime! An act, perhaps even a series of acts, against the people! And what could have made this boy so criminally irresponsible? He had been given everything! The Yankee Chinese were even less likely to be allowed into universities than pure-bred Yanks like Castor himself. The boy must have been something special—and had been given special privileges; for such a person to have betrayed his trust was almost unbelievable!

The whole courtroom was tense now, with stirrings and whisperings. Castor could hear no sound from the penned spectators, but he could see them leaning toward each other in excitement; body language was not screened out by the glass. In the front of the room the head judge was peremptorily recalling the old slaughterhouse boss to the stand, and his body language, too, was clearer than words. Head down, face stricken, steps slow, he took his seat and waited for the blow to fall.

"Did you know that Apprentice Feng was missing from his post?"

The old man took a bitter breath and flared, "Of course I did! He was my grandson, how could I not know?" Two seats down from Castor, the baseball-playing boy began to cry.

"And you did not report his absence?"

"I didn't have to!" yelled the old man. "I knew! Always in trouble, never satisfied! He had stolen a gun; he was going to attack the radio-telescope. I followed him; I begged him not to—" And then as, at a signal from one of the judges, Tsoong Delilah and the other police rose to approach him, he bawled, "I didn't mean to do it, but he gave me no choice. He would have destroyed us all..."

* * *

So the day in court was over, the courtroom emptying. Castor sat waiting for someone to tell him what to do, glumly contemplating the long bus ride back to the village and the scolding of Fat Rhoda and the endless stoop labor of the rice paddies, when he heard his name called.

It was the policewoman. "Well, Scholar, what are your plans?" she asked, her face bright. Obviously she was pleased with herself over the easy solution of the case. He shrugged.

"Back to the village, I suppose."

"Back to the village, of course," she agreed, "but there is no reason to hurry. The buses run every day, and you might as well stay here tonight."

"Really?" He began to feel pleasure: the rest of the day in the city, some quick shopping in the morning, the pleasures of the transient hotel that night, this time with money in his pocket. "I can watch some Indian programs in my room," he said happily.

"Return to that slum? Certainly not!" she scoffed. "No, I insist. Dinner at my place, and we will find a bed for you there. No argument! It is decided."

IV

Tsoong Delilah's "place" didn't mean her place of residence—"My city apartment! No! That's not much better than your damned transient flophouse!"—but the "place" she kept for herself on the water, way down the Delta to the Gulf Coast. It took more than an hour to drive, even in Tsoong Delilah's zippy little sports car, while the afternoon darkened into full night.

Castor, sitting next to her in the two-seater, was alternately glowing with delight and sick with envy. How skillfully her gloved hands turned the wheel, dimmed the lights, operated the radio, sounded the horn; how briskly the little car slipped through gaps in the stream of trucks and taxis! The envy was just as powerful. Castor had never driven anything more exciting than one of the village trucks. What must it be like to have a machine like this for one's own? And under the excitement and the envy, another feeling, partly sexual, partly fearful, as he wondered what this woman had in mind for him that night.

When they were out of the city traffic she rummaged in her pocket and passed him her little lacquered pipe. "Fill it from the pouch in my bag," she ordered, not taking her eyes off the road to see that he did so. When he started to hand the filled pipe back to her she scoffed, "Oh, Scholar, what's the use of a pipe not lighted? The plug on the dash—use it!"

When Castor succeeded in figuring out how the plug lighted, he took a reckless deep puff. Mistake. He was sent coughing and strangling, head down, almost dropping the pipe. When he recovered, the policewoman was laughing. He passed it over, wondering what he had inhaled. Not tobacco, certainly, but if it was marijuana it was something orders of magnitude more potent than the homegrown from the private plots of the village.

Still, it certainly did make one feel good. Relaxing, he asked a question that had been on his mind: "What will happen to the old man?"

"The murderer? He will be convicted in the people's court, of course, and sentenced no doubt to many years of reeducation," said the policewoman righteously; and then, "But if I were the judge I would suspend the sentence."

"Because he is so old?"

"No. Because he did nothing malicious or evil. I almost admire him, Scholar. He saw something that threatened the people, and he took steps to stop it. He did not mean to kill Feng Avery. When he saw what had happened he grew frightened and careless. It's too bad you found the head; he would have got off clean otherwise."

She took a deep draft on the pipe and handed it back to him in silence. Then she exploded: "You Yanks! How many of you secretly hate us?"

"It is natural to hate one's conquerors," Castor said boldly, sucking at the pipe.

"But we are not conquerors! We came here to help, when you and the Russians had stung each other to death— and nearly killed the whole world, too! We brought you doctors and teachers! We helped you rebuild your land!" When Castor was silent, she turned her eyes from the road for a moment to look at him. "Don't you know that?"

she demanded. "Don't you know that without us you might all have perished? We did right to come!"

The pipe was burned out now. Castor turned it over in his fingers thoughtfully. What the woman said was true enough, or almost true enough, except—

"Except that you are still here," he said at last.

The moon was setting, on the heels of the sun, as they pulled into a parking space overlooking the waters of the Gulf of Mexico. Castor got out and waited while the policewoman rummaged in the trunk of the car, gazing about. There were four or five houses, most of them dark, in this little colony. They were on a bluff, and that was strange. There were no bluffs there. Mud from the old course of the Mississippi River had made all the land within a dozen kilometers or more, and mud does not heap itself into hills. It took Castor only a moment to realize this, and to realize that Police Inspector Tsoong's home was built on the heaped-up ruins of what had once been some sort of town. From the reek of petroleum in the air he realized another fact. No matter what Tsoong Delilah had jokingly promised, there would be no tandem skin diving for them this time. There had obviously been an oil surge from the rickety old wells a hundred kilometers out on the Gulf, and swimming would be no pleasure.

Still, it was a delightful place. The sliver of a moon did not obscure the stars. "There's Jupiter," he said suddenly. "And Vega and Altair—this would be a marvelous place for a telescope!" Tsoong Delilah looked at him curiously, but said only,

"Here, take our dinner while I get my bag. The house is just up that path."

If Castor had thought the transient hotel splendid, Tsoong Delilah's country retreat was simply awesome. A private kitchen! A fireplace! A bedroom that contained neither working desk nor dining table, but only those things that went with the bed—and such a bed, big enough for six!

She also had a bar, and the first thing she did was to make him a drink. She took her own into the kitchen, leaving him to sit in a deeply enveloping soft chair and gaze out over the Gulf while she put their dinner into the slow cooker, then disappeared again, into the bedroom, coming out in black silk pajamas, her feet bare. Not for the first time, Castor wondered just how old Renmin Police Inspector Tsoong Delilah was. Uniformed and interrogating him at the rice paddy, she had looked middle-aged, maybe even *old*, say as much as forty or more. At lunch that afternoon, a handsome woman in perhaps her late twenties. Now, curled up on the rug before the fireplace (so great a waste of fuel in this balmy air!—but so cheerfully relaxing, too), she seemed no older than Castor himself. Certainly she did not seem as old as his recent twenty-year-old wife, Maria, who had always had an inclination to seem more mature than her years . . . Maria! It was the first time that day Castor had thought of her!

"What's the matter, Scholar?" the policewoman demanded. "Did someone just walk over your grave?"

He shook his head without answering. He didn't want to think about Maria just then, much less talk about her with this woman. What he wanted to think about was why Tsoong Delilah had brought him here. For his body? Oh, yes, very likely, and that might prove very interesting. But he could not help feeling that there was something else. He could not begin to imagine what a Renmin police inspector could possibly want from a peasant. It was difficult to think of such subjects in this place, with this pleasant-smelling woman close to him and his blood-stream full of cannabis and alcohol. He didn't speak; and the woman misinterpreted his silence.

"I think," she said, "you are mulling over what I said in the car. Well, I, too, have been thinking. Do you know what China was like in the old days? We were conquered by one invader after another, over and over, through thousands of years. When we ran out of nomads from the west we had the Americans and the British, and then the Japanese. They stayed too long, too, Scholar, but at least in our parks there are no signs saying: 'No dogs or Yankees permitted'! Now," she said, rising, "I think our dinner is nearly ready, if you will help me set the table."

Castor had never dined by candlelight before except when there was a power cutoff. The dinner was delicious—it was a mixture of Yankee and Han Chinese, a stew of pork and beans and a salad. And wine. They sat facing the dark Gulf, and with the room lights dimmed Castor's eyes began to pick out a pale flicker on the horizon. He knew what it was. Oil spills were usually controlled in a day or two, but the old natural gas wells cracked and leaked everywhere, and when there was a steady bubbling up of gas from the bottom over a period of time, sooner or later something set it off and the sea blazed for a few weeks. The gulls were dining by candlelight, too, feeding at night because there were so many dead or stunned fish, choked by the hydrocarbons in the water, helpless at the surface. He could see the birds diving and soaring, silhouetted against the distant glow. "Do you blame us for that, too?" the policewoman asked, and Castor shook his head.

"I don't blame you at all," he said. It was true. Nearly true. He didn't blame the Han Chinese for what had happened to the Gulf. Everyone knew that it was a couple of H-missiles that had wrecked the American fuel supply, the hydraulic hammer of their blast snapping off the pipes and pylons of the oil rigs. The Han Chinese had capped the worst of them almost at once and were still working on the hopeless myriad of others. He did, perhaps, blame them for other things, not excluding the desertion of his wife.

Tsoong Delilah did not pursue the subject. She tapped her wineglass with a long fingernail to signal Castor to refill it and began to tell him the story of her life. It was an interesting enough story. She had been born in San Francisco, grown up in a mixed neighborhood, Han Chinese and Yankee, mostly prosperous, mostly professionals. Her father, an economist specializing in trade matters, had sent her to a preparatory school in Guangzhou; then her two years of national service, as an MP in Africa and later in such romantic places as London and Marseilles and Zurich, serving the Han Chinese embassies in what were, after all, basically Indian protectorates. Then back to college, this time in Beijing. "I liked being a military police," she said as they cleared off the table, "so I majored in criminology and police procedures—and here I am."

Castor stepped back to observe how she fitted the dishes into the automatic cleaning machine—another marvel! "You never married?" he asked.

She looked up at him quizzically. "Who said I never married? Do you think you are the only one who has ever been divorced, Scholar? I married my professor, and when he retired he decided to spend the rest of his life at Home. So we divorced. Now," she said, turning on the machine

47

and leading the way back to the living room, "let us have another drink while we hear your story. You are an interesting young man, autodidact. You took courses in physics, three years of that. And in physical chemistry; and in mathematics, also three years, all the way up to calculus and even a survey course in matrix mechanics which, however, you did not complete. I do not mention astronomy, navigation, astrogation, a survey of space medicine, planetology and orbital ballistics." While she talked she was seating him at one end of a deep couch and freshening their drinks; when he accepted his glass he said,

"Your investigation left out a couple. Chinese and English literature, history—"

"I left out all the ones which appeared to be only compulsory courses required for a degree, which you did not, after all, apply for. Why?"

"I just wanted an education," he said sulkily.

"You wanted a special kind of education," she corrected. "Space. All of your courses point to space. Is that it, Scholar? Are you longing for the old days, when you and the Russians dominated space, and everything else?"

"I want to go there," he mumbled, his tongue loosened by the wine and the dope. "My great-great-great-grandfather—"

"Yes? What about this honorable ancestor?"

"He *was* honorable, damn it! He was an astronaut!"

"An astronaut," she said, but for a wonder her tone was not mocking.

"That's right. My grandmother told me— Well, he was killed, I think. Probably in the war. But he was in the space program, that is definite."

She nodded slowly. "It is not shameful to want to match the brave deeds of your ancestors," she said, and her tone was almost kind. He shrugged. "And is that what you want to do, Scholar?"

"What chance do I have?" he demanded.

She thought it over. "Very little, I admit. You Westerners cost the world a great deal with your wars. There has not been much left over for a space program."

"And what little there is, do they take Yankees?" he asked bitterly.

"Perhaps not," she conceded, but as though she had lost interest in the discussion. She looked into the fire for a minute. Then she turned to him, and she was neither sexually alluring nor police-arrogant. She said, "I was not truthful with you at lunch, Castor. There is something you can do for me, and it has nothing to do with the River of Pearl Livestock Collective." It was the first time she had called him by name.

Castor sat up. His head was woozy, but he knew a point when he came to it. "What can I do that you can't do for yourself?"

"Not what you can do. What you know." She swirled the ice cubes in her drink moodily. "I have a puzzle. It has nothing to do with a police case, because I would know that. It does not involve high party members or politics with India—I would know if either of those were so, too. But information is being kept secret, and I don't know why."

"Then what can I do?"

"You can lend me some of your wisdom, Scholar." She reached over to the table at the end of the couch and lifted one edge. It exposed a keyboard. The tabletop, erected, became a screen. "For instance," she said, punching in commands, "see here." A table of numbers wrote itself across the screen, faster than the eye could follow:

SELECTED POWER ANOMALIES

Bermuda	Drain 0335–0349Q	Standby 0350–0450Q
Arecibo	Drain 0500–0514Q	Standby 0515–0615Q
Gulfport	Drain 0605–0619Q	Standby 0620–0720Q
Goldstone	Drain 0720–0734Q	Standby 0735–0830Q
Mauna Kea	Drain 0940–0954Q	Standby 0955–1055Q

"This is from the energy collective," she said, "and it shows an extraordinary power consumption for about fifteen minutes and then a period of an hour when all major electrical machinery is silenced for quite a large area. It is only these areas that show this, and although this is for yesterday, the same thing has been going on all week. What does it tell you, Scholar?"

He said promptly, "Well, they are all radio-astronomy observatories. The times are Q times—World Standard Time, based on the Beijing meridian—"

"Scholar!" she warned.

He grinned, for almost the first time in their relationship confident. "I did not know how much you knew," he explained. "The times correspond to about the rotation period of the earth. Presumably all observing the same point in space."

"Excellent, Scholar."

He admitted, "I had help, Inspector. We've had these power blackouts every night in my village. I didn't know till now what they were for. I suppose the same thing is going on in the observatories in the rest of the world."

"Very likely," she agreed, "but the records for the energy collectives outside the North American grid are less conveniently accessible for me. What else can you tell me?"

He was getting enthusiastic now. "Well, hell! Obviously they're radaring something—the heavy power drain, then the waiting period for signal return. Since they require so much power, it must be pretty small. Also pretty distant—but not more than, let me see, about five A.U. Because of the round-trip time for the signal at light speed," he explained, answering her frown. "Say seven or eight hundred million kilometers. That would be way past the asteroid belt, almost to the orbit of Jupiter. If," he added with some bitterness, "we had probes in space, we wouldn't have to worry about surface radar observatories to see things like that."

Tsoong Delilah was scowling, but it didn't look like anger, only concentration. "If the People's Republics have no energy to waste on space travel, it is not their fault, Scholar," she reminded him. "What else?"

He said, keeping the reversal-of-role superiority out, or largely out, of his voice, "If I can use your screen, I think I can show you a picture of it."

The look she gave him was sardonic again, but she moved aside for him—and raised her pencil-thin eyebrows a few minutes later when he looked up, blushing. "Well, Scholar? No picture?"

"It's your system," he said defensively. "I can't access SKYWATCH or the IAF net, or even the current-projects file for the Bama scope. I could probably get something through the Transient Phenomena Center in Mukden if you want to pay for an overseas line—"

"No. Not Mukden," she said sharply.

He spread his hands. Trying to make the position clear without being definitely disagreeable about it, he said, "Your system doesn't seem to have much science capability."

"Why should it? I'm a police inspector, not a professor. I can access anything I like through the police net—but that," she added swiftly, to forestall him, "I think I will not do in this case. There is some delicacy here. I don't know what is being such a mystery, but there must be a reason." She gazed thoughtfully into the fire for a moment, then snapped the screen down decisively. "It is just as well," she announced. "I have told you nothing that is not public record, so there can be no criticism."

She stood up, satisfied, and moved over to the bar. "Another drink, Scholar?" she called over her shoulder, but didn't wait for an answer. When she brought Castor's new drink back, her appearance had changed; she was neither police inspector nor puzzled citizen, and once again she looked much younger.

Castor found his face warming once more. Robbed of his position as lecturer in astronomy to a class of one, he was a rice-field Yankee in the private retreat of a seductive and worldly-wise woman. "But aren't you curious?" he asked.

She sank down next to him. "If I am curious tomorrow, I will have one of my sergeants access the IAF net or SKYWATCH or the Transient Phenomena Center in Mukden through the police net," she said, demonstrating how well she had learned her lesson. "But perhaps I will think it over for a day or two first. In any case, Castor, there are other things I am curious about. How did you come to make that woman pregnant?"

He almost choked on his drink. "You mean my wife."

"Wife, of course," she shrugged. "Did she not receive an implant at twelve?"

"Implants are not compulsory, Inspector," he reminded her and this time did not even get a shrug. He went on, with some embarrassment, "It's hard to explain, because it's a religious matter."

"Ah! Religion! Of course. But I did not think all Yankees were religious."

"Well, personally I'm not, but my wife is. Was. It has to do with, uh, what they call the sanctity of life giving. It means that before you have intercourse you're supposed to have to, well, pause for a while—that's when she puts the thing in—so she can reflect before deciding not to have a child. Only then she said she really wanted one."

Delilah sipped her drink, regarding him over the rim of her glass, while Castor tried to read her expression. Was she going to tell him how quaint these barbarous practices seemed? Or remind him of the duty to control population while the carrying capacity of the world's land was still so low? She did neither. She leaned forward suddenly to brush his cheek with her lips, then stood up. "What we do," she said, slipping loose the cord that held her pajamas, "is to receive an implant just before puberty. Then, if we want children, we have it removed. It is in the fatty part just where the buttocks join the thigh, so it really does not appear in most circumstances. I'll show you, Castor. And then you can show me if you are able to perform without such a preliminary pause to consider the sanctity of life giving."

At daybreak she woke him with her gently, sweetly stroking hand, and they had another bout—the fourth, perhaps, or maybe the fifth or sixth. She seemed inexhaustible. He was twenty-two years old; and besides, what happened in Tsoong Delilah's perfumed and gently resilient bed was light-years away from frantic grapplings at the edge of a rice paddy or even the marriage chamber. She was a *marvelous* lover, denied him nothing, demanded (it seemed) only his pleasure, and let that magnify hers.

Nothing that passed in that night led Castor to suspect that he was any more to Tsoong Delilah than a one-night stand, and he was wholly sure that he was only one of many. Still, he came out of the shower to find she had made breakfast for him. And when, in her turn, she finished her toilet and came out uniformed for the day, she sipped tea with him as he finished his rice and crab. "Well, Scholar," she said, puffing on the little pipe—it was tobacco this time—"you've had an interesting time, but now it's good-bye. Perhaps we'll meet again."

"I hope so," he said, surprising himself with the warmth he felt. Embarrassed, he added quickly, "Do I go back to the village now?"

She said indulgently, "You can if you want to, but maybe you'd like another day or two in the city. They will have kept your room at the transient hotel, and it's all paid for by the court."

"I'd like that!"

"Of course. Don't stretch it too long, Castor. There's a limit—ah." She frowned in annoyance as her screen beeped for attention. She clapped twice sharply; the satellite screen over the breakfast table blinked alive, and a face looked out at them.

It was the famous scientist and high party member Fung Bohsien, and the reason he was called Manyface was instantly apparent. His face was twitching convulsively, as though he could not make up his mind what expression he wanted to wear. Even less did he seem able to decide what he wanted to say, because his words were jumbled, interrupted, terribly confusing:

"I am looking for—*no, I'm not*—PLEASE!—for Bama Repub—**shut up**—lic citizen, Pettyman Castor—*aw, he's not there*—PLEASE! LET HIM FIN—of Production Team—**I want to watch the opera**..."

54

"He's right here," Tsoong Delilah cut in, for the first time in Castor's experience showing consternation. She waved furiously to Castor to take her place before the screen. The old man looked at him, face working, his voices muttering to each other.

"Ah," he said. "Come to—*no!*—my office at—**not to-day!**—noon today because—" The voice faded to inaudible mutterings, while the expressions chased each other across the old face before, triumphantly, he finished in a rush: "My fourth part wants to see you!"

And he clicked off.

V

The university grounds sprawled over a dozen or more hectares. If Tsoong Delilah, silent and withdrawn, had not dropped him at the right building, Castor would have been lost beyond prayer. Even so, he had to ask directions twice before he found the correct wing of the Center for Neuroanatomy and Brain Studies. Then it was easy. Fairly easy.

All of the offices had nameplates on the door, CHEN Litsun or HONG Wuzhen or, rarely, BRADLEY Jonathan, but Castor recognized the one he was looking for instantly. It could have been no other, for the nameplate was three times regulation size and it said,

FUNG - HSANG - DIEN - POTTER - SU - ANGORAK - SHUM - TSAI - CORELLI - HONG - GWAI Bohsien - Futsui - Kaichung - Alicia - Wonmu - Aglat - Hengdzhou - Mingwo - Anastasio - Ludzhen - Hunmong. Evidently Manyface had, at least, a sense of humor!

When Castor let himself in, he discovered that Manyface's secretary did too. She was an elderly Han, far past the age when most Chinese went Home to die, but not past a jocular glint in the eyes when Castor explained he had an appointment with Professor Fung. "Do you now?" she asked. "They didn't tell me, though that's no surprise. Hold on a minute while I see where he is." She punched keys for her desk screen, gazed a moment, and shook her head. "He isn't on campus. I'll try the professor's home to see if he's left yet."

"I don't want to disturb him at home," Castor ventured. The secretary laughed. It was a friendly laugh, and Castor decided that what was amusing was the concept of Professor Fung Bohsien's being any more "disturbed" than he usually was. Encouraged, Castor edged forward to peek at the keyboard as she switched to comm mode, and his mouth watered. What a keyboard! This put the inspector's puny little rig in the shade, not to mention the rudimentary teaching screens at the Heavenly Grain Collective. There were hard-wired single-key functions for tasks that would have taken long and complicated programming instructions back at home. If they could have been done at all. He had seen setups as complicated as this on the village screens, and his heart had yearned for them. Here one was!

He could hear the *wheep ... wheep* that indicated ringing on the other end of the line. It seemed to go on a long time. The secretary read his expression and said kindly, "He's probably there. It takes them a long time to get themselves together to answer when there's no servant, and they always have a hard time keeping them." She let it ring at least fifty times. Long past the point when Castor would have given up, she leaned forward abruptly and spoke into the phone. "Professor Fung, Pettyman Castor is here for his appointment with you."

Castor was only in the fringe of the directed sound from the screen, but he could catch what sounded like several voices babbling at once. It did not disconcert the secretary. She looked up at Castor. "He wants to speak to you himself. I'll put it on the wall screen." Castor turned toward the screen wall, and Manyface peered out

at him. The old face creased and twitched and managed
to spit out words:

"Welcome, Pettyman—*hell if he is*—Castor—WHO'S
HE?—I'm sorry I am late—*am not sorry!*—but—**ooh, it's
him!**—I'll be in at three—NO!—*but I wanted to*—
PLEASE!—**please wait, Castor**—" There was more, but
it got worse. Castor could understand almost nothing of
it. What made it worse was the look—the looks—on the
old man's face. It was not a handsome face to begin with.
The huge football helmet was gone, but replaced by an
equally huge turban of white toweling. When the screen
clicked off Castor turned bemused to the secretary.

"What did he say?"

"He said to come back at three," she reported sym-
pathetically. "Maybe he'll be here. Maybe not. I advise
you to get something to eat while you're waiting. It might
be a long time."

In spite of the secretary's directions it took Castor
half an hour to find the student lunchroom in the Liu Piao
Center. He made several false starts, got lost twice, wandered through the Astronomy & Astrophysics building
with his heart hungry, took a shortcut through the Foreign
History Institute lobby, with American Revolutionary War
army uniforms in glass cases. He did not ask directions
until the hunger gnawing at the pit of his stomach forced
him to. But it was not only hunger that knotted his belly.
It was envy, sick envy, and regret. If things had gone just
a little differently, he might have been a student at this
very university! He might long since have earned an honorable degree—might even have been allowed to go on
to graduate school—to a doctorate—even to a profes-
sorship, right here, to teach new generations of the stu-

dents he saw thronging the halls and walks. He pushed his tray along the steam-table line, caught between a giggling group of Han girls and a covey of Yankee ones, exchanging the same confidences in the high tongue and in English. He was pop-eyed at the wonder of being there. When he found a place at a table to eat his dumplings (two turbaned Indian exchange students sat across from him!), every mouthful tasted of what might have been. If his grades had been a little better in the village school— If his teacher had fought for him a little harder or been a trifle better connected— If he had been born Han Chinese instead of Bama Yank— If the Russians and the Americans hadn't blown each other away a century before and left the world to the surviving hundreds of millions of China and India—

If the world had been a different world, then he might have been here, not by an old freak's caprice and the chance of blundering onto a severed head, but by right. And then even Maria would have been impressed by her scholar husband!

It occurred to him that that was only the second time in forty-eight hours he had thought of Maria.

Anyway, he told himself truly, it was a wonder to be here at all. When he had finished his dumplings he watched the others to see what they did with their trays and where they went afterward. Moving after random knots of students, he prowled the student center, the snack bar, the screen rooms, the beer hall, the study lounges, the supply stores, the auditoriums. Pure heaven! What it must be like to have the right to use these facilities any time you liked...

And, after all, he thought suddenly, who was to stop him?

He looked around to get his bearings, then headed straight for the nearest screen room.

The screens for students were nearly as formidable as the secretary's, but Castor was thrilled to be able to practice on one. When he had got it into communications mode, the first thing he did was to call Professor Manyface's secretary to make sure the strange old creature had not decided to come in early. He hadn't. Reassured, Castor tinkered the screen into data-retrieval mode and punched up *Directory—University*. He found the entry for Fung Bohsien easily. The cursor poured out fifty characters a second, and in no time at all Castor had Manyface's vital statistics:

> Fung Bohsien, b. Sinjiang Province 2019. BSc Sinjiang 2037. MSc Beijing 2039. MD Tokyo Prefecture 2042. PhD Stanford 2046. Fellow Academica Sinica—

Fast-feed. Castor humped the crawl ahead, past dozens of lines of honors given and positions held—then, with a growing puzzlement, past a much longer roll of major papers published. It was a perfectly ordinary, if unusually distinguished, academic vita. There was not one word to suggest what made him talk so funny or have such weird nicknames. The only unusual thing about the biographical entry was a postscript that said, "See also Hsang Futsui, Dien Kaichung, Potter Alicia, Su Wonmu, Angorak Aglat, Shum Hengdzhou, Tsai Mingwo, Corelli Anastasio, Hong Ludzhen, and Gwai Hunmong."

Castor frowned in frustration at the screen, then doggedly rolled it back to the beginning and reread every word. And in the list of papers for the year 2057 he hit pay dirt.

The title was "Personality Retention after Brain Tissue Transplant," and the authors were given as Fung, Shan, Tzuling, Gwui, and Gwui.

Fortunately the journal cited was in the university library memory. It was the answer. Not easily found, because Castor's autoeducation had not included much anatomy. He had to force his way through thickets of fornices and corpus callosa and tangles of epiphyses and hypophyses, but the story was there to read. At the age of only thirty-six, Dr. Fung had developed a brain tumor, and it was malignant. Worse, it involved areas with names like the "basis pedunculi" that involved the basic functioning of the body; to lose them was not merely to lose a few memories or the sense of smell, it was a loss incompatible with life. The only hope was a transplant. The operation was successful ... except that, coming out of his druggy post-op doze, young Dr. Fung Bohsien responded to the surgeon's questions clearly and positively. Who was he? Why, he was Fung Bohsien, of course, and in the next breath identified himself equally certainly as Hsang Futsui, the young Han student killed under the wheels of a trolleybus who had donated the brain stem.

Castor stared at the golden characters on the screen, thrilled and revolted. Revolted to find that the famous scientist and high party member did not merely perform experiments but was the subject of one. Thrilled to be, at last, in the place where such wonders could happen. Revolted, and thrilled, and desperately, desperately sick with longing to stay there.

*   *   *

"No," the secretary said good-humoredly, "Professor Fung isn't here, and I have no idea where he is. He did call. He said he would be greatly pleased if you would remain in the city for a few days. All the necessary papers will be arranged."

Castor's heart throbbed joyfully. "In the transient hotel?" he asked hopefully. The secretary pursed her lips.

"If you wish that, I suppose it could be arranged, but Professor Fung suggested you stay with Police Inspector Tsoong. It is more convenient to the university. I promise the inspector will not object," the secretary grinned. "I have informed her already. So stay in the city, enjoy yourself—but first you should see the professor. He may come at any time."

Never since the feast days of childhood had Castor had so many wishes granted at once. "Can I wait in the student center?" he asked with stars in his eyes.

"No, why? Are you hungry still?"

"I would like to use the screens," he confessed.

"Do you know how? Well, then! Why use a public screen when you can use the professor's?"

And so for three hours and more Pettyman Castor lived in the very heart of heaven, seated at the huge keyboard belonging to a famous scientist and high party member, with what seemed nearly unrestricted access to all the world's scientific data. The keyboard, of course, was formidable. He studied it for ten minutes before he dared do anything more than turn it on. Then he repeated the searches he had conducted in the student center, adding a cross-lookup instruction to find later papers, and easier papers, to describe what Fung Bohsien was and had done. The screen was a marvel. It seemed to think for him, once instructed in what he wished. By the time the secretary came in with a cup of tea and word that the professor was still missing, he had learned more than he ever wished to know about Fung Bohsien. He had part or most of the brains of ten other human beings, all dead of things that wrecked their bodies but left their brains intact, installed within his own skull—well, not his own skull anymore, because one cranium could not hold so much tissue. Bone grafts and later noble-metal plates had expanded the cranial capacity. He seemed—now it was perhaps they seemed—to have no limit to his desire for added personalities; it was not lack of will that kept him from adding a dozen more but the difficulty of finding proper tissue matches. Most of the conventional series of antigen factors were no problem at all, because immune-reaction suppressants handled them well, but the brain was tricky stuff. Fewer than one cadaver in a hundred could live comfortably inside Manyface's pumpkin-sized skull.

Then, emboldened, Castor threw a wider net. Was there any progress in solving the mystery of Ursa QY since his last course in astronomy a year before? No. There was not; it was still an anomalous black hole. Had the Earth-based telescopes any new pictures of the massive eruptions on Callisto? Yes, they had—good ones, considering that astronomy was all back on the surface of the planet again, with the adventure into space a forgotten chapter a century old...

He might have gone on forever if the secretary had not appeared to say, "The professor is in his laboratory; go there. Out the door, down the stairs, room 3C44—don't worry, you won't have any trouble finding it!"

Castor had no trouble at all. The laboratory announced itself by its sounds and smells before he reached the open door. Sounds of chirping, cheeping, squeaking, yowling; smells of animal cages by the dozen. Most of the cages were full. A good half of their occupants were monsters. A capuchin monkey, intact and lively, chattered as it bounded from perch to floor in one cage; next door another monkey squatted sullenly in a nest of rags, its huge head braced by a leather collar, its eyes fierce. The dominant freakishness of the animals was the big head, but there were others—a snake with two bodies joined to a single skull, a steel band reinforcing the joint as the creature squirmed and twisted in its own coils; a piglet's head on a puppy's body; a guinea pig that seemed to have no proper head at all, just a nose and a mouth that seemed to come right from its shoulders and eyes that peeped pleadingly at Castor. He was shaken. When he saw the great football helmet of Manyface past a row of cages, he looked at the animals no more, but kept his gaze on the scientist as he approached.

Three or four normally formed human beings were with Manyface, a couple of them Yankee, Castor saw with surprise. They listened patiently to the internal debate that confused every statement that came from the mouth of Fung Bohsien; they seemed skilled at disregarding the minority voices and extracting the instructions and comments of the boss.

Castor did not have that skill. When Manyface's gaze fell on him he shrank back. Not only was Fung Bohsien a freak, he was *old*. The face was wrinkled; there were age spots on the hands; the voice (voices?) tremulous. There was a faint musty smell that managed to register itself even through the miasma of the animal pens. It was the smell of old age, Castor thought, wondering. Old Yankees were nothing new. Old Han Chinese, however, were exceedingly rare on North America. Why had this man not gone back to the Mainland to live out the last years of his life like everyone else? "Who?" demanded the scientist, and Castor licked his lips before he answered.

"I'm Pettyman Castor. You sent for me. You saw me at the hearing, I think."

And all the voices tried to respond at once: "What hearing? *That hearing, damn it, the one Alicia dragged us*—I didn't drag anybody, I simply wanted—Oh," said the least confused voice of Manyface, "I remember. You're from the Heavenly Grain Village—*what village?*—please—SHUT UP—and one of us has a special interest—wait." The massive head turned aside for a moment while the voices muttered to each other. When Manyface looked back at Castor the voice was different:

"I'm the one," it said. "Potter Alicia. Do you know the village well?"

"I've lived there all my life."

"Well, then—*ah, let's go*—SHUT UP!—well, then, do you know a little girl named Grootenbart Maria?"

"Maria? Certainly I know her, but she's not a little girl. She's my wife."

More confused internal argument among Manyface's personalities; it lasted for a half a minute, and then the twitching face settled into an expression half-joyful, half-pleading; and the voice said:

"Well, I'm her mother!"

VI

The city apartment of Renmin Police Inspector Tsoong Delilah was even grander than her beachfront place and a lot more lived-in. To begin with it had *five rooms*. What any single human being could do with five whole rooms Castor couldn't imagine, but the quiet Yankee maid who let him in assured him they were all for Tsoong Delilah—and, of course, for her "guests." No other guest was in sight this evening. Neither was Tsoong Delilah because, the maid explained, she was detained on duty but would be with him in time for dinner.

In fact, she was earlier than that. She came in behind Castor without warning while he was gazing at an extra bedroom, larger than the whole apartment he and Maria had shared, complete with closets and washstand and screen. "Like it?" she said to the back of his head. "You can have it—to keep your things in, anyway." When he turned she was smiling. If there was a touch of rue in her smile, at least she did not seem angry at having him thrust on her. He started to apologize, but she shook her head. "A request from Fung Bohsien is an honor for me—I think a pleasure, too," she added, looking at him boldly. "I must shower and change before dinner—make yourself at home. Although I see you have already done that."

Dinner was interrupted twice by faint beeps from the screen. Each time Tsoong Delilah got up to take the call in another room, and the second time she returned, frowning. "You don't have to worry about the old man from River of Pearl anymore," she reported. "He committed suicide in his cell."

"Oh," he said, startled. It had not occurred to him that even a convicted murderer might want to take his own life. "What a pity!"

"It is a pity, Castor. He was a good man," she said softly. He was silent for a moment, thinking about the old man and about why a police inspector should care about a felon's death, and then he forgot about the old man. What was much more interesting was what had happened to him that day—above all, what might yet happen! Tsoong Delilah let him do all the talking while she picked at her food. Then, when the maid had put the dishes in the washer and departed, they sat at opposite ends of a huge couch and the policewoman smoked her little pipe and let him go on talking. Castor did not object. There was so much to say!

"Manyface likes me," he boasted. "He even asked if I might be willing to work for him, what do you think of that? That could be a very good deal, although working for a freak like Manyface isn't my idea—what?"

Delilah was smiling, but only just. "Not 'Manyface,'" she corrected. "'Senior Party Cadre Fung Bohsien.' And not 'freak' under any circumstances."

"Oh, hell, Delilah," he said scornfully, "there's no need to be so formal." He observed the smile chill and changed his mind. "But you're right," he added quickly. "One has to respect authority, of course! He does like me, though. Or part of him does. Do you think I could stand working for him? I'm to see him again in the morning. Will you take me there?"

"Of course," said Delilah, watching him.

"But he's so hard to talk to! Not so much when he's quiet, but when he gets excited. Then they all try to speak at once—of course, he's excited a lot of the time . . ." He remembered, "And, oh yes, I punched up my own dossier. I'm qualified for the observatory! If Manyface will just put in a word for me—"

"Why the observatory?" the policewoman asked. "The telescope is only a tool. If you wanted to run your farm collective, would you assign yourself as a plow?"

He paused, blinking. "What do you mean?"

"If Fung Bohsien would help you get transferred to the observatory, he could just as easily get you admitted to the university."

Castor sat up straight, gasping. "The university?"

"Why not?"

"Can he do such a thing?"

She only laughed. Obviously he could. Perhaps he would! Perhaps that great sullen dream might come true after all, and all because he had had the dumb luck to kick a dead man's head one afternoon in the rice paddy!

He realized the policewoman was smiling at him indulgently, almost fondly, and he recollected himself. "I forgot!" he cried. "I brought you a present."

Tsoong Delilah actually looked startled. "A present?"

"They let me use their screen," he said, getting up to rummage in his backpack, "and—may I use yours?—I remembered what we were talking about last night." He sat before the small living-room screen, studied it a moment and then punched for display mode. "They can access *anything*! SKYWATCH didn't have what I wanted, and neither did the IAF, but the university's astronomy department had all the plates—all the way to the big Lhasa scope, and some Indian ones, too. So I took the best radar scans from each, corrected for rotation and tumbling and scale—it's coming toward us—and programmed a comparison mode to pick the best features of each—it was easy, really," he boasted, though that wasn't true, and pushed the button for display. On the screen an object took form, surrounded by blackness pierced with tiny dots of blinding white.

It was a spaceship.

Tsoong Delilah gazed at it wonderingly. "But we don't have any spacecraft out there," she said, her voice husky.

"Exactly! Isn't it wonderful?" Castor was thrilled.

VII

The morning sky was blue and fine; the odor of hydrocarbons from the Gulf was no more than a suspicion; even the New Orleans traffic was no more than a challenge to the rapidly evolving Pettyman Castor, who became an order of magnitude more sophisticated every day. He did not even get lost on his way to Manyface's office. He made his way unerringly to the proper building, floor, and even room. The only thing that went wrong was that Manyface was not there, nor even expected.

The faithful secretary said so. She was picking desultorily at her screen with a cursor rod when Castor came in. She did not seem either surprised or particularly apologetic when it developed that Senior Party Cadre Fung Bohsien had forgotten to mention Castor's arrival. She was friendly enough, though. "You have to allow for him at times like this, Pettyman," she said absently, eyes on the screen. Craning his neck, Castor caught a glimpse of what was on the screen. The secretary was playing a game of Go with the computer. She made her move and then went on: "He's always this way when he gets a new implant."

"I didn't know he had a new one," said Castor.

"Oh, sure. Five weeks ago. Do you think he's always this way? Would I be working for him if he was?" She shook her head, glancing distastefully at the screen. Perhaps, Castor thought, the computer was beating her. Suddenly she threw the cursor rod down on her desk and asked, "Have you eaten?"

"What?"

"Eaten breakfast," she explained. "You know? In the mouth? Chew? Swallow? No? Then pull up a chair and we'll order some soup and rice from the faculty club."

Actually, the woman seemed to want to be friendly! She called in the order and, waiting for it to be delivered, put her feet up on the desk to regard Castor appraisingly. "So, young man. You think you would like to work for the professor?"

Castor nodded.

"But you don't know if you can stand his craziness, is that right? Yes, well, do not worry too much. Now his whole personality is out of balance. They all start fighting among themselves when a new one is added—it is *terrible*! But it ends." She looked up as the messenger from the faculty club came in and instructed him in where to lay out the dishes. "Eat," she ordered Castor. "You may ask questions of me while you eat, if you wish."

Castor was caught with chopsticks halfway to his mouth. He watched the woman nimbly alternating soup and rice while he formulated his questions. "Well—what is it like for him to have all those people in his head? Is it like split personality?"

"No, not at all. Split personality—or as Professor Fung's colleagues describe it, 'multiple personality disorder,' is a psychological thing. It is trauma, usually from early childhood damage, that in some way causes a retreat from reality. Manyface is very real. So are all of his voices."

Castor scooped rice into his mouth, dampened it with a porcelain spoonful of soup. He managed to say, "But how?"

"How do they operate within his head? Let me see. There was a psychologist named Hilary Roberts who published work many, many years ago—when there really was an America, even. I will give you his example, by asking you a question. What are we doing now?"

"Why—" Castor swallowed, to be able to say, "Talking?"

"Exactly. Now, young Pettyman, how did you know that was what we were doing?"

"Why—" Castor swallowed again. This time it was not to clear his throat of food, but to assist in thought. "I guess I thought about it?" he offered.

"Right. So, while we were 'talking,' you were also 'thinking' of 'talking.' You are now probably 'thinking' of 'thinking' of talking. That second thinking is what Roberts (and I) call 'meta-thinking.' But, look at this, Pettyman! Now we are 'thinking' about 'meta-thinking'! What does that mean we are doing?"

"Wow! Meta-meta-thinking?"

"Precisely." The secretary grinned, crushing the empty disposable cups that had once held her rice and soup. She tossed them neatly into a disposal basket. "You can go on doing that forever, Pettyman. You can do it through infinity."

"Wow!"

"More than that! You cannot tell which thinking is the 'ultimate' thinking, because there is none, it being infinite. You cannot even tell which kind of thinking is at the bottom—is the 'real' thinking—because infinity is a closed loop."

Castor was frowning, trying to find a way of applying this airy-fairy metaphysics—this meta-thinking!—to the reality of his life. "Do you mean that Manyface is infinite?" he demanded.

"Not infinite, no. But a closed loop, Pettyman. There isn't any 'real' Manyface any more. They are all real."

Following her example, Castor picked up his own empty containers and disposed of them. He reached for the remains of the rice, but the secretary was ahead of him, scooping out the last little bit to eat. "How do you know so much about it?" he asked.

She gave him a disliking look. "Because I am a secretary, you mean? Even a secretary has a brain, Pettyman. Also, how do you think I got this job? I was Professor Fung's research assistant before I was his secretary. Then, for a time, it was proposed that I be his wife. Then he found companionship inside his skull and no longer needed a wife . . . but I remained his secretary." She balled up the last of the containers and pitched it after the others. "Well, Pettyman, how would you like to amuse yourself till the professor comes? With his screen? To follow these spacecraft that fascinate you so?"

"Don't they you?"

She shrugged. "Outer space is less interesting to me than inner space, but yes, it is interesting, I admit, that there is talk of radio signals that have not been decoded."

"Radio signals!" And mystery ones at that! Castor felt the sudden pull of the screen, but the secretary smiled.

"A great mystery, yes," she conceded. "But perhaps not a very interesting one, since most likely it is only that the decoding algorithms have been forgotten."

By the time Castor established, regretfully, that the secretary had been right, it was midafternoon. The first he knew of the arrival of Fung Bohsien was a gabble of voices from the outer office. Manyface was talking in tongues again—at least four of his personalities contrib-

73

uting their share to the dialogue. He was also being followed by a group of citizens, some young, some old; some students, one or two obviously senior executives of one kind or another. What they had in common, Castor realized, was that every one of them seemed to want something from Manyface. Manyface was not merely a curious physiological preparation. He was indeed a high party cadre. And thus, Castor perceived, able to grant boons or withhold them.

Castor moved out of the way as the whole procession entered Fung Bohsien's office. He was studying the old man, for in addition to checking out the disappointing news from space, he had spent his waiting time at Manyface's screen in looking up the physiology of Manyface.

The brain is in some ways the most delicate of the body's organs and in some ways the sturdiest. What anatomists call "the blood-brain barrier" is a mighty shield against the outlaw cells and organisms that circulate through the rest of the body. Cancer of the brain rarely metastasizes to the torso. Cancer of any other part rarely invades the brain. Immunologically speaking, the brain is exempted from most of the body's threats. Of all the secret corners of the human frame, it may be the very least likely to reject an implant.

And yet what a wonder it was that Manyface's huge buff-watermelon head should hold eleven minds! It became obvious to Castor that each of the occupants of Manyface's head had his own personal identity—or hers; that sometimes one did the speaking, sometimes another, depending on the subject on which they were addressed. Or depending on the consensual will of the majority within Fung's head. Or depending on which shouted loudest.

When the clients and hangers-on had been sent away, Manyface sat down at his desk and, for a moment, examined Castor silently. Castor prepared himself for the babble of competing voices that he had heard before. Surprisingly, when Manyface spoke it was with only one voice—the one Castor supposed to be his own. "So, Pettyman Castor," he said, "do you want the job?"

"To be your houseboy? Cook your meals, clean your house? I do not know if I can do that well. I have no training in these skills, apart from my compulsory help-out duties as a teen-ager."

Manyface's mouth spoke, but this time with a different accent. "He means yes," it said. "Get it over with. Let's get out of here."

"We will get out of here," Manyface told himself solemnly, "when we have finished. Pettyman Castor! Do you want to enter the university?"

"Oh, do I!"

"That means yes, too," said the second voice disagreeably, and Manyface's own overrode it again:

"Do you know what courses you want to take?"

"Not really," Castor confessed. "I mean, after all, the semester has been running for weeks now. I'm not sure which ones will still admit me—"

Manyface looked surprised with all his faces. "Admit you?" he said uncertainly, as though testing whether the words had any meaning in that context. "Of course they'll admit you!" He gestured at the screen. "Display the curriculum lists," he ordered. "Pick what you want, and I will put my chop on your application—no, no more discussion, boy! Do it. Then go to my house and make dinner. It has been too long since I have had a home-cooked meal! And I want something special tonight—let me see, I think some fried fish—*no, not fish, too much oil in the water*—STEAK, PLEASE—*no, shrimp*—*no, damn it, remember the oil*—Oh, hell," shouted Manyface furiously, over the noise of his own skullmates, "cook anything you can! But do it well and serve it hot! Now get on with it!"

So Castor prepared for himself a dream menu of all the hands-on and advanced courses his village screens had been unable to supply. He munched his way through the various classes with delight—astrogation, solar ballistics, space medicine—everywhere he was welcome, and the instructors unfailingly made sure he caught up quickly with the classes. Castor was awed. To him the concept of "high party official" had been one of those abstractions that you knew people thought about. But he had never before seen the power one such (or, in Manyface's case, perhaps several such) could display.

And Manyface's status was very high indeed. He was a powerful figure even at Home, when he chose to visit the old Han cities of Beijing or Guangzhou. In the Chinese society of North America, where Home was only an ideal, he was at least first among equals.

After the first day of school, Castor was addicted. He decided that no price was too high to pay for these joys! After his first full day as Manyface's houseboy, however, he began to think that some prices were at least extravagant. For one thing, he had not expected that he would be required to sleep at Manyface's house. That was not bad. The room given him was large, comfortable, even luxurious. All it lacked was the presence of Tsoong Delilah. Castor had rapidly become accustomed to that most appreciative of bedmates, was jolted to find his sleeping arrangements had been altered without consulting him, was startled to learn (from Manyface's secretary) that the change was at Inspector Tsoong Delilah's own request. It had to be some sort of feminine tact, he decided. No doubt she was giving him the opportunity to find some younger woman to relate to among the female students at the university. No matter. That he would straighten out when the time was ripe—when the question arose—when his glands recovered from their exercise in her busy bed.

There was also the question of Manyface himself. Or themself.

It was not that any one portion of Manyface's collective personality was unduly abrasive—well, not *intolerably* so, anyway. It was just that they were eleven individuals. With eleven different sets of habits and preferences and interests and dislikes. Usually it was Professor Fung who did the talking, as "chairman" of the committee that lived inside his skull. But that was only custom when there was no serious competition; what Manyface's secretary had told Castor was true. There was no "real" Manyface. When one of the others had some special interest in talking to Castor—when, one might say, the chair of some subcommittee needed to discuss a matter of particular interest—the other voices gave it freedom to speak. Sometimes for minutes on end. "It's quite difficult, yes," said Potter Alicia, through lips of the old man. "But we rub along somehow together. We have no choice, after all. Hsang is always complaining that we never play golf. Shum gives us the most trouble, I think—I do not!—oh, be still, Shum. I'm not criticizing you, I'm only saying that you have very strong sexual drives. There's not much we can do for either Hsang or Shum, actually. Shum least of all—not counting that the idea of physical intimacy with a woman quite disgusts me—" A warning grimace of the lips as Shum gathered himself to rebut made her change the subject—"anyway, we do the best we can to humor each other. It makes for peace inside the skull. Tell me, are you going to see my daughter soon?"

Castor cleared his throat. "I'm really very busy here," he temporized. He had said, or as much as said, that he and her daughter were divorced. If his putative mother-in-law had trouble remembering that, it was certainly not his business to remind her. It was a good time to change the subject. "As to dinner," he said, "I think we're all agreed on chicken, is that right? And with it rice?"

"**Rice with onions, correct**—*no, plain*—WHAT RICE? PILAF!—*plain rice*—I think," said Potter Alicia's thoughtful, ladylike voice, "that you should cook what you like, dear Castor, and we'll eat it anyway."

It was all a dream for Castor. Acceptance to the university! No need ever to go back to rot in the damned rice paddies! A skilled new mistress—temporarily unavailable, yes, but sure to be restored to him before long. It even occurred to him now and then to miss his wife. (But she had left him, after all. There was no need to feel guilt, and thus no obligation to miss her.)

And most delightful of all was the chance to look out into space through his new classes—not as a stubborn student at the end of a computer tie line on a collective farm, but as a regular member, indeed a privileged member, of the academic community.

And there was news. His astrogation class was full of it. First, the Party had ordered a speedup in the desultory space program. The instructor was as thrilled as Castor to be able to tell the class the news. He displayed the dozen or so rockets that had been designed long since, some of them even built; but there had been no muscle behind the program. Now the tempo was picking up. Why? asked the class, and the instructor gave them an opaque look. "It is the wisdom of the Party cadres that must answer such questions," he said. "At certain times it is necessary to wait and regroup, at others to move ahead."

And now was a time to move ahead.

Castor said boldly, "Has this anything to do with the new spaceship that has been discovered?"

The instructor hesitated, looked around the class for support, finally dared a "Perhaps."

"And have any of the messages from the spaceship been translated?"

To that not even a perhaps; the instructor took refuge in indignation. "Pettyman Castor! If such information were available, do you not know that the high Party officials would let us know at once? Think rightly, Pettyman Castor!"

But he had not said the message had not been translated. Nor did he pretend that the spacecraft was some burned-out hulk left over from either the Russians or the Americans.

That night in his room at Manyface's house he slaved the screen in his room to Manyface's own and systematically searched the files for further information on the spacecraft. There was none. So there was a secret, that was clear; but he was not going to find out what that secret was. And that, too, was clear.

As, bored, he snapped the screen off it suddenly blinked into his attention signal: Someone was calling him. When he opened the circuit he discovered it was Manyface's secretary. Her expression was frosty. "Orders," she said. "You are to report to her apartment for duty."

Though Castor knew it was not decorous, he couldn't help himself. He laughed out loud. "Duty, she said? Oh, to be sure! I know that duty well."

But the secretary was not sharing the joke. "You would

be well advised," she said seriously, "to take an order from a Renmin police inspector seriously."

"I will," he promised, suppressing the smile. Then, as he thought things over, he wondered just why the Renmin police inspector passed on her orders in just that way. Puzzlement became irritation. He waited until he was sure she would be home. Then, when Manyface was well asleep, Castor stole out of the house, hailed a taxi, and in ten minutes was in front of the building that contained Tsoong Delilah's apartment. He was smiling as he entered the elevator. He had calculated that the light traffic of late night would make the trip trivially brief. So it had. Ten minutes cab ride each way. Say sixty minutes in bed— no, better allow ninety—why, he could be back in time for a good five hours' sleep before getting up to start the rice steaming for Professor Fung's breakfast.

But when he knocked on the door the errand was not what he expected, and in fact it was not Delilah who answered the door. It opened no more than halfway, to show a tall Han Chinese youth, Castor's age or nearly. The young man gave him a hard-eyed look. "You are the peasant Pettyman Castor?" he demanded.

Castor didn't pay him the compliment of admitting it. "And who are you, then?" he demanded cuttingly.

"I am the son of your lover," said the youth. "I have orders for you. This urn here by the door contains the ashes of the murderer Feng. These are to be returned to his collective. It is my mother's order that you take them there tomorrow morning."

VIII

When the bus stopped at the Heavenly Grain Village Collective, Castor got off grandly. The conqueror of the city returns to the humble place of his childhood. Only the humble place did not seem to care. Though Castor was ready to smile and to grasp the hands of his old neighbors just as warmly as though he were still no better than they, no old neighbors were there. No adults at all were in sight. The only person around was little Pettyman Benjy, the five-year-old son of Castor's cousin Pettyman Pendrake. The boy was sucking his thumb in the doorway of the village school—thrown out again for wetting his pants in class, no doubt.

Castor had no time to seek more of an audience. "Citizen!" remonstrated the bus driver. "I have a schedule to keep. Which bag is yours?"

The injury to his vanity was only grazing. Castor shrugged, picked up the boxed urn, dangled his overnight shoulderbag from the other hand, and went into the assistant director's office. There his reception committee was waiting for him: Fat Rhoda, with more than the usual bundle of complaints to deliver, starting with, "Your bus was late!"

But at least it turned out that Fat Rhoda had really missed him. Well, that was not quite true. She had not missed Castor in particular, but she certainly was deeply aggrieved that her production team had been left a worker short. When she had finished reproaching him for the fact that their plan had, therefore, not been more than 83 percent completed in the past week, she gazed down at the screen on her desk and punched out orders for the plot of available housing. "What a nuisance," she grumbled, eyeing the plot on the screen. "I suppose you want a bed? And a meal tonight, no doubt? Although, since you're not on the ration strength anymore, everyone will suffer?"

Well, that was nonsense. To serve one more meal out of three hundred would certainly cause no suffering for anyone. At most, it would mean only a little less scraped into the cans to feed the tilapia. Castor did not dignify the statement with a reply, nor the next proposal—which was that he share a bed with one of the children that night. "Your own apartment—your *former* apartment—" she said with pleasure, "is of course being repainted for the next tenant."

"Of course," said Castor, wondering how she could lie so. Fat Rhoda had never charged a can of paint against her team's profit and loss in her life. "Keep your food," he said cuttingly. "Keep your pissed-in bed, too. Let me only charge out a bike, and I will go to River of Pearl and stay there tonight."

Fat Rhoda stared at him resentfully. "There's no need to take that tone," she said. "Still—well, yes, I suppose there's a bike in the transportation pool..."

There was also at least one human face glad to see Castor again and happy to talk over the small talk of the commune since he left. No, said Pettyman Jim, nothing had been heard of Maria. Yes, they still had the blackouts. Something to do with the radio-telescope, wasn't it? No, there wasn't any reason he couldn't take any bike he liked—only, see, Castor, he said apologetically, since

Castor wasn't on the ration strength anymore, he'd have to pay tourist rates for the rental...

Castor had not expected the hole left by his departure from the commune would heal so seamlessly and fast.

It was dark when he reached the River of Pearl. Bawling cattle and snorting, snuffling pigs filled his ears—nose, too. Since he had phoned ahead, at least this time someone was waiting for him.

The waiting person was a girl, slim, dark, short. She wore blouse and shorts, but fashion was not a motive. The blouse was khaki and stained—with, Castor supposed, pig slop. The shorts were no better. As she moved into the light to greet him he saw her face and realized he had seen it before.

It was the face he had seen in photo exhibits at the inquest. It was the same face on the same head—though a more gracile version of it—that he had kicked against in the rice paddy, to start all his troubles. And triumphs. "I'm Feng Miranda," said the face, unsmiling, even unwelcoming. "Thank you for bringing Grandfather's ashes home. No, no. Don't hand them to me now. A memorial service has been arranged and the people are waiting, so come along."

As they walked into the lighted catwalk to the community center, Castor found that Feng Miranda had every reason to look like the murdered youth. She was his sister. Twin sister, and she shared more than genes. "He died a hero," she said matter-of-factly. "Who, my grandfather? Of course not! My brother was as dedicated to freeing America from the yoke of the oppressor as I. A martyr to America." Gee! Castor moved half a step farther away from her and let her guide him into the hall.

The point of not taking the old man's ashes from him at the bus, Castor discovered, was that they were to be handed over at a ceremonial, when appropriate remarks would be delivered. Why not? It would be interesting to see how these peasants conducted funerals; Tsoong Delilah would be amused, perhaps. But the ceremony was a surprise. It was a one-woman performance, and what she said in the hall was worse than she had said outside. She stood there before the gathering of forty or fifty villagers, mostly elderly, and let Castor hand the unboxed urn to her. She did not treat it reverently. She glanced casually at the nameplate to see no impostor was receiving her grandfather's funeral oration, then put the ashes down on a table—a kitchen table, Castor saw, though at least someone had troubled to cover it with a red cloth that drooped to the floor on both sides. She kissed the urn absentmindedly, as though she were brushing itching lips against some handy surface while her hands were full, and turned to the audience:

"This old man, Feng Hsumu, was my grandfather, who killed my brother. Feng Hsumu was a good father to our father and I mourn him for that, but he was a murderer to my brother—only because my brother wanted the Han Chinese to leave America and let it be free again."

Castor sidled off the platform, shocked a little, more sorry for the girl. She did not seem to have a good grasp of reality. Although the Chinese had preserved the forms of the old People's Republic, they were most of all just Chinese. America's lack of "freedom" interested them very little. The Han Chinese didn't look on themselves as occupiers of America (or of Eastern Siberia or Japan or Indochina or Australia, or all the other non-Chinese places they dominated). China—"Home"—was the China of the emperors. It included most of Indochina, part of

Korea, and part of Siberia; that was their China, and they simply did not think of arguing the point. The rest of the areas under their control were foreign lands.

She was still speaking, and Castor glanced around the room. Surprisingly, no one seemed to take offense. No one seemed to agree, either; even the young faces seemed placid as the cattle they tended.

She was reciting ancient history now. Much of it was true. When the nuclear war was over there were a couple of hundred million Chinese still alive, and a couple of hundred million Indians. They inherited the world. There wasn't anybody else still around big enough to challenge them. So they chopped up the world—Western Europe and the Near East for India, most of the rest for China. Nobody was in any position to challenge them effectively. Nobody even tried. The big power centers didn't have anything left to try with, not even much population.

But what this woman didn't seem to realize, Castor thought, was that the Chinese weren't *conquerors*. Han China never tried to conquer anything outside of Han China. Han China didn't want to add non-Han races to its empire. Han China was willing to *own* whatever was valuable in the demolished lands—but they didn't want the people in those areas to be Chinese; and the Chinese born and raised in those areas certainly didn't regard themselves as natives, either.

Except for the oddballs like Feng Miranda.

It did not do one good to be too close to oddballs, and so while Miranda was still speaking, Castor edged, slowly and as though abstracted, to the back of the room, where the River of Pearl director was standing, as impassive as the rest. "Sir?" whispered Castor, meaning to ask if the man saw anything strange in the funeral oration. But when the director's eyes met his, Castor changed his question. "Sir," he said, "have you found me a bed for the night?"

The director's expression remained placid. "Of course, Pettyman Castor. I think the Renmin policewoman intends to have you share hers." He nodded toward the side of the hall—and there, in a seat in the last row, inconspicuous apart from her sardonic expression, was Tsoong Delilah.

He did not ask her what she was doing in the cattle collective. She did not volunteer, only took him by the hand and led him firmly toward the guesthouse. He suspected that he knew the answer anyway. He suspected that the Renmin police kept hotbeds of insanity like this under surveillance—that was logic—and maybe that Delilah had arranged for her to do that and for him to be ordered to bring up the old man's ashes, for obvious purposes. Perhaps because she did not want to invite him to her own bed while her son was there. (That was vanity, but at least that part was right enough.)

When they reached the guesthouse and the door on the crude, small room was closed, he stammered, "Will you arrest her?"

She laughed. "Don't be foolish," she said, hanging up her civilian trousers and pulling a nightgown out of her bag. "We watch these silly kids, but we don't make any arrests—unless some wiser person murders one of them. Come to bed."

TSOONG
DELILAH

not only astonished herself but displeased herself very much. It was degrading to the dignity of an inspector of Renmin police to allow herself to be sexually attracted to a man younger than her own son! And a Yankee at that!

Even in her self-criticism, the term she was careful to use to herself was "sexually attracted." Not even in those morning periods of reproach, while she squatted over the toilet and balefully gazed into her own hostile eyes in the mirror on the bathroom door, did she admit the term "love." Such a word was simply out of the question.

Delilah, she reminded herself, was a woman with a fine career and considerable power. They were what her life was organized around, not "love." If Castor ever interfered with either (she told herself) she would discard him instantly. More than that. *Kill* him, if necessary. She knew that that was true; and, therefore, the word "love" was wholly inapplicable. All she cared about, really, was his strong, lean, lanky body that covered hers from toes to temples and made the entire inside of her torso tingle and convulse when he entered her. Sexual power, of course. Love? Not in the least!

So when, next morning, Castor dared to ask her, grinning, "Is that why you had me bring the ashes up here? So we could get it on, even though your son's home now?"—Delilah responded, quietly and firmly,

"My son's presence is an inconvenience, yes. So I preferred that we meet here, yes. Do not attach any special importance to those facts."

"Oh, very well," he said, still grinning. The words were satisfactory if the grin was not, so Delilah elected only to notice the words. He went on: "I suppose I'd better get the bike back to Heavenly Grain—"

"The peasants can pick it up themselves, Castor."

"Well, I suppose so, but then I've got to get the bus back to New Orleans, and it doesn't stop here."

"Bus!" she scoffed. "How foolish it would be for you to take the bus when I must drive the same route today! Almost the same route," she qualified. "I must stop at the observatory to pick up some material—but you won't mind that?"

"Oh, no," Castor said, obviously pleased; and that annoyed Delilah. Why was she trying to please this boy? Why ask him what he minded? Why, for that matter, offer him the car ride when the bus was available? "Get in the car," she ordered and was silent until she turned off on the sea road that passed the observatory. The thoughts she was thinking were dark. It was true that one tried to be considerate to one's lovers, but all the same—

All the same, simple "sexual attraction" was running thin as an explanation. At the observatory she braked peremptorily. "You will wait here, Castor. It will be best to stay in the car. If I need you to help carry anything I will call you."

"Right, Delilah," he said cheerfully, looking around the parking lot. It was the first time he had been inside the observatory's perimeter fence, Delilah knew. That no doubt accounted for his happiness, but what accounted for the light way he addressed her? "Delilah," forsooth! It was all very well to call her so in bed, where one could not reasonably demand "Renmin Inspector Tsoong," but here the guards were watching and listening. No. It was impudence, or very nearly. As she presented her ID to the guards, Delilah thought that the boy needed a lesson.

"You may enter, Inspector Tsoong," said the NCO of the guards. She nodded and passed through the heavy doors. She sat in an anteroom and waited for the director of the observatory to bring her what she had come all this way to receive. That cassette would be very important. But in her thoughts it was taking second place.

Delilah was thinking about her lovers. In the eight years since her elderly husband had gone Home to die, she had had—how many? One a week?—several hundred bed companions, at least. They had been of varying ages, and all available ethnicities. They had each one been different from the others, too. Some had been nasty or inept or— worst of all—seeking mastery over her. Quickly gone, all of those! Not one had ever taken her as lightly as Pettyman Castor. That was annoying. It could not be overlooked, because it might cause a scandal. It was also unworthy of her position and, of course, wholly inappropriate to the gravity of her errand here at the observatory.

The boy was going too far, she decided sternly. He should be corrected, she thought, and wondered if the sun was going to be too hot for him out there in the car.

Then she found out what it was that the director of the observatory was bringing her.

Castor did not mind being left to loaf in the sun. After all, he was inside the grounds of the observatory, where for so long he had so longed to be. Where he had, almost, a right to be, he thought with a sudden thrill of joyful realization and pulled out his university student ID. He showed it to the guards and wheedled nicely in the high tongue. "As I am a student of space science," he pleaded, "I have a natural right to be received at space installations."

The guards looked at each other, then the NCO grinned. "Not inside the building, Yankee student," he instructed. "However, you may walk around the parking lot if you wish."

"That's fine," cried Castor, beaming. He construed "parking lot" to mean the planted area that surrounded it—everything up to the chain link fence that cut off the nearest of the great pale radio-telescope dishes. Altogether well over a hectare. Plenty to explore! He made a beeline for the marching line of RT dishes, almost pressing his nose against the fence. How huge and handsome the telescope was! He could see the parabolic shell that caught the radio waves, the little helium-cooled nut in the middle that trapped them and converted them into signals that could be read. It was magnificent!

Then he returned to the observatory building itself,

skulking along its walls, peering into windows. Most were disappointing because blocked—instruments, drapes, stored cartons, whatever. But now and then a glimpse of a shadowy room, even of a couple of Han observatory workers running up data on a bank of screens. Some day, he promised himself, he would be in one of those rooms! They would have to let him in if he completed the university courses—into the observatory, at least. Into the actual space program—if ever there really was an actual space program again—well, not so likely. It was true that the all-China space authorities seemed to be picking up a little speed under the spur of the unknown spacecraft, but if ever there were manned crews again, the Sinonauts would not be Yankee Americans. They would be Sino...

"Castor! Pettyman Castor!"

The voice was Delilah's, but the tone was one he had never heard from her before. Castor turned quickly. He was astonished that Delilah had come back out so soon. Not only soon, but rapidly; she was hurrying, almost trotting, to the car. Not only hurrying, but carrying a flat black metal box. And, in spite of what she had said, she did not let Castor carry it. When the boy reached for it she jerked it furiously out of his hand. "In the car, Pettyman," she snapped. "Move! We must get back to New Orleans at once!"

At once meant at once—not merely quickly, but as near to instantaneously as the car could be made to move. Speed was her only concern. Safety did not seem to matter at all. All the way down the coastal highway she drove at top speed, the blinking Renmin lights atop the car ordering people out of the way, the wheee-*wheep* of the siren commanding compliance.

All the way back, Delilah did not speak a word.

When they got into the heart of the old city Delilah slowed. Not much. Just enough to let civilians scurry out of her path. She spoke briefly into the car radio, and in a minute two other Renmin police vehicles appeared, leading the way for their inspector. But the way was not to her own apartment building. Castor was astonished to see her take the turnings that would bring her to Manyface's home and even more astonished when they reached the block the house was on. It was filled with cars. The curbs were crammed with limousines with official license plates—and with other vehicles so big and new that they didn't need to display official plates to show that they belonged to people of power. Half the power of New Orleans seemed to have parked its cars outside Manyface's home that night. Police. Renmin officials. University leaders.

"What is going on?" he demanded, staring around.

"It should not tax your intelligence, student, to deduce that for yourself," Delilah said as she pulled in to park. But though the words were her hard-edged standard, the tone was not. Castor was astonished to see that she looked upset. No, it had not taxed his intelligence to figure out that something worrisome had come in that box from the observatory; nor to realize, from the assemblage of cars, that the high party official Fung Bohsien was entertaining a leadership and cadre group summoned to discuss it. All that had been quite obvious all along. But to see that Delilah's face was drawn and her lip was being nibbled by her teeth—Tsoong Delilah, the tough-minded police inspector!—that was a surprise!

And she went on surprising him. Castor started to get out of the car. Before he had his feet on the ground he heard the door on her side slam. Before he had closed his door behind him, she was already up the steps of the walk, thumping impatiently on the knocker of Manyface's door. The box was clutched firmly under an arm, and as Castor hurried to catch up with her she gave him a frosty glare. "You will go to your room," she ordered. "There is to be a private meeting, which you may not attend. Do you understand?"

He said, "Yes, Delilah, I understand quite well. Delilah? As I am not inside to answer the door and Manyface never does, there is no use standing here. Push it open and we'll go inside."

It was a petty victory. There was no joy in it, either, because Delilah had not responded with that faint pulse of indignation that greeted most of his jokes at her expense. She was past that point, Castor realized. Which meant that whatever it was that had upset her, it was not likely to be trivial.

Castor followed instructions at least up to a point. He did go to his room. There he turned on his screen, hunted for news of something from space, found none. When he interrogated the data files they informed him only that electromagnetic emissions had been detected. What the emissions were was not stated—they could have been radar, they could have been automatic IFF pulses, or leakage from some telemetering systems—or a message. The news channels said no more. Even the interactive ones, where it was possible to search for key terms in the headlines and then to summon up uncut reports on any aspect of the story—even they had nothing to say that clarified Castor's mind. He left the screen set to continue the search, sat on the edge of his bed, gazed out the window at the chimney-pot skyline of the French Quarter, and pondered.

The Han Chinese did not bother to keep secrets, as a general rule.

If there was a secret, it had to be in some way political.

What could be political about a spacecraft in orbit?

Castor stepped to the door of his room and opened it. Manyface's house was nearly two hundred years old, built on the lavish scale of Louisiana gentry at the beginning of the twentieth century; the corridors were wide, the stairway broad, the ceilings high. Unfortunately the doors were also solid. Castor could hear a confusion of voices from the drawing room where Manyface and his guests were discussing—whatever it was they were discussing. But to pick out any individual words at this distance was hopeless. He drew back into his room as a pair of grim-faced young men, later arrivals to the meeting, pushed in the front door and entered the sitting room.

If he was to go down the stairs and listen at the door, he realized, some other latecomer might catch him at it.

Well, why not? What harm could that do? He lived in the house; it was his right to move about it!

Having convinced himself, he slipped silently down the stairs and pressed close to the regrettably thick door. It wasn't soundproof, quite. Voices came through. They were all talking in the high tongue, which was not a problem; the problem was that they seemed all to be talking at once. Most of the voices were strangers to him, but he recognized Manyface's treble and Delilah's deferential, but agitated, contralto.

He could not make out a single word of what they said. He pressed his ear to the crack—and heard, a moment too late, the opening of the unlocked front door. He straightened up quickly, but not quickly enough to avoid criticism. "Yankee!" shrilled a female voice—it belonged to a wrinkled old woman in Home blue. "What are you doing there? Go away at once!"

Castor gave her a sulky look. He tarried long enough to show her that, if he was going, it was because he had decided to go, not because he was ordered. All the same, he did as he was ordered. He complied with the letter of the order. He went away; but not to his own room.

His curiosity had become too great an itch to remain unscratched. He glanced back at the closed door, then stole into Manyface's private study.

What Manyface had that Castor did not was a hundred-channel receptor. Even slaved to it, Castor's satellite screen did not have the range of options that of Manyface possessed. He closed the door of the study behind him and made a systematic search for further news.

There was none. Not on the local channels. Not on the ethnics for the few Amerindians or Mexicans. Not on the ionosphere-relay channels from Home. Not anywhere on any of the scores of stations that Han China broadcast on, for any purpose.

Of course, he told himself irritably, that only meant that it was more interesting! If the news of whatever it was that the highest officials in New Orleans were huddling over was kept from the public, then it must be tremendous news indeed. Frowning, Castor reached to turn the screen off—

Then he thought of something. Han China could control every one of its broadcasts absolutely; but there were parts of the Earth where China's writ did not run.

Even on Manyface's hundred-channel screen, getting one of the Indian channels was hard. Their satellites were weakly powered and their antennae often savagely out of line. When the image came in it was grainy, and the indexing capricious—Castor had to try more than a dozen times to get the story he wanted.

But the story was there.

When at last the index retrieved the proper clip, Castor saw an Indian youth, pomaded hair and dhobi, wearing the sneery kind of smirk that the Indian propagandists always wore when they thought they had something discreditable to say about China. Behind the speaker was a patched-in space shot. Although it was breaking up in the poor transmission from the Indian satellite, Castor recognized the scene. It was the unidentified spaceship. The image was poor, indicating that the picture had been either taken through inferior Indian telescopes or stolen by one of their spies from Chinese sources.

It was what the man was saying that riveted Castor. "The People's Republic of China," he sneered, large lips wrapping themselves around each word before they spat it out, "is once again concealing the truth from its people." Since the satellite was time-locked to the western hemisphere, the announcer was speaking in English—almost accent-free, Castor noticed. "That a message has been received by the Chinese is undeniable, though they have made no announcement of it. We now present you the text of this message—in English, just as you hear it now."

There was a pause, while the sneery face pursed its lips to listen. Then came a recorded voice. "Attention!" it said, tone deep, hoarse, whispery.

There was a pause. The pause filled itself with pictures on the backdrop—a woman in what seemed to be military uniform; another woman, nearly naked, with what looked like a kind of stuffed animal doll on her shoulder, standing next to a sort of great bat or small dragon; a great city, glassy towers all the colors of light, with some of the same creatures wheeling above it.

Then the voice again: "We have a demonstration to offer you, since you doubt our powers."

The sneery face of the Indian announcer nodded and pursed its lips to listen.

"Choose an island," said the other voice. "We will show you our capabilities by annihilating all life on it. Then you will understand that we are serious and that the Chinese invaders must return to their own country. But we will discuss this with only one person, the president of the United States."

The pictures faded. The voice stopped. The Indian announcer was smiling disdainfully. "The 'president of the United States,'" he repeated. "As though there were any such person! No wonder the Chinese warlords have concealed this message! It will be fascinating to watch them wriggle as they attempt to deal with this challenge to their evil hegemony!"

An hour later Castor heard the sounds of the meeting below breaking up. He raced downstairs in time to catch Manyface in sober conversation with Tsoong Delilah. The other great leaders had gone. Castor dared demand, "Is it true, what the Indian satellite broadcast says?"

Tsoong Delilah gave him a look of compassion and fatigue. "It is, Castor."

"And there is a spacecraft that wants the Chinese to leave America?"

"So it seems," she said heavily.

"And they have the power to destroy life on Earth somehow?"

She did not answer. Neither did Manyface. And for Castor that was answer enough.

II

Once the news had been broadcast on the Indian satellite stations, there was no longer any use trying to keep it secret. It was electrifying news. The surge of its power flashed all over the Renmin. Sparks flew in command posts along the Indian border, haloes flickered over the Central Committee, arcs flared about the great Space Center on the island of Hainan. First the high councils knew. Then the middle-level civilians with access to Indian TV.

Then everyone.

The outpost centers in New Orleans and Sydney and Acapulco and everywhere else were sizzling with the electricity of the message from space, and so were all the anthill cities of Han China itself.

When Indian satellite TV broke the story, the leadership was already in session in the Great Hall of the People off Tienanmen Square, though it was nearly four in the morning in Beijing. They received the word at once. "Hindu pigs!" snarled the commissioner for culture, fox-faced and long-haired, descendant of a hundred generations of Kwangsi peasants—and five generations of high party cadres. No one listened to him. What did culture have to do with a threat from space?

Threat it was. Dire. Dangerous. Wholly unexpected and unprovided for, for who could have guessed that that comic and extinct monster the "United States of America" might have spacefaring allies after all these years?—and armed and belligerent ones! Dangerous, unexpected, and sickeningly unfair, too, for what "invasion" had China committed? China had never attacked the U.S.A.! The U.S.A. and the U.S.S.R. had committed a messy and mutual suicide, and China had simply spilled over into the hole they left.

The meetings of the high leadership were formal—ritualistic, in fact, as elaborate as a consistory of cardinals. Each cadre had his own page, secretary, and bodyguard, and the debate was usually stately.

But then the debates had always had time to be stately, calculated to the long time spans of ancient China itself. Now there was no time. There was an ultimatum: "Do they mean it?" "Of *course*, they mean it, pig's dung!" "But can they *do* it?" "Who can tell?—" There were fears: "If they take America, what next?" "If there is a next, then maybe China itself?—" There were greedy notions born of fear: "But if they *are* so powerful, and if we *can* make terms with them, then vis-à-vis the Indians we can wipe them out! If we wish, of course."

So the Highest Councils met and tried to plan and told each other it was *unfair* . . . and decided at last what every such nation and person must decide, which was that fairness had nothing to do with it. They didn't decide that easily. They needed help. The mule moves along when you tell him to, but you first have to lay the club across his nose to get his attention; what got their attention was the missile that streaked in out of space across the Sahara and the Indian Ocean and Indochina and the Philippines, and exploded fifteen hundred meters over a Western Pacific Island named Shihiki, just north of Truk. It wasn't a very big island. It wasn't even inhabited, really—not

99

by Han Chinese, at least. But everything on the island died at once.

And after that the Highest Councils were unanimous in their resolve. The trouble was that they couldn't find anything very promising to resolve to do.

When Tsoong Delilah deigned to visit Renmin Police Headquarters these days, even the commissioners leaped to open the doors in her way. She didn't do it often; she had too much to do to waste time with routine police matters, and everyone in the Renmin administration knew it. Promotion? She could have had any promotion in the commissioners' power by the snap of her fingers; she was above promotion, she was an insider in the Highest Circles.

That was all an accident, pretty much. Because Delilah had been the one whom chance (and a little help from her glands) directed to bring to New Orleans the tapes that were too secret to transmit, she was present at that first emergency meeting of the New Orleans Renmin. Because she was there then, she was the logical choice to be assigned to the committee permanently. Why should the committee need a permanent policeone? Because anything might happen! Nearly eight million Yanks were still alive in what used to be called the Lower Forty-Eight, and who knew what craziness some of them might get into? Even serious and dangerous craziness, if they were not watched. They seemed placid, true. Placid people, all the same, sometimes blew up for no good reason at all— look at the Cultural Revolution. Quiet subject races went insane with religion or patriotism or tribal loyalties—look at old Iran or Ireland or South Africa. The most prosperous and peaceful state could be ruined by riots and bloodshed—look at everywhere. No. The police had to be ready at an instant's need. A police liaison had to be there always.

So Delilah sat silent at the back of the New Orleans People's Hall, listening to the debates and diatribes.

It was as bad, almost, as the first meetings of the Highest Councils in Beijing—in fact, there were a lot of Beijing all-highests there in New Orleans, for the leadership had split off a chunk from itself to send to America. They could not conduct secret meetings by satellite—the alien spacecraft would be listening. And New Orleans was where the action was; it was the United States that was the problem, and the United States was the best place to look for an answer.

No one had any idea what that answer might be, of course.

Castor was allowed into the meetings, too, as the page of the high party member Manyface; from her seat at the back of the room Delilah could see him, sitting at Manyface's knee, his eyes turning from speaker to speaker. Half the remarks were addressed to her: "Increase surveillance!" "Certainly, Cadre Hsu; I will notify Renmin headquarters at once." "Arrest known 'patriots' like that Feng Miranda." "With all respect, Comrade Fiscal Director, I advise against it. It suggests we are afraid the masses will follow them. At need we can conduct many arrests very quickly. We know who they all are." She was extraordinarily busy, Delilah was, and formidably competent; but all the same those qualities did not, when she caught sight of Castor on his low stool, prevent her knees from moving an inch or two apart. They moved wider than that, of course, when she could find an hour or two to be alone with him. What a pity that he wanted to spend so many of their scarce hours together talking! And what mad ideas he had of what constituted pillow talk! "Will the spaceship really attack China?" he would breathe in her ear, just as her ear was softening for some sweeter breath; and she would push herself erect and tell him not to be a fool. No one would dare attack Han China! And a precious quarter of an hour would be lost while they settled that question and went back to what was important.

To what was important, at least, to her.

What was important to Pettyman Castor was not at all the same. Oh, certainly he enjoyed the use of her body! But certainly he had other things on his mind as well. For a time Delilah had the worrisome suspicion that Castor was secretly praying for a great victory for the alien spaceship—real freedom for "America," laughable as that notion was. But that fear dwindled and disappeared. Castor was not political at all. The idea of a rescue mission to liberate America from the Han struck him as bizarre enough to be fascinating, but he did not take sides—go it husband, go it bear; the quarrel was interesting to him to contemplate, but he was not interested in who won.

What interested him—no, what excited him far more than freedom for America or the soft, sweet recesses of Delilah's body—was space. The idea of actual human beings in orbit excited him. The possibility that something important might happen in space excited him. The vagrant, hopeless hope that somehow, some day, he himself might have a chance to climb out there into the void beyond the air excited him most of all.

And they all, Delilah reflected, stung, excited him much more than she did.

He did not in the least appreciate that the hours she spent in his bed carried a heavy price tag for her. She had to steal that time. She had a son at home now, and a son who did not in the least approve of liaisons with arrogant Yankee peasants who did not know their place. When at last Delilah got to her own home each night, young Tsoong Arnold was always waiting up for her, almost sniffing at her for the stink of sex that would confirm what he already was sure she had been doing with Pettyman Castor. He was his father's son, was Tsoong Arnold. The old man had also been puritanical and righteous, though Delilah had given him no cause for jealousy—well, not much, anyway, and not very often.

What was most annoying to Delilah was that the boy did not ever charge her with what, in fact, she was doing. He only engaged her in conversation—at midnight and later, when what she desperately wanted was sleep.

Sometimes the conversations were of some importance, for indeed there were questions to settle. Questions, for instance, of Arnold's future. He had been discharged from his compulsory service in the Militia only a week before coming home. It was not the best time to be discharged, he told her, because for the first time there might be a reason to prolong his service. He was fidgeting around with the notion of reenlisting—quickly—while he could still keep his rank and assignments. So, "What do you think, Delilah?" he would demand. "Will there be trouble with the Yankees?"

"Not a chance, son"—wishing he would go to sleep—or reenlist—or miraculously drop sixteen years off his age so she could pack him off to nursery school again.

"But there might be! There might be pacification missions. There might be fighting! Chasing aboriginals into their mountain fastnesses, capturing their leaders, bringing criminal outlaws to justice—"

"There are no mountains to speak of in Louisiana province," his mother reminded him, yawning longingly.

He set his jaw. His fingers were working, as though curling around the butt of a gun. "What is the Council going to do about the ultimatum?"

"They will send the American president to meet them in space, of course," his mother said with a flash of humor as she slipped out of her polished boots.

Her son had no sense of humor. "President? What president? There is no American president," he said, and his mother said,

"Then we will have to invent one. Go to bed."

She did, too. But she remained upright on the edge of the bed, staring into space, for some time.

There was one good thing to ease the scary tension, and that was the law of orbital ballistics. The alien ship had first been spotted on the far side of the Sun, many millions of miles away. It took time for it to approach the Earth. Between the first messages and the ultimatum it actually passed behind the Sun. When the ultimatum was delivered, it was spiraling in. It continued to transmit, but it did not, could not, expect the "conquerors" to deliver the actual, physical body of the president of the United States until it came much, much, closer.

So there was time. Time to think and plan.

So Delilah sat at the back of the Council chamber and listened to the debates and went out to implement them when police action was needed—prophylactic only, of course. The masses were interested, but a long way from uprising. She got her son attached to the security forces at the administrative section so he could be near her—and had a word to see that he was put on night duty so he would be far. And she watched.

They were cowards, the high party cadres, she thought

judiciously. They were afraid for almighty China, when all the ship was known to be able to do was boil off one tiny island. China had survived the all-out Soviet-American exchange. It would surely survive any hit one ship could deliver from space. What damage could be delivered to the ground Delilah knew quite well. In her youth, doing her national service, she piloted aircraft that sprayed five-year sterility drugs on African villages. That was in the airborne MPs; that was what decided her to continue police work when she was discharged, though no longer in an airplane. The sterility drugs killed no one, of course, but the job made her want to know more, and so she had read and studied: Airborne warfare could annihilate, yes, and it could damage and kill, certainly. But it could never *win*.

Manyface knew that. Of all the comrades in the green-and-gilt room, he was the only one who consistently said, "This is not a cause for fear alone, it is also an opportunity if we know how to seize it." The old man was recovering from his last implant—the spur of urgency no doubt helped his recovery along. Manyface was a committee—thought of himself as a committee—but in times of crisis the committee spoke with a single voice.

Manyface was, for instance, a great deal more sensible than Tchai Howard, the director of Taxation and Enforcement, a tiny man with a mean disposition whose favorite refrain was: "Prevent local trouble! Disarm the Yanks. Open camps."

"And who," asked Manyface, "will feed us then, if we put them all in camps? They *are* in camps, Tchai; they *live* in camps in their communes."

"But Comrade Tchai is right," the district commandant squeaked, moving restlessly in her silk-brocade chair. And so the wrangling went on. Delilah watched Castor's face

105

turning from one to another and wondered what he was making of it.

And then Manyface said, "All we need is a president, comrades. A president whom we can trust, who has demonstrated his loyalty to the Han Chinese, who knows enough about space to talk sensibly to the aliens. Whom we can control."

And Tsoong Delilah glanced at Castor, slipped silently around the rows of armchairs, bent down to Manyface's great, bulging head, and whispered in his ear.

Manyface looked startled. For a moment the icy control wavered, and others of his voices tried to speak, then he got back his chairmanship. "Pettyman Castor," he called, "go back to my home and get my briefcase. The red one. Do it now."

That afternoon a message went out to every village, collective, farm, and factory in what had once been the United States. It said,

> It is necessary to elect a president of the United States to deal with the bandit spacecraft. Poll your people. Report immediately the total of the voting in three categories, as follows:
> a. Total voters in your community.
> b. Total of votes for the candidate.
> c. Total number of voters who failed to understand instructions.
> Categories b and c should equal a.

While it was on its way Castor hurried back to Manyface's house, found the briefcase, started to return—and was interrupted by a message: "Don't bother to come back. The Council is recessing." A few hours later Many-face returned, uncommunicative, retiring to his room with instructions not to be bothered; and Delilah followed not long after. She was communicative enough, but only on the level of biology. "We will eat, my young friend," she announced jovially, "and then we will have a few drinks. My son? He is on duty tonight. All night. He will be kept on duty until the Council resumes, and so I will remain here with you tonight."

Castor would have preferred to talk, but he could not talk with his mouth full of food, or full of wine, or later full of Delilah. He fell asleep with all his curiosity un-satisfied—intellectual curiosity, at least.

At 6:00 A.M. the phone rang in his room.

He reached for it, but Delilah scrambled over him to take it. She identified herself, listened, hung up, then turned to Castor, grinning. "Mr. President," she said, "good morning."

III

When the Council resumed its deliberations later that morning there was no stool at Manyface's feet for Castor. A high-backed gilt chair occupied the middle of the room with all the brocaded armchairs surrounding it; and Tsoong Delilah managed not to smile as she conducted Castor to his new place. Back at the wall of the room she saw with amusement how ill-at-ease the boy was. It was a place of honor, but not a comfortable one; he could see only the upper portion of the Council and craned his neck uncomfortably now and then to peer at what was going on behind him.

But it was the front of the room that had taken over. The chairman was Wa Fohtsi, head of the delegation from Home, the power figure in the room. He peered nearsightedly at Castor and said:

"Do not worry, Mr. President. No one will hurt you." Castor stared at him—almost impudently. Delilah thought: Please, don't let the boy get himself into trouble now! But Wa went on ponderously: "As president of the United States, there will be only some very simple things for you to do. Your main job, if not your only one, will be to communicate with these bandits and persuade them of the realities of the situation."

"What—" Castor began eagerly, and the old Buddha raised his hand.

"What those realities are," he said, "will be explained to you before you begin communicating. There will be no 'conversation,' Pettyman Castor. You will have a prepared script to tape for transmission to them. Basically, you will convince them that we Han have done no evil thing. That we are, indeed, America's benefactors, if the situation is understood properly. Your ultimate objective will be not only to cause them to withdraw any threat against China, but indeed to lend support in convincing the Indians that they must abandon certain outrageous and damaging practices, such as transmitting propaganda broadcasts to Han areas. However, all that will be explained to you. Meanwhile there will be some delay until the bandit spacecraft is in position to communicate again. There will be plenty of time for your reeducation."

"I see," Castor said, dampened.

Then his spirits rose again as Wa said, "Inspector Tsoong will remain with you to aid in your reeducation, and you will give her an official title." ("I, Castor? Give Tsoong Delilah a title?") "You will be provided with suitable quarters and staff." ("Quarters? *Staff?*") "It will be useful as well for you to put together some sort of mock government apparatus," Wa went on thoughtfully. "At least a cabinet. In that way, when we prepare your transmission to the outlaw ship we can have you appear with your cabinet around you to show that it is official."

"Of course," Castor cried and then, "What's a cabinet?"

Wa glanced humorously at Delilah, who frowned, though her heart was suddenly melting. The poor, innocent, uninformed kid! "A cabinet, Citizen Pettyman," she said severely, "is a group of high officials. The most important one at this time is what is called secretary of state,

109

and Comrade Wa has been generous enough to propose that I assume that post."

"Ah, not generous, Inspector Tsoong," the old man protested modestly. "It is what is required by the logic of the situation." He closed his eyes for a moment to try to think if he had forgotten anything and decided he hadn't. He opened them and extended a hand, Western-style. "That will be all, Mr. President," he said, his eyes twinkling. As Castor left with Tsoong Delilah he heard the old Buddha chuckling.

In her car, en route back to her apartment building, Delilah indulgently let Castor chatter. The silly boy was almost believing all this was real! Not real, exactly—of course it was real, or as real as the presidency of a nearly imaginary country could hope to be. But he thought it was substantive!

In certain senses it almost was substantive. As Delilah took Castor up the elevator to the floor of her apartment she greatly enjoyed showing him one of those senses. She led him past her door, to the door of the even larger corner one just beyond, pulled the key to the new apartment out of her bag and handed it to him. "Mr. President," she said grandly, "with the presidency comes a presidential mansion, and Castor, here's yours."

How pop-eyed Yankees got sometimes! The expression on his face would have forced her into hysterical laughter if it hadn't forced her into tenderness instead. The face was sweaty with joy and confusion as he unlocked his very own door and looked in on his very own apartment. He didn't walk in. He trotted in. He didn't wait for Delilah. She followed, smiling at his glee, as he peered into the kitchen—"It's bigger than yours!"— and the master bedroom—"A *water* bed?"—and the view from the window, and the little toy fountain that plinked

into the rock pool built into a corner of the sun porch.
Delilah was not at all surprised that he loved the apartment. It was a very good one, better than her own, and
the previous tenants had been very surly about leaving
it.

At the bed he clutched her to him and fell back with
her, the cold water underneath rippling back and forth
and jouncing them. Crossly, Delilah tried to pull herself
free, but he was too strong. Laughing, he pressed his face
into her neck and then pulled it free to stare into her eyes.
"Madame Secretary of State," he chortled, "what a hell
of a fine cabinet meeting we can have right here!"

She jerked free, squatting on the hard edge of the bed,
stern with him: "Have a care, Castor! It is all right to
make jokes because in a way this whole situation is no
more than a joke. But it is also in some ways very serious,
and if you joke it must only be with me. Not with the
high cadres. Certainly not when you talk to the spaceship
people!"

"Aw, hell, Delilah," he grumbled. "I wouldn't do anything like that. Please, do I get to keep this when it's
over?"

"Something of it at least, perhaps," she said, softening.

"How much?" he begged. "No, don't tell me. I will
enjoy it while I have it and earn it as best I can."

She looked hard at him, but the look on his face was
without guile—inside his heart, perhaps, something entirely different. She got up, slapping back her wandering
hair, and sat more decorously on a gilt bench before a
makeup table. "Now. There are practical matters. The
cadres have caused research to be done into the old American cabinet, and it seems that there are twelve major
posts. Most of them will of course have no function, even

111

as a joke—there is certainly no need for a secretary of labor. But we will fill all the posts anyway."

"Of course," he said earnestly, so earnestly that she looked at him warningly.

"For instance," she went on, "we will use some of them for political purposes. To the post of secretary of the interior you will appoint Feng Miranda."

That one, she saw with pleasure, jolted the prepared expressions off his face. "But—But—"

"But she is a revolutionary, yes. I know that, of course."

She patted his head, relaxing, and sat down to take off her boots. What a good student this Castor was, after all! Unruly. Vain. Inclined to be impudent. But educable— more than willing to learn, quick and eager to learn. He was watching her with complete attention as she lectured, "To deal with a revolutionary group, the first thing of importance is to keep the channels open. If you stop them saying what they wish they will say other things you do not hear; trouble begins that way. What does the girl want, after all? Freedom for 'America'? But there is no America. The expulsion of us Han Chinese? How silly, since she is purebred genetic Han herself. So we will give her a title and the illusion of a national government to satisfy her illusion of a nation. Also," she added, smiling as she reached to undo the buttons of his shirt, "it is really quite amusing, and a joke is always worth having. Come try out your new bed."

It was not up to Tsoong Delilah to select a cabinet for Castor to appoint, but she was permitted to make recommendations and to be in on the discussions—which was more than Castor was. They could not find twelve that were worth the naming, but Delilah assured them the people from space would not notice a few shortages.

When the list was complete Delilah returned to her own apartment to think it over. It was not her responsibility in any formal sense to do that; nothing she had done had been done without the approval of higher authorities than she. But Tsoong Delilah did not need to be given responsibility. She *was* responsible. If things went wrong in any project with which she was concerned, it was never because Renmin Police Inspector Tsoong Delilah had failed to try to anticipate problems and try to avoid them. Delilah knew that of herself. It gave her pride. In that respect she was irreproachable—not counting the occasional reproach or fleeting thought that she might deserve a reproach over the way she had let Pettyman Castor occupy a measurable part of her concerns...

She dismissed that thought peremptorily. It wasn't hard. She'd been practicing it for months.

Tsoong Delilah dropped a chip into her home screen and studied the list of high officials in the American government. (Or American "government"? Or "American" government?)

They were:

President: Pettyman Castor, age twenty-two, nonpolitical, docile (not counting youthful impudence). A satisfactory choice, with watching.

Attorney General: Sebastio Carlos, poli-sci professor at the university; Yankee whose family had been in Chinese government for two generations—very loyal. Very loyal in the ways that could be counted on, because the Han Chinese could give him more than anyone else. An excellent choice for attorney general, Delilah thought sardonically. If this "government" should ever succumb to the wild impulse to pass any laws, Sebastio would make sure they didn't matter.

Secretary of Defense: Tchai Howard, small man with a mean disposition—but a former comrade commander in the Air Defense Corps and well able to plan military actions. Killing did not frighten Tchai Howard. Like Tsoong Delilah herself, he was American-born; also like Delilah, he was in no sense an "American."

Secretary of the Interior: Feng Miranda. There was nothing Delilah needed to think over about Feng Miranda, for she had thought it all already. The possible gains outweighed the losses. It was only necessary to be watchful so that the losses did not occur.

Secretary of Agriculture: Danbury Eustace—nonentity—regional director for rapeseed and oil grains for all of the New Orleans area. That didn't matter. What mattered was that when Delilah called up pictures of American statesmen, the most statesmanlike of them were middle-aged, iron-gray-haired, wide-eyed, strong-jawed—exactly like Danbury Eustace. No problem. Didn't even have to be watched, because it would never occur to him to do anything at all not ordered in a party directive.

Secretary of Health, Education, and Welfare: Manyface. An obvious choice. A comic one, too, because what experience had Manyface had, these last twenty years, of health?

Vice-president: Delilah frowned. How had they forgotten to name a vice-president? Should she call Wa and mention it to him? Did it matter? She could not decide that and resolved to think it over more carefully later on. Perhaps, she thought, unable to leave the subject, it was too late for that, for wasn't the vice-president what they called elected, like Castor? Another election would be easy enough to arrange, of course—No. Let it go. She went on to the last post:

Secretary of State: Tsoong Delilah.

That completed the roster, and that one, at least, she thought, smiling to herself, would never ever, under any circumstances at all, do anything harmful to the People's Republic of China, by accident or design.

It was a good list.

It only remained to get them all together and rehearse them in their roles.

The rehearsals—which Wa, grinning sardonically, instructed her to call cabinet meetings—were in fact political reeducation sessions. Wa himself sat in on some of them, Buddha-grin, absolute certainty of control over them all. For him it was voluntary. For the others it was compulsory—for almost all the others, at any rate. Sebastio was never at the cabinet meetings because he didn't need reeducation; his work was elsewhere, anyway. Delilah certainly didn't need it, either, but the meetings needed her—she was the one who kept one eye on Feng Miranda to see that she didn't get any troublesome ideas and the other on Castor to see that he took the matter seriously. That was not easy. Castor could stand about five quotations from Marx, Lenin, and Mao Tse-tung in one morning, she found. After that he began to scowl and whisper sardonic remarks into the ear of Feng Miranda. At the end of the second session she took him firmly by an arm. "You must be more serious," she scolded as soon as they were out of the chamber.

"For what?" he demanded angrily. "Shit, Delilah, I don't care about all this stuff. It's costing me time at the university—I'll never catch up with the classes!"

"The president of the United States," she said firmly, "does not need to attend a class. You can have tutors. You can become a research fellow. You can order your own degree and it will be given you—all this, providing you do the task the Party has assigned you, will be yours."

And the funny thing was, she realized she meant it. Whatever else happened, Pettyman Castor could never go back to being a peasant on the Heavenly Grain Collective.

What the implications of that were, Delilah could not decide, but a queer burning feeling in her belly told her that they were going to be important to her.

When finally they were all sufficiently indoctrinated to be trusted, a taping session was set up. Castor read his lines handsomely:

"My friends from space," he said, gazing benignly into the camera, "I am afraid there has been a mistake. The Chinese are not our conquerors. They are our friends. Let us both put down our weapons and meet in peace and friendship, and—"

Peace and friendship. Put down our weapons! While the president was delivering his canned message, his secretary of state was doing her very best to keep a dignified expression. The idea of *America* having any weapons to put down was ludicrous.

The idea, or more accurately the fact, that even Han China had no weapons that might prevail against the spacecraft was not funny at all.

The taping was successful; the technicians all checked in, one by one, with their assurances that sound was good, color was good, no one had a bad shadow to hide his face, all the cabinet had managed to look sufficiently cabinetly; but Delilah was quiet as she and Castor started back. It was only when they were nearing home that she began to grin. The grin came when Castor asked, "Say, Delilah—there was scaffolding around the building when I left this morning. Do you know what they're doing?"

"I know," said Delilah smugly, "very well." But would not answer him. Would not tell him how all the other tenants in the building had been persuaded to move out, how all the "Americn cabinet" had been provided with suitable quarters; would not speak at all on the subject until they rounded the corner and saw what had happened to the building. The pastel lime green was gone under two coats of quick-drying paint the color of rice flour. The workmen were just removing the last of the spidery struts and platforms they had worked from. Castor turn to her in puzzlement, and Delilah snickered. "Mr. President," she said, "behold your White House!"

Living in the same house with Tchai Howard and Feng Miranda and Danbury Eustace and Tsoong Delilah and Tsoong Delilah's son—especially with Miranda and Delilah and the boy—was not a relaxing existence for Castor. For a lousy secretary, Tchai was pretty peremptory with his president. Delilah was peremptory enough, too, with her bed demands—which, it was true, Castor greatly enjoyed meeting. (But why did it always have to be *her* idea?) Miranda was the most troublesome, for what she saw in Castor was hard to figure out (certainly she treated him as a silly delinquent), but that there was something was clearly demonstrated by the way she hung around.

Life had been a lot less confusing back on the collective.

What it had been back on the collective was boring, and even now there were boring parts. Most boring of all were the "cabinet meetings," where nothing ever seemed

117

to be discussed except why it was dialectically essential to maintain proper political and economic attitudes and what those ordained attitudes had to be. It was so often explained to Castor that the Chinese were not aggressors in America that Castor, who had always assumed that was true anyway, began to doubt it. Miranda fed that doubt. Miranda had no doubts. When one day the meeting was abruptly terminated without explanation and Delilah and Manyface went hurriedly off in her car the same way, Miranda clutched Castor's arm. "We'll walk home," she informed him. "I've got a lot to say to you."

Inside, Castor groaned; he knew what that lot was. After half an hour or so he was groaning audibly, because the lot was just what he expected. "You're a traitor to your country," she lectured. "You make a fool of yourself with that old Han policeone! You have the title, and the title gives you the power—have the courage to use them!"

Reeducation had not worked well on Feng Miranda. Argument did no better: "What 'country'? What is the harm in making love with someone I enjoy? Use the title for what?—and what good is the title when it can be taken away in a minute?"

"You're a silly child," spat Feng Miranda, and the argument could have gone on forever. It lasted more than an hour. Could have lasted for three, but just as they were crossing Canal Street a Renmin police car made a violent U-turn, its siren suddenly ascream, and pulled up beside them. "Are you Citizen Pettyman? Citizen Feng? Get in at once—you are needed!" And no questions answered as they screamed through the streets to the mock-White House, where Delilah was tapping her foot at the door.

"Where have you been?" she demanded; and, without waiting for an answer, "They finished the secure link and transmitted the tape. The answer has just come in."

"Answer?" said Castor, not quite able to follow. "What kind of answer?"

Delilah's face was like thunder. "They won't talk to you by radio. They want you to meet them in space."

IV

Castor had never been in an airplane before. When the takeoff thrust jammed him hard against the seat back he swallowed and grinned weakly and wondered if airsickness disqualified a person for spaceflight. Feng Miranda had never been in the air before, either, and hissed resentment into Castor's ear: "These airplanes should have been *ours*!" Tsoong Delilah had been in aircraft a thousand times—all types of aircraft, all over the world—and mostly she was watching Miranda and Castor in the seat ahead with cold eyes. It was of course certain that she was not jealous of the way this Overseas-Chinese vixen had set her sights for Castor, since Castor was merely a machine she used to produce good sensations inside her body. There was no question of "love." Therefore there could be no question of "jealousy." When she disciplined Feng, as she intended to do very soon, it would be for none but the most correct political reasons: the woman could not jeopardize this most vital of missions.

What she would do to, or with, Castor was less clear in her mind.

Still, she thought indulgently, the boy was so *very* thrilled by it all! It was flight and adventure that made Castor's eyes sparkle so, not the presence of a skinny girl child with crazy and destructive notions.

So thinking, Delilah let herself drift off to sleep. All

the same, hours later, when they were in the limousine to take them to their housing, she made sure that it was she who sat beside Castor.

In truth, Delilah was nearly as excited as Castor, for everything was almost as new to her as to him. The island of Hainan hung from the southernmost tip of Han China, out of the way, not very interesting except for its climate (but Hawaii's was just as good) and for its Space Center. That was very interesting, of course, but generally speaking that interest was discouraged by the high party officials. Delilah had been Home a dozen times, the last time to escort her aged and ailing husband to his dying place (when *would* the old man do it?). Hainan Dao she had never seen.

From the air there had been tiny and unsatisfying glimpses of coast, palms, rivers, villas; even, a minute or two, everybody craning to get a corner of one of the tiny aircraft windows as they approached the landing over the Space Center itself, a giant man-rated ship towering over its own gantry, with the meteorological and communications and sky-eyes rockets dotted across the rest of the field pencil-thin and wheatstalk-high by comparison. Everyone on the plane shouted when they saw the ships. Even Delilah.

And everyone, even Delilah, stared excitedly out of the limousines as they purred toward their quarters. Hainan Dao was rather like a combination of the old Waikiki and Palm Springs, with Midwest car racetracks and stately California mansions thrown in. Castor's eyes popped as they passed groves of ornamental trees and swimming pools tucked into the formal gardens of homes. There were joggers along the road and children playing games in meadows; there were old people taking the sun between holes on the golf courses and lovers holding hands. And

121

all the cars! Hainan Dao was a rich place. Except for the Han Chinese, none of the "American cabinet" had ever seen a rich countryside before, and when they pulled into a long, pine-lined drive, Feng Miranda began to swear bitterly to herself. Delilah grinned. She knew what the silly child was thinking.

"What is *that*?" Castor demanded in her ear, and Delilah peered to see what he meant. They were approaching an immense house with balconies and pillars and a fountain playing in the center of its circled driveway, and just before the fountain was a pole. The pole bore a flag: white stripes and red stripes, blue field and white stars.

Delilah could not help herself, though others might have seen. As she leaned toward the window she touched her lips to his cheek in pleasure at his openmouthed stare. "Have you never seen it before, Mr. President? It is the flag of your United States of America."

Exhausted though they were and spacey with jet lag, the first thing they did was have a meeting. To Delilah's surprise it was Manyface's face Dien Kaichung that took charge. "You, Tsoong Delilah," he snapped, "you will study pilotage."

"I already know pilotage," said Delilah, and heard with surprise the tone of her voice. It was not a good tone to take with a high party member. But in fact it was not really the high party member Fung Bohsien who was speaking, but only the implant Dien Kaichung, or the implant that had once been the human being Dien Kaichung before he became an implant, and thus only one member of the committee that was Manyface. Delilah found herself confused, not only by jet lag. Yet one thing was clear to her: it was not only politically unprofitable to take that tone, it was also likely to make problems. In fact it did. The face of Manyface twisted in a grimace that was almost pain. For a moment it was the eye of the real Fung Bohsien that stared accusingly at her out of the face they held in common. "I'm sorry," she said, as graciously as she could. "I am tired, and careless. I will of course do as you instruct, Comrade Dien, since you are our director of training."

He frowned at her, moving his lips as though holding an internal conversation—no doubt he is, thought Delilah. She looked away from him to minimize the confrontation and fell into another. Feng Miranda! Saucy little Overseas-Chinese slut, she was sitting far too close to Castor and whispering far too intimately into his ear. And—oh, what unfairness!—it was not the slut who got reprimanded, it was Delilah herself. "Do pay attention, Comrade Tsoong," Manyface snapped. "We have much to cover, and little time to do it. Now! You will of course all be required to take extra-atmospheric training. There will be centrifuges and bouncing chambers, spinning rooms to test for space-sickness, underwater maneuvering to simulate zero-G. These courses are of the utmost importance for those who will be part of the mission! If anyone fails any of these tests," he added severely, "he will of course be disqualified from the mission at once, so do not take them lightly—oh, what is it now?" he demanded irritably as Feng Miranda raised her hand.

Her expression was innocent enough, but her tone was not. "I only wanted to ask, what if it is President Pettyman who should fail the tests?" she said sweetly.

That nasty little man Tchai Howard interrupted then. "Shut up, Feng," he ordered roughly. "Let the briefing proceed." Delilah could have kissed him . . . almost.

In fact the rest of the briefing was more interesting

123

than the assignment of tasks, for the Space Center teams had produced computer simulations of the alien vessel's orbit and projected deltas; there would be eighteen days at most before it would be in position to meet the launched president of the United States in orbit. "That is at most," Manyface warned. "It may be as little as fourteen. So there must be no delay in training! Is that understood?"

The party all nodded, and Manyface allowed himself a grin. "In that case," he declared—and this time the voice was Fung Bohsien's own—"I will tell you what has been decided. Three of you will be aboard the rocket when it is launched for the rendezvous—always assuming you pass the tests," he added, looking meaningfully at Delilah. "I will now give you their names. Pettyman Castor. Tsoong Delilah. And Tchai Howard."

Castor looked thunderstruck, then ablaze with joy. The mean little face of Tchai Howard froze, then split in a predatory grin. Delilah herself felt nothing at all—nothing but a sort of subliminal sting of fear, then a rush of pride at having been selected . . .

And then, as she caught a glimpse of the jealousy and rage on the face of Feng Miranda, an exultation of triumph.

The house they stayed in had twenty-nine rooms. Castor counted them and reported the result to Delilah with awe. No one else had counted, because it was not the kind of house that announced its status with numbers. It was far too grand for that. It was a manor, almost a palace; in the queer, archaic terms of its butler (for it had, among many other unprecedented luxuries, a butler) it was "the Residence." Whatever it was called, it was impressively huge. It had the Master Suite and the Green Jade Suite and the Mao Wing, with six handsome bed-sitters, each complete with bath and tiny sitting room and hot tub. It had a library and a drawing room—actually two drawing rooms, if you counted the one that completed the Master Suite. It had a dining gallery and a billiard room; it had porches and conversation chambers and a huge green lawn.

It also had, as noted, servants. What servants! Delilah had never seen their like. These were not peasants hired out of the pig slop. The butler was Singapore-born and Shanghai-bred, but his genes were pure English countryside six generations back and so were his accent and his manners. Not to mention his warm, pale blue eyes and his curly blond hair. All eight of the maids were from New Zealand, mixed Anglo and Maori ancestry. The kitchen help, which had been hired away from the rich suburbs around Benares, were every one French by ancestry and training. All these people contributed all they could to the material well-being of the party from America—such food! Such wonderful, warm, soft, perfumed beds! But they were not what the party was there for; that was training.

And training they got.

First there was pilotage. That was not hard for Delilah, with six thousand flight hours on her log, and not too hard for Castor, with all his lonely hours in front of the teaching screens. For Tchai Howard it was hard, because he had to start from scratch. There were scuba lessons—because scuba diving was the closest easy thing to zero-G—a breeze for Castor, not too hard for Delilah, again a starting-over for Tchai. Martial arts was quite the opposite. Tchai not only didn't need that, he was their instructor—as he was in hand weapons and the concealment thereof, a course that they got whether they needed it or not. Tchai didn't need it, clearly, but he put himself through the same loading and firing and marksmanship and stripping and cleaning drills as the other two.

Almost all of that part of the training was on the Space Center grounds itself, half an hour from home. A smell of petroleum products hung over everything—not from the rockets, but from the crackers that made the liquid hydrogen fuel; by and by no one noticed it anymore. The rest of the cabinet was not required to take any part of the training. Most of them hung around anyhow—especially envious Miranda, who complained endlessly that she was excluded. Even to so unsympathetic an ear as Delilah's: "I *deserve* to go into space. I want to!"

Rough good humor from Delilah: "No chance, Yankee. You couldn't stand the centrifuge."

"I'll bet I could," Miranda said. It wasn't just her tone that was resentful. Her whole body was tense and angry, thumbnails digging into the nails of her forefingers.

Delilah felt a flash of anger. "No chance anyway! You are disloyal, Feng. What fool would trust you in space? Earn trust, then you may have some chances—possibly!" And flounced off to try her space suit with Castor and Tchai Howard while Miranda glared after her.

The rocket that would carry Delilah, Castor, and Tchai into space was still the tallest object on the field, but as they came out of the space suit workshop Delilah frowned at a second gantry. What were workmen doing there? And then she saw that preparations were being made to install a second rocket, not one of the lesser utility craft but a big one. "What's going on?" she demanded of Tchai Howard, who shrugged.

"Backup," he said.

"Backup for what?"

He looked at her, and then at Castor a few steps away earnestly listening to the complaints of Feng Miranda.

"None of your business," he said and left Delilah to wonder.

Since training was arduous, there was not much time for Delilah to worry about Castor, who shared her bed every night anyway. There was even less time to think about the rest of the world until, waiting for Castor to come out of the shower one night, Delilah absently thumbed on a newscast.

The rest of the world was not idle.

When Castor came back to bed Delilah was sitting upright, glaring at the screen. "Look!" she cried. "The wogs are making trouble!"

"Trouble" was the word for it. It wasn't crisis, wasn't a threat, exactly—certainly wasn't a danger of warfare or anything like that. Well, not immediately, Delilah thought savagely; but perhaps the Indians needed to be taught a lesson! The newscasts were showing "spontaneous" demonstrations against China, not only in Delhi and Calcutta but in the rebuilt cities of Rome and Moscow and a dozen other places. It was hard to piece together, from the voiceovers and statements of public figures, just what was going on; but the outlines became clear.

India had got suspicious. They suspected what was quite true, that the Chinese were in secret contact with the spacecraft. They could not know exactly what the contact meant, but they were worried—hence the "spontaneous" demonstrations to denounce China's "attempt" to "revive" the imperialist United States.

The night went badly for Delilah.

In the morning she demanded admittance to the daily Steering Committee meeting. That was not her right; she was not high enough to have such rights. It was not her duty, either, because her time was taken up with training; but the morning was free, as part of the carefully prepared recreation schedule, and anyway her blazing eyes would have let her in regardless. "I hope," said Tchai frostily, "that you have a good reason for this!"

"The best!" declared Delilah, seating herself on one of the half-dozen chairs in the study—there were only three people present, Tchai and Manyface and the Space Center chief, Mu Dailen. "Why have you not instructed us on the Indian situation?"

"There is no Indian situation," said Tchai frostily. "It is only a nuisance, not important. What is important is your mission."

"You think you can get the spaceship to help you against India, is that it?"

"It is our intention to explore that possibility, yes," said Manyface, smiling at her. "Please, Delilah. Your training is your first priority. We had no wish to disturb it with outside factors."

Tchai was having none of the smiles or pleases. "Enough," he barked. "We are in the middle of important decisions. Tsoong must go."

But Manyface smiled at him, too. "She can stay, Howard. We may want her advice."

What they could possibly want her advice on, Delilah could not guess, since what they were discussing had to do with Tchai's specialty and no one's else. Weaponry! Delilah sat seething as they displayed holograms over the bamboo fireplace. Explore a possibility! An unimportant nuisance! And what was important to them? Was it these weapons that they were hiding inside the spacecraft? Delilah looked at them with disdain. So this was how high party members conducted themselves! Why, they were no more than foolish children! Even the tai chi class of seven-year-olds she could hear faintly beyond the pine grove would not imagine that these peashooters could prevail against a spaceship that had the power to annihilate an island—that claimed that it could annihilate a continent as easily, or a planet! Delilah believed that claim. No. There would be only one useful weapon on that ship, and that would be herself. Castor, a silly figurehead boy. Tchai, a sillier, older one. Their carefully camouflaged guns were as idiotic as the fireplace of bamboo, in a room that never needed a fire, that would burn the house down at the first touch of flame. "I am not useful to you here after all," she said frostily, "so I will go supervise the others."

"Of course," said Manyface, this time managing not to smile, and Delilah managed not to slam the door. It was, of course, not true that she needed to supervise the others; there was nothing to supervise on a free morning. It was unquestionably true, on the other hand, that she had not seen Castor since he disappeared into the shower that morning. Where could he have gone?

He was not in the gun room, though he liked the old one-over-one shotguns the Chinese craftsmen had made and the mean little Uzis that could cut a man in half. He was not in the library—no surprise there, Delilah thought darkly. She walked through them, and the breakfast room, and the halls, as though absentminded in thought. Her eyes were focused, though, and they saw nothing she was looking for.

Where was the boy?

She stepped out onto the eastern sun deck as though for a breath of air—who would want that? Steamy, sultry, it stung her nose. There was no one there, no one on the long, green lawn, no one visible in the piney grove or around the water-lily pool. "Sawyer," she called harshly over her shoulder. The butler appeared at once. "Sawyer, have you seen Pettyman Castor this morning?"

"Yes, modom. In the conservatory. With Comrade Feng Miranda, modom," he said, and Delilah whirled and glared at the tone of faint amusement in his voice. How terrible if even the servants thought she was jealous of the boy! Delilah was in no good mood as she stormed through the rooms toward the conservatory.

Before she saw them she heard the voices, Castor's good-humored growl, Miranda's angry soprano. It was not only Miranda's voice that annoyed Delilah, the voice that had always grated on her nerves—pitiful bird-chirp, how could a sensible man like Castor stand hearing it? The words were far worse. She was denouncing Castor: "You're a honey-ball! Rice-flour white on the outside, Han yellow inside—you're a traitor to your country!"

And Castor's placatory "Aw, sweet, you're as Han as Delilah is. What are you carrying on about?"

If only he had not said her name, thought Delilah as she stormed into the doorway, glaring at them with frost and flame. "You have no country, you fool," she shouted at Miranda. "You had a desert, and we Chinese came and brought it back to life for you!" She blasted them while she froze them. They stood petrified, Castor with a foolish grin on his face, hand still uplifted in mock-defense against Miranda's attack; the girl with her mouth still open to deliver it. And what a nasty little mouth she had, lipsticked to make it worse!

Whatever Miranda was, she was no coward. "We hate you for it!" she cried belligerently.

And that was fine! How stupid of the girl to let it become a debate, Delilah thought, for at debate she was confident of winning. She advanced into the room, the fire and ice controlled. "I see," she said, seating herself between them. "You and those other madmen the Russians, you did your best to destroy the world, did you not?"

"We did not! We were simply defending ourselves—a network of antimissile satellites that could not possibly be used to attack—"

"Ah, yes," nodded Delilah. "You erected your nuclear laser defenses, yes, so that the Russians could thereafter do nothing to hurt you. But you could hurt them. And you were terribly surprised when it all failed."

"They attacked us without warning!"

"Yes," sighed Delilah. "The naked warrior saw his opponent putting on armor, so he attacked while he thought there was still a chance to win, is that not right?" The girl was angrily silent. "But let us consider this question of hate, Comrade Feng. You hate us because we brought you law and order. You hate us for helping to get your farms clean again. You hate us because you insanely destroyed what used to be your country and your people were unable to put it together again. I understand that. It is natural to resent help. The wounded dog snaps at the master who tries to bind its wounds."

"Tsoong," Miranda said, "the British brought law and medicine to India long ago. Did that make the Indians love them? Or want them in their country?"

Delilah shook her head indulgently, though the frost and fire were still in her voice. "The cases are entirely different. There it was a few thousand Englishmen running the affairs of a hundred million Indians. Now there are almost as many Han Chinese in North America as aborigin—as persons of North American extraction."

"Do you think that makes it *better*?"

"It makes what you say unfair!"

Miranda said doggedly, "You're Han, Tsoong. You don't understand."

"You're Han, too!"

Miranda shook her head. "I'm an American, Tsoong. So is Castor if only he knew it. And," she added, rising and moving toward the door, "this conversation is at an end."

The Indian unrest grew. The alien ship was moving into position. The training went on. The man-rated ship was tested and fueled and stocked.

And armed.

Only Delilah and Tchai Howard, of the crew, knew about the armament. Castor was kept away from the ship while the weaponry was installed and so, of course, were the other "Americans." Castor objected only out of annoyance, because the ship was so fascinating to him; Feng Miranda objected out of the reasons she always had for objecting to anything the Han Chinese did. "You stole our space program from us," she shouted at Delilah, and Delilah snapped back, "You have no space program. There is no 'you'! In any event, you have neither the training nor the aptitudes to be of any use."

"You said I couldn't stand the centrifuge, either, but I did! I won twenty yuan from Tchai Howard because I took more Gs than he could!"

"Tchai Howard will be spoken to," snapped Delilah. "Go about your business!"

But at last the great day dawned.

To Tsoong Delilah's astonishment, she found she was frightened. Going into space was not, after all, like getting into an airplane. Going into space was like entering an immense, hostile, and unknown place where human beings—even Renmin police inspectors—came at their peril; and the burden of the responsibility (and the fear) of meeting whoever was in the alien spacecraft was terrifying. She let her dressers put her space suit on her and attach the vulgar and uncomfortable little pipes and slip the mating collar around her neck, and she was in a daze.

It all went so fast! Out of her dressing room, into the White Room, up the elevator with Tchai and Castor in their own suits next to her, as silent as she. She glanced into their faces and saw only what they saw in her, the opaque light-shutter faceplates and no humanity behind them; they didn't talk; the technicians and helpers talked, kept on talking, talked endlessly, but it was only orders: "Through the door, please!" "Sit down in your seat, please!" "Move your arm so I can see if it's free—"

And then the great belly-busting thrust from below and the queerest moment of sick terror and wild jubilance Tsoong Delilah had ever felt.

And they were in space. Forty kilometers up in six hundred seconds, dropping the boosters and the tanks, and Delilah was too busy to think and Castor too drunk with delight to stop talking. They were in space! Naked hairless apes, spurning the planet that had borne them! What a clod you are, Tchai Howard, Delilah exulted as she matched her board for the lifting thrust—not a word out of you in this great moment...

The words did come from Tchai then, but not from the space-masked figure still beside her. They came from the space control radio, and they said,

"Tsoong! Pettyman! Arrest her at once! She must be shot! She knocked me out and took my suit!"

Delilah and Castor turned to stare at the figure between them.

"I told you I could get into space," said the shrill, vindictive voice of Feng Miranda.

V

It was impossible to turn back, of course.

It was ridiculous to "arrest" Feng Miranda, though of course Delilah did so. But what did "arrest" mean when there was nowhere to go?

It was inevitable, though, that rage and frustration exploded on the girl, and her nose was still bleeding from the back of Delilah's fist when they sighted the alien spacecraft. If Castor had not got in the way, there would have been more than a nosebleed, but he took Delilah's karate chop harmlessly on his forearm and managed to squirm out of the way of Miranda's retaliatory kick. "Don't kill each other, damn it!" he shouted. "How'll I get rid of the bodies?"

Delilah breathed hard for a moment. A moment was all she had; the spaceship needed to be piloted or they were all dead and the mission wasted. "I will deal with you later," she said through gritted teeth, and devoted her attention to the board.

"Later" was indefinitely deferred, to Delilah's serious regret. There simply was no time. There was less time than anyone could have calculated a need for, because when Miranda stole Tchai's space suit she stole from the spacecraft a large fraction of its utility. Tchai was the gunner. The hidden weaponry tucked into the spaceship was no longer a counter in the game unless Delilah herself could operate it, and how could she do that? and pilot at the same time? and keep an eye on the vicious little bitch's machinations and for that matter on Castor, and—hardest of all—simultaneously think and plan and be ready for what terrible and unexpected things the alien ship might produce? Delilah's mind fluttered like a limed bird with the trapper closing in; and then there was no time, no time at all, because the alien ship appeared on their radar, and a moment later Castor squawked in excitement as he picked up the faint dot of it through the starboard glass.

The radar said nothing useful about the alien: the read-outs along the edge of the screen gave mass (three hundred metric tons, close enough) and dimensions (easily forty meters long) and shape—shape more like a can of fruit than anything else, with bits of odd metallic shapes stuck onto it. The visual to the naked eye was not even as useful as that, except that there was color to the naked eye, purply, violety color that did not seem material. Delilah snatched the twelve-centimeter glasses out of their felt-lined pocket and stared through them at the stranger. Behind her Castor and Miranda were demanding and pleading and exchanging quick words of explanation of how Miranda had got there; behind her Tchai Howard's radio voice was still screaming demands and questions. Delilah blotted them out. She had enough attention available to keep her own board dressed and her ship on course; all of the rest of it went to what was in the glasses.

The ship was metallic, but not shiny-chrome metallic. Thirty years at relativistic speeds through the diffuse dusts and gases of interstellar space had dulled the shine and pitted the surface. It looked mean. It looked like a storage tank for some unpleasant liquid waste or like one of the first primitive nuclear weapons. It was barrel-shaped rather than truly cylindrical, with here and there a scarred fin or incongruously bright (because long retracted from the buffing of dust) paraboloid dish. The whole thing was longer than the radar had displayed because of its angle of approach, perhaps as much as a hundred meters long.

"What's that purple?" Castor screeched in her ear.

The purple. Good question! The squat cylinder wore at one end a ring of faint violet light. Faint? That was not the right word. The glow hurt the eyes. Plenty of photons were coming out of whatever it was, but perhaps only a small spillover into the visible band. Puzzled, scared, Delilah let the bitch Miranda snatch the glasses away from her and reached to thumb on the ship-to-ship radio. "Unknown spacecraft," she said, "this is the ship of the president of the United States. He is aboard and ready to meet with you."

She released the thumb button and waited for acknowledgment to speak again.

There was no acknowledgment. There was no answer at all. "Call them again, damn you," Miranda shrilled, struggling with Castor for the glasses, and without will of her own Delilah repeated the call.

No answer, and the two spacecraft were moving volitionlessly toward each other, hindquarter to forequarter, not as though they were planning it, but as though some large Caliban were stirring minnows together in a pool. "Back away," whispered Castor, his nerve failing.

Delilah's nerve was also failing, but her finger would not tell the keyboard to take them away. Her duty was assigned. It was not to flee because she was scared or because the aliens were impolite about replying; it was to make contact.

Anyway, she thought, there was still plenty of distance between them, and if they tried anything funny the secret panel to Tchai's weaponry lay within the reach of her right hand, just under the bulge of Miranda's shoulder as she squirmed to stare out the window.

There was not still plenty of distance, though. All of a sudden there was no distance at all. The two ships did not accelerate toward each other; it was something unexpected and worse.

The violet ring slipped free of the alien ship.

It spun around on its axis twice, like a coin on a tabletop. Then it rushed toward them.

Tsoong Delilah slapped quick fingers on the board, and their spaceship bucked and tried to turn away. Thrust forward, she reached out despairingly toward the weaponry board. Miranda was on top of it in her hard and unmoving suit; she wouldn't get out of the way and got a backhanded slap again for her trouble—would have got worse if there had been time—did get worse, verbally at least, with Delilah screaming fury, promising punishment for leaving them without a gunner . . . There was no time for punishment. There was no time to solve the riddles of the arming and aiming and launching of Tchai's missiles, either.

The ring was on them.

The ring swallowed them. It slipped past the plunging stern quarter of their ship like a hoop over a stake. Delilah had not permitted herself to vomit in years, nor did she feel ill; but for the tenth part of a second something in her stomach lunged toward her throat.

Then it was over.

The ring sailed away from them. They were floating in space. The star-sprinkled black of the sky was all around them.

But the stars were different stars.

*   *   *

Instinctively Delilah cut the thrusters and switched on all sensors: Were they in orbit? was it stable? was there a terrible crash threatening at any second? While the ship's autosystems were reaching for data and trying for solutions, she had a moment to see that they were not alone in space—quite—for behind them and below was a planet, blue-white and huge.

It was not the Earth. Beyond it, its sun was redder and larger and nearer, and under the planet's white blobs of cloud the continent at its sunlit edge was none she had ever seen before.

Doubly they were not alone, for radar squawked the word that a ship-sized object was near. It was on the side of Delilah's spacecraft away from the ruby sun, therefore brightly lit. It, too, was nothing they had seen before. A spaceship? Well, certainly it was a spaceship; that followed from the fact that it was a ship and in space. All the same it was queer that the vessel was lined for air. It was wingless, yes, but its bedbug-shaped contours were those of a lifting body; and it had control surfaces that meant nothing in a vacuum.

Not only bug-shaped. It had a bedbug's claws. Tiny blue-white jets flared on the ship. It turned, till opposing jets halted it in a posture aimed directly at them. Behind it a swell of golden flame showed main-thrust engines, hurling it toward them, and the claws opened.

Delilah could have escaped the claws. This bedbug was a mere rocket, not some mad and inescapable wheel of violet light. There was plenty of time for Delilah to run. There was plenty of time, too, to go through the steps of the weaponry board. *Arm*, and the ready lights on the lid of the secret board blinked green. *Aim*, and the sighting reticle flashed a solution.

Launch—

But she did not launch the missile.

Delilah didn't have a chance to launch the missile, actually. Miranda saw what she was doing and swarmed all over her, pinning her arms, wrestling her away from the board—Castor trying clumsily to help one or the other, or to decide which one to help—yelling and shouting of *Let go, bitch* and *Don't be a fool, Tsoong* and *I'll kill you* and *You'll kill us all!* in hisses and grunts. It was almost impossible to tell which one was shouting which . . . but then it was all moot. The alien shuttle was too close. The grapples closed. And at once they all went flying in a sudden surge of acceleration as the alien towed them away.

Reentry was no faster than on Earth; all of a sudden they had plenty of time. There was time, thought Delilah, to power-up the main engines, blow every drop of fuel, break free from this steel-clawed bedbug—

But where would they go?

There was time, at least, to try to make sense of where they were and what was happening, although it did not seem that all the time in the world would suffice for that. The sensors read out data on the planet they were spiraling in on. It was a fatter and flimsier planet than the Earth, with a surprisingly dense atmosphere—thus the lifting body instead of wings on the shuttle. It was warm where the continent lay, Hainan temperatures or better, and hardly cold enough to matter even at the poles.

It was inhabited.

Well, of course it was inhabited! Delilah snapped at herself—where else would the shuttle come from? But all the same it was a startlement to see the crystalline lights on the dark side and the glitter of what could only have been cities on the bright. What cities! Beijing was a mud-hut village by comparison.

And the other way they knew it was inhabited was that the planet reached out and told them so.

"Look at this!" squawked Castor, playing with his communications equipment, and it was something indeed to look at.

Pictures were coming in, and sounds.

None of them were clear, of course, and none of them lasted. The photons in a slice of electromagnetic radiation are the same on the Earth and out past the farthest quasar. But the way technologists count and measure and decode them depends on chance and the accident of somebody's handy piece of equipment when the first vacuum tube is built. The aliens did not use the same bandwidths or screenline parameters or even the basic choices out of the electromagnetic spectrum that were doctrinal on Earth. The comm equipment in Delilah's ship was marvelously resourceful. It could seek patterned transmission anywhere and then puzzle over the patterns until it congealed them into data. But it could not do it easily, and sometimes its solutions failed.

So what they got were snatches and glimpses and glitches. Some were patterns of meaningless color; most were not even patterns. But now and then, for a moment at a time—

Pictures. What pictures!

There was a city—maybe the city, or one of the cities, that popped into glittering life below them as they spun around the planet. Bright green and shockingly brilliant pink, all colors, all intense.

There was a machine that pumped out thick, syrupy goo—why and how and for what they could not guess.

There was a cluster of creatures—buglike? molelike? there were no real standards to judge by—tumbling over each other and pausing to move their lips; but the sound channel did not go with the picture, and what sounds they made were lost.

There was another creature—a statue of a creature, perhaps?—in a sort of niche of glowing gold, more like an ostrich than anything else, but with arms instead of wings.

There was their own ship, blipped onto the screen, flashed away.

There was a planet, and the planet was Earth.

There were a thousand other things; and there were sounds on the audio frequency—chatters of facsimile and code and telemetry; whispers of, almost, voices, but whose and saying what they could not tell.

The sounds were as bad as the pictures, in fact. Every now and then there was a sound that seemed almost to make a sort of sense, a whisper of an English phrase ("—rescue you"—was that one?) or a name: Was "A-Belinka" a name? And Castor would capture all those fleeting bits and pour them back through the secondary screens and speakers so that Delilah and Miranda could puzzle over them while he hunted for more . . .

And all the time, all the time, they were swirling down to whatever was kidnapping them.

All the time in the world would not have been enough to try to understand, or to feel terror, or to scheme what steps they might take against whatever might befall. That didn't matter. They didn't have all the time in the world. Suddenly reentry began, and there was no time at all.

Reentry was no gentler than on Earth, either. Fortunately they'd managed to strap their battered bodies in again. Whether that would be enough to save them, Delilah could only guess; there was a lot of danger here. The claws on the alien shuttle had grasped their ship any which way. The ablative surfaces were no longer where they could do any good.

But their captors had thought of that. The thermal shock was minimal. The bug-tug blasted, blasted continuous retrofire. There was no time for their ship's skin to soften and burn away before they were down to a crawl— Mach 4 or less—and then it was a long, gentle glide to the surface.

They bounced—but not hard, and surprisingly slowly— and stopped.

When they realized they were down and safe—momentarily safe—they scrambled out of belts and harnesses. Castor was quickest. Before she could stop him— before she had quite realized that it might be a fatal act— he was at the door, opening it to their new world. All their reflexes were like molasses. The pull of gravity was distinctly less, and their heads unhinged. Delilah had only time to scream, "Be careful!"

The air did not kill them.

It smelled—strange all right, but good. A little like distant frying mushrooms. A little like the sea. It was raining, slow fat drops like peppermint jelly, and the breeze was gentle and quite hot. The astronauts clustered around the port, staring out at a maroon paved plain. The port, unfortunately, was facing away from the city they had seen, but out at its farther edge were lesser buildings, a cluster like crystals grown in a saturated sea, green and blue prisms, golden needles, ruby columns.

And it sounded as though they were being met.

"Put it away," snarled Miranda, and Delilah realized her hand had reached inside the waistband of her suit for the weapon Tchai had given her.

"Yes, please, Delilah," said Castor nervously. "Let's not start a fight."

She didn't answer. She put the gun back, and that was answer enough. She jumped down bravely from the port to the maroon paving—how strangely slowly one fell here!—and began to shuck out of her suit. They would look less threatening out of the suits, she reasoned. Besides, she was sweating terribly inside it.

The sounds of Someone Coming got louder. By the time Delilah had struggled out of her bottoms and stepped out of her jonny-drawers the sounds were just around the other side of the rocket, and then they were whirling around toward the three half-naked people.

There was a hoverplatform. It slipped and skidded in its turn, and more slowly came toward them—two or three others were following after, and the whine and screech of their air pumps was deafening.

They all carried passengers. What passengers! Alien passengers, as alien as you could ever wish! with their buggy, feelered faces and the ridge of glossy spines along their backs. Monsters from space! Deadly creatures that made childhood nightmares seem tame!

But Delilah had expected monsters, and besides, these monsters were no bigger than cats. Some of them wore clothing and ornaments of one kind or another—fabric ruffs around the places where their necks should have been, cloaks, jewelry, as well as what Delilah thought might be the equivalents of wristwatches, communications pendants, and so on. Most didn't. The naked ones were the ones who seemed to be hanging onto the floats any way they could and sometimes falling—children, perhaps?

Some one of them did something, and as the three hovervans dropped to their knees around the Earth spaceship, a great glowing hologram sprang into the sky—on one edge one of those ostrich-things; on the other what

143

Delilah recognized as a bird clutching lightnings and leaves; in the middle a globe that might well have been meant to be the planet Earth.

All these shocks registered only peripherally in her eyes, because the thing she saw most clearly was a woman. A bare-busted, bulgingly pregnant, saber-wavingly grinning and huge woman who stood triumphant among the aliens as though they belonged to her—or she to them—and bawled at the three undressed visitors, "Welcome! Be brave! We'll save you yet!"

"Oh, my God," whispered Miranda from beside her, and Delilah could not guess what she meant to say. None of them knew what to say. They were in shock.

It was only a little less startling, and not reassuring at all, when the aliens on the second platform twitched themselves into a sort of regular cluster and raised objects before them. Some they blew into or rubbed against; the most common were things like horizontally held xylophones, and they struck them.

It was music that came out. Approximately music, anyway.

Delilah had no way of recognizing it, but beside her Miranda caught her breath and sobbed, "Oh, Castor! They remembered! It's 'Hail to the Chief!'"

J U P E

was out hunting when the great day arrived. He didn't plan it that way. The event caught him by surprise. The Real-Americans weren't due for days yet, he thought. But he was wrong, and so he missed it all, the landing of the Presidential yacht, the welcoming ceremonies by the first-contact party, the whole thing. He'd stopped off to shoot an inkling on the way— he was always fond of inkling roasts, so succulent and sweet once you leached the iron salts out of them. He never enjoyed inkling again. When at last he strolled into his home nest—sweating profusely in the hot, dank air of World, picking up a fuzzy leaf on the way to towel off the sweat—his senior sisters greeted him with jeers and

145

reproaches. "You missed it, Jupe, you fool." "It's just like you to be off killing something when—" "He's really the *President*, Jupe, and—" "And, oh, Jupe, he's so *handsome*!"

"Ah, *no*!" he bawled, making sense at last of what they were telling him. He dropped the inkling on the floor, causing Senior Sister Marcia to boom complaints at him for dirtying her clean mats with inkling blood. He didn't listen. "They *came*?" he demanded in outrage at the unjust universe. "No one *told* me?" But of course no one could have, as several of his sisters took pleasure in explaining to him. Other sisters, especially the more pregnant ones, flinched away from his reddening face and flailing arms. Jupiter would never hurt one of them on purpose, that was certain. But sometimes when he windmilled his arms in excitement and rage someone got in the way. That was just temper, and Jupe had a lot of it.

"Please, Jupiter, hold still," one of the junior sisters begged, approaching him from behind. She was a bright ten-year-old named Susify, and she carried the softest of toweling leaves to rub him down and oil away the spatters of inkling blood from his bronzed skin. She edged him gently away from the mess on the floor. Marcia was already kicking a crew of dumb erks toward it, to the task of mopping it up and taking the fresh meat to the kitchen, while Jupiter stomped and swore at the bad news.

No—not bad news! It was all good, really. The only bad part was that Jupe himself had been off adventuring in the woods instead of being in Space City for the glorious moment, or at least clustered around the index-viewers with his sisters. The greatest thrill a lifetime could provide! And he had missed it! Had missed seeing the Han Chinese launch the Presidential yacht, as relayed by the spy-eyes in orbit around Earth's sun. Had missed the yacht's bursting into near-space when the spaceway transporter whirled it out of one universe and into another. Had missed the capture of the yacht, the landing, the first greeting by the bursting hearts of the loyal Yankees of World.

Had missed it all!

His sisters told him about it, of course, one or another chirping her bit to fill out the mosaic for him. The President was alone—malewise he was alone, anyway. Of course, there were two sisters with him—but such funny-looking ones, Jupe, the old one sallow and lined, the young one sallow and angry! Who had met them at Space City? Why, the Governor herself, of course, Big Polly. Yes, she had made a speech. Yes, of course they had recorded it, had recorded every minute of every event; would he like to watch the replay?

No, he would not like to watch the replay! His place was there! He was going there, as soon as possible!

It was not just that Jupe was a blazing patriot (they all were that), or even that he'd taken combat training. They all did that, too; it was their most important social function other than childbearing, from which Jupiter was biologically exempt. But the tiny minority of males were not merely combat-ready; they were combat-*prone*. Everybody knew that. Sisters were ready to fight because they must. Males were ready to fight because they were warriors. Most of Jupiter's discontent with the universe— and he had plenty of that—arose from the fact that no one was conveniently near to be a warrior against. You couldn't fight the erks, either the dumb ones or the smart, if only because there were too many of them. (Besides, it was their planet, sort of.) You could hunt and kill inklings or wild carry-birds, of course, and that was pretty good, although the foolish creatures never fought back.

But what Jupiter had longed for since he got his first set of pugil sticks at the age of five was an *enemy*.

There was a guaranteed enemy for every Yank, of course, but they had never been near enough to actually fight.

Until now.

So, "Feed my carry-bird," Jupe ordered the stablehand sisters, and, "Get my uniform!" to the twelve-year-olds detailed to housemaid duty, and, "Fix me a light lunch for the trip!" to the kitchen staff. He threw orders in all directions, in fact, and the nest bustled, as it always bustled, around its one and cherished male.

It is a proud and a scary thing to be an emigré, to spend your whole life knowing that there is a Homeland that has been stolen from you. To want it back. The emigré mentality fueled the aspirations of every Yank on World. It was the same fire in the belly that kept generations of Cubans and Poles and Jews forever consecrated to the lost, the never-seen, the semimythical Home. The more improbable its recapture became, the hotter that fire burned.

Jupiter wanted to fight for that Homeland. He wanted it very badly, and that was not his fault. It was the product of his age and life. And, yes, of his gender; an ancient named Daniel Patrick Moynihan once said that every society gets invaded by its own barbarians once in each generation—those barbarians it generates itself, the young males from seventeen to twenty-three. Jupiter was a large-size, prime-quality barbarian. He was looking for cities to pillage or foes to slay; that was what his glands made him. He was also an emigré, third generation on a planet forty-some light-years from Home, so the combative urge

148

was focused. Recapture! Recover! Revenge! Those were the key words in the litanies he had learned with his first lisped baby words.

Because there was only one human male to every one hundred and seventy human females on World, naturally the invading force could not be exclusively male. The females would fight, too. They were trained for it. They were dedicated to it no less than Jupiter. They could be as deadly as he and would be when the battles began. But they did not have Jupiter's glands. So all the sisters admired and chirped around him, even the ones who were as eager as he for the fray. Dumb erks scuttled around the nest to get out his uniform, sponge off stains, iron in creases sharp as knives. Sisters came running in from all over to praise and admire as he bathed and shaved and practiced fierce military expressions before a glass. Senior Sister Loyola even left the nursery, abandoning the fifteen nestlings not yet old enough to talk; they would be fed by a dumb erk crew under the supervision of a twelve-year-old. "I wish I could go with you, Jupiter," she sighed. "You don't want to wait until I put the nestlings to bed?"

He didn't say no. He only laughed and gave her one of the fierce military expressions because she knew the answer as well as he. Jupiter did not want to wait for anything... except, of course, his mandatory interview with the Mother Sister before departure.

And that he was putting off as long as possible.

When at last Jupiter had the entire nest organized to the task of getting him ready for his trip, he allowed the kitchen sisters to feed him. There was an inkling steak— not from the beast he had brought home to the nest, but one out of the freezer. There were crisp vegetables from the garden and a chilled glass of fruit wine. Jupe's nest was one of the oldest and, all of its nestlings thought, one of the best—particularly as to the splendid way it fed its members.

Of course, every nest thought it was special in some way. That wasn't unreasonable of them. There were not so many of them that each could not claim some special distinction; there were not that many humans on World, even after half a century of intensive child breeding.

The places where the Yankees lived on World were usually right outside one of the huge old erk cities. Humans seldom lived in the cities themselves. The cities were too hot and muggy, too much trouble to air-condition against the steamy air of World. The air in the nest was not really any cooler than the ambient outside. The Americans had got used to a steady eighty-some degrees over the generations, and the erks, of course, had been evolved to thrive on it. The big difference was that the inside air was a good deal dryer than out. Little bags of hygroscopic salts in the nest's ventilators sopped a lot of the water vapor out of the air. When the bags were saturated, the dumb erks took them out and dried them in ovens—or in their own body heat, as they clustered in sleep or companionship or sex. None of the erks, dumb or smart, minded being wet.

The other reason the Americans lived in nests rather than in the half-empty cities was that the smart erks didn't want them there. And, after all, it was their planet.

Sort of.

Lunch over, Jupiter squared his military jaw and faced his interview with Mother Sister Nancy-R. He couldn't postpone it any longer. So as soon as his uniform was ready for him to carry out and the handlers reported that his carry-bird, Flash, was eating its dinner nicely, Jupe left the big nest for the pleasant little cottage under the Joe tree that belonged to the Mother Sister and her wife.

Mother Sister Nancy-R was a woman of fifty and some. She was still strikingly beautiful. All of the women of Jupiter's nest were above-average good-looking; when brothers from other nests decided to wander for a time, they often tarried a week or two there, sampling a different sister each night. They were always politely enthusiastic about their beauty when they left. A dozen or more brothers had offered bedding to Nancy-R, age notwithstanding, but she was wholeheartedly les. Monogamous les. She and Suzi had been mated for thirty years, proud parents of fifteen children already and another on the way. And every one of them their own—no implants out of the freezer for the wife of Nancy-R!

Between Jupe and Nancy-R there had always been a jockeying for position. Jupe was The Male. Nancy-R was The Mother Sister.

Nancy-R's own host-mother had been one of the Original Landers. That did not mean one of the original flight crew. Those women had been well past even the age for bringing implanted embryos to term, much less conceiving their own, by the time they landed on World in the year 2047. Not surprisingly, Nancy-R had inherited her mother's life-style. She was a little old-fashioned. Spottily old-fashioned, anyway—her decision not to bear a child elevated a lot of well-shaped eyebrows when she reached menarche-plus-four and all her age-cohorts were starting their first pregnancies. Not Nancy-R. She was radical about that if nothing else. She did not want to become pregnant except through love. Of all things! But you could tell her old-fashioned ways just by looking around her cottage. Item, Old Glory waving on a wall screen. Item, signed pictures on every flat surface, pictures of most of the Original Landers, personally autographed to her. Item, in her dooryard, as a bow to their hosts, a figure of one of the long-necked, tadpole-bodied, two-legged Living Gods of the erks. "So you're here at last," she called to Jupe as he came swinging through the Joe tree archway, his uniform bag over his shoulder.

"I didn't know!" he snapped. He nodded to the Living God and impatiently waited for Nancy-R to get out of the way so he could enter her cottage.

Between the nest's senior female and only male there was a permanent jockeying for position. Jupe won his rounds by staying out of her sight when he was doing things he thought she would disapprove of. Nancy-R won hers by outguessing him when she could. She knew what he was there for. Even the nest's male needed permission to leave the territory. Of course he wanted to go to Space City! Hell, what American didn't want to see her—or his—President? And she knew what storms would follow if she didn't give permission. So her first strategy was to make it her idea: "Why are you still here, Jupe? I want you to greet the President at once!"

Jupe's tentatively sullen expression melted immediately. "Oh, thanks, Nancy," he said, sliding out of his breechclout and beginning to pull on his uniform pants. He had a fine body, Nancy-R thought with aesthetic appreciation. A fine body for a man, of course. He added, "The erks are getting my kit together—I'll be set to leave in ten minutes."

"Good, dear. Are you taking Flash? But she's ready to come into heat. She'll be chasing birds all the way." The smile-corners drooped down, the eyelids went to half-mast. Nancy-R added quickly, "But of course you can handle her if anybody can, Jupe. Would you like to give your report before you go?"

"That's what I came in for," he said. He waited good-humoredly enough while Nancy-R called for her wife, Suzi, and Suzi, belly protruding far before her, waddled in to handle the recorder. Jupe patted her belly amiably. "Lucky Nancy still has a viable ovum at her age," he commented, and Suzi giggled as she dropped the needle in the machine and nodded for them to go ahead.

What Jupe had been doing was scouting a new nest site. (The detour to hunt inklings was an afterthought.) With a hundred and thirty-one sisters over the age of eight in their nest, it was ripe to fission. Everybody wanted a new nest when possible. A new nest meant one of the seniors could become a Mother Sister without waiting for Nancy-R to die. It meant even more that another male could be born, without upsetting the established 170-to-1 ratio. It meant most of all that America was alive and well on World, and growing!

Jupe's report was quick. The lakeside site had good farmland. It was near an erk city in good repair. There were plenty of dumb erks in the vicinity for stoop labor and quite a few smart ones for company. There was water from the lake—samples already delivered for testing—there was drainage, there was even pretty scenery, with soft hills on the horizon and the lake clean and broad. "So we can fiss whenever you like, Nancy-R," he finished, and was startled to see her purse her lips. "What's the matter?" he demanded.

"I'm only wondering if we want to," she said.

"Want to? Of course we'll want to! Why wouldn't we want to?"

Nancy-R winked at Suzi. A point won! Obviously Jupe had not thought the thing through. "Because we might all

153

go back to Earth now instead," she said, and enjoyed the shocked rapture that flooded Jupe's face.

Jupe looked grand in his uniform. He knew it. It was tailored by smark erks, with loving and faithful attention to all the old pictures and the American Senate's new design: trousers, visored cap, jacket with epaulettes, holstered sidearm. The sidearm even worked, although its accuracy was poor and range small. All Americans had uniforms, tailored to them as soon as they were ten. They were for parades on Veterans Day and the Fourth of July; they were for dress-up whenever anybody thought of a good excuse to do it. Jupe's usual costume was no more than a breechclout and a thin coating of oil. But, as he had seen in Nancy-R's mirror, in uniform he did look grand!

Because the carry-bird Flash was near her time, she wasn't in the paddock when he got there. Dumb erks were tumbling over each other in excitement, squealing and gesturing at the sky. That's where she was, aflight, pursuing birds for dessert after her meal, to build up her protein store for her next mating. When at last she settled heavily into the paddock, great thin wings beating majestically, there was black blood on her mouth. But when Jupe stroked her pouch she opened it willingly enough.

"Jupe, man! Hey, Jupe? A ride?"

Jupe turned, one leg already into Flash's soft, warm pouch. It was the smart erk, Ike, loping toward him on his stubby little legs. Ike was uniformed, too—as uniformed as an erk could get—with uniform colors painted on his body and a cap with a visor as shiny as Jupe's own. "Can I come?" he begged. "Have you got room?"

"He's our President, not yours," said Jupe suspiciously.

"No, no!" the erk squealed. "Our President, too, Jupe! Anyway, I want to be in the parade, please, come on, Jupe, please?"

"Oh, well," said Jupe, only it sounded almost as much like "Oh, hell." But the erk got his wish. Jupe liked Ike, as a matter of fact. They had even gone hunting a time or two together, and though Jupe was miles stronger, the erk was miles better at scenting the inklings and freezing still until they came in range. Ike was old for an erk, even a smart erk. He was a good ten years older than even the Mother Sister; he had seen the Original Landers, too.

He was also big for an erk, nearly the size of a collie. Flash grunted in annoyance when she saw that she was going to be expected to carry double, even though one was only an erk. It was only an annoyance. It was not really taxing to her strength. Evolution had designed Flash to carry a whole litter of six or eight juveniles at a time, and in the gentle gravity of World, her muscles were well up to the job.

Quarters were cramped in her pouch, though. She moaned a couple of times as she was jabbed by the hard-soled shoes, the stiff belt, the rigid holster. "Watch it," Jupiter said crossly to the erk, and Ike pulled in his tree-climbing claws apologetically.

Flash grunted and twitched her pouch muscles. Still, when Jupe seized her nipples in a firm grip and tweaked them upward, she launched herself willingly enough into the soggy air.

Like all carry-birds, Flash had been trained along with her rider. Tiny Jupe had squirmed his way into the barely fertile pouch of the young carry-bird when both were very young. They had grown together. Flash followed Jupe's hand with the ease and familiarity of long practice, although there were times when the hand needed to be firm. Flash's hungers were becoming acute, and so when a bird flock passed incautiously near, Jupe had to check her strongly. The rest of the time she flew steadily enough on her own. There was time to relax and chat with the smart erk, Ike, and to gaze out at the countryside below. Mostly to talk. "You haven't *seen* the index tapes?" Ike demanded, scandalized.

Jupiter helped the erk to peer out over the lip of the pouch. "I haven't had time," he said stiffly, but the erk waggled his jaw reprovingly. In erks, the jaw was about all that could waggle; the head was fixed to the torso, like that of a whale or a bedbug. Ike was indignant.

"You missed the most important thing that ever happened!" he said, and fumbled in his belly pouch for a pocket viewer. The carry-bird squawked glum protest as a corner of it snagged the tender lining of her pouch. Neither Jupe nor the erk paid attention. "Look here," the erk commanded, coding for the reception of the President.

"No, no, earlier," Jupiter pleaded, and the erk compliantly coded back farther still. Jupiter gasped in excitement as he saw the Presidential yacht burst out of the spaceway, right where planned. The yacht offered no resistance. The shuttle's hooks caught it neatly—blur, click, as the erk switched forward to the landing—then he saw Big Polly, the Governor of all American World, ride triumphantly out to greet them. The erk was peering over Jupiter's shoulder. "He's really little, though, isn't he?" Ike asked, and Jupiter stiffened.

"Little? He's quite *normal*," he said in his stern, military voice—no erk was going to criticize a Real-American in his presence! But it was true that Big Polly towered over her President.

That didn't matter. What mattered was that the President was on World at last. Now things could begin! Even now, the news index said, the President and the two sallow sisters who were with him were in a meeting with the Senators already on hand. More Senators, more Congressones, more military officers and leaders like Jupiter himself were trooping into Space City every minute—"So hurry," pleaded Ike. "We don't want to miss the parade."

"Flash is flying as fast as she can," Jupe said sternly, but surreptitiously he gave her guidance nipple another little tweak. She groaned protest again, but did manage to put on a little more speed. As much as was possible, Jupiter knew. He resigned himself to staring out of the pouch beside the erk, daydreaming; and a great slow grin spread over his face and stayed there.

From below, Jupiter and Ike would have looked very strange to, say, Castor or Delilah. The two little heads were a bizarre contrast—Jupiter's dark and stern, but human, under his visored cap; the erk's less human than a star-nosed mole's. Erks were mammals, more or less. At least, they were warm-blooded and generally rather soft-skinned. But more than anything else they looked like insects the size of terriers; and their faces were not like anything earthly at all. Flash was bizarre enough, too, with her stubby body that carried the pouch they rode in under her eight-meter dragonfly wings. Any earthly stranger would have gaped or fled in terror. But there was no stranger below them to see. Field erks glanced up from the farmland, and a few of the dumb ones tumbled over themselves to wave—until nipped and threatened by the smart erk foremen. Jupe kept the carry-bird low to avoid bird flocks, just high enough to clear trees and buildings. They could hear sounds from the ground clearly, especially when a smart erk or occasional human called to cheer them on: "Give honor to your Living God President!" "Free America forever!"

Flash grunted interest, and Jupe saw that they were approaching Space City. Other carry-birds were converging at low altitudes, and more worrying to Flash, aircraft were sailing in from farther places. It seemed that every Yank in the World wanted to be in Space City. There were seventy or eighty nests within a thousand kilometers of the center, and nearly every one of them had sent its own male or senior sister to greet their President. Under the spires of Space City, bright and new—though, really, it had been in just that place, looking just like that, for nearly three thousand years—the ranks of the parade of welcome were beginning to form.

"We're in time, we're in time," the erk screeched, and Jupiter's heart leaped.

What Jupe had expected when he landed he didn't know. Falling to his knees before his President, before a crowd of a million cheering erks? Instant battle-stations to repel a Chicom attack? Something dramatic and martial, surely!

What he got was a quick order from his nest's Senator Martha-W: "Get in the hall, there, Jupe! Clear it out! We need a room to greet the President in!" So what Jupe did for an hour after he landed was kick and cajole giggling dumb erks out of the long-unused auditorium at the base of Space City's tallest spire. The President was somewhere around—so people said. Resting, maybe. Waiting for the parade to form up and the hall to be ready. The hall was a human-built auditorium, added to Space City in the days when every adult man and woman on World could assemble there at once. Dumb erks liked to den in it because it was so peculiar. Getting them out was like herding mice. The dumb erks let themselves be driven, but the minute the Yanks' backs were turned they slipped back in, squealing happily at the fun. It wasn't until a team of hard-bitten old smart erks arrived with electric shock prods that the dumb ones gave in and, still giggling, retreated out onto the broad yellow-green lawn.

There remained the problem of cleaning up after them.

And all the time the rumors flew. The President was being entertained by the Governor, the Lieutenant Governor, and the head erks. The President said they were going to liberate America right away and everybody was being issued real weapons. The President had decided that there wasn't enough transport for an invasion; consequences of that unknown.

But nobody had actually seen the President.

And the President of the United States, Pettyman Castor, had on the other hand seen far too much! He was in shock. He was very nearly in fugue, running away within his head from externals too bizarre and scary to deal with.

His "party" was in no better shape than he. Tsoong Delilah spoke only in monosyllables, her face frozen in an expression that mingled dislike and disdain; Feng Miranda babbled uncontrollably. They sat in a triangular chamber filled with flowers (what strange flowers! what sickly sweet or foul-smelling aromas!), and listened, and hardly heard what was said. There was too much of it! They had a whole world's history to hear, and Governor Polly and the "erk" called Jutch would keep on talking and talking so!

It was, to begin with, the worst kind of shock to find

159

that creatures like the erks could talk at all. There was nothing like that on Earth, nothing to prepare them for the dizzying dislocation of being politely welcomed by an animal—or an insect?—no, a *thing*!—with more legs than it ought to have and a face that sprouted cat's whiskers out of a body like a bug's. Even the human beings (why were they almost all women, for heaven's sake?) were hardly reassuring. They were so grossly *large*. They towered over even Castor, and the two genetic-Han women together would not have made one of these giantesses.

Worst of all was what they said. For it seemed that here on this place (they called it "World"—what arrogance!) a colony of lost human beings had been for generations breeding like maggots, arming themselves with weapons more terrible than Castor had ever dreamed possible—allying themselves with these outrageous-looking creatures, the erks—readying themselves to invade the Earth at whatever cost in life or destruction!

There had been human beings on World for fifty-eight years, the Real-Americans were told. They came from an interstellar mission, sent off in those last spectacular days of the space adventure just before the missiles flew and ended space adventures for the foreseeable future. The astronauts had known that was possible; tensions had built steadily from the mid-twentieth century until the hour of their launch. All the same, the actual outbreak of nuclear war caught them unawares.

Then they no longer had a future.

By the time the astronaut crew, fifty-five strong, healthy, smart, young (but aging) men and women, realized there was not going to be a good world to return to, it was far too late to turn back.

They went on as ordered, to Van Maanen's Star.

And there was another shock. Two of them. The first

shock was to find that none of Van Maanen's pebbly little planets had either air or water; there was no place to land.

The second shock was both better and worse. Better because it meant their lives might yet be lived to the end— a very big plus, for fifty-five men and women who had faced the probability of whirling around a dim, unfriendly sun in a steel coffin, waiting for the last of themselves to die. But worse because what they found were the erks.

"I don't mean the actual erks," said Big Polly graciously, smiling at Jutch and the other creatures chirping and twitching around the table. "They didn't send manned—I guess you'd say 'erked'—probes out. What they sent out was automated exploration ships. Each one of them had a spaceway. And that's what the Original Landers found." She chuckled fondly. "What a surprise that must have been!" she said.

A great surprise indeed, for the erk spaceway had captured the interstellar spacecraft as unceremoniously as Castor and his crew themselves had been snatched away from Earth's solar system—whirled through the dizzying tunnel between real-spaces—thrust into orbit around World—grappled—tugged down to the surface—caught.

Their interstellar voyage ended on World, and they were greeted by the erks.

Language was a problem; the erks had never heard of English, of course. But they had skills developed all through their racial history for learning to speak with new races, for they had done this thing many times before. In a week the Original Landers were able to speak to their hosts, or captors.

To understand what they heard in return took a great deal longer.

At first the Original Landers did not see that there was a difference between smart erks and dumb erks. They looked identical, after all, except that the smart erks usually wore more clothing or ornamentation, and it was generally of more sensible patterns. (But the dumb erks liked to play dress-up too.) This led to some confusions, especially when they were feasted by the smart erks and the dumb erks kept climbing up from their laps to their tables to lap at their food. The natural conclusion the Original Landers came to was simply that erks had terribly bad manners.

The erks were almost as confused about the Yanks. They found that the Yanks came in two distinct generations, with a third generation already swelling the bellies of all the females. The eldest generation comprised the females from the original flight crew, all clustering close to fifty years in age by then. The erks did not know enough to be surprised at finding swelling bellies on post-menopausal women, but they knew enough to see that something was odd. Then there were the twentyish females—so very many more of them than men in that generation—and all of them pregnant, too.

It took some explanation before the Yanks began to understand the erks and the erks the Yanks—a little bit.

For the Yanks, it was all sensible and understandable, once you understood the basic needs. The trip to Van Maanen's Star took thirty-one years Earth time, twenty-nine relativistic—far too long to expect the fifty-five original crew to arrive in dewy-fresh condition. If they had all paired off and started raising families about the time they passed the orbit of Neptune, their kids would have been of a prime age to explore on arrival—if there had been anything to explore.

But nobody wants dozens of squalling, diaper-dirtying kids cluttering up an already cluttered spaceship. Besides, the psychodynamicists predicted an absolutely appalling divorce rate . . . if they bothered with marriage.

So they didn't. They enjoyed themselves in such varying ways as each conscience (or pair of consciences—or sometimes larger group of consciences) directed. And once each month each of the women clambered up onto the cot with the stirrups and allowed to be teased out of her private plumbing that month's new ovum. And once each month, in strict rotation, one of the men received somewhat higher kinkier gratification than usual so that he might provide a few cc of spermatozoa to make the ova blossom when wanted. The blossoming was all in vitro. That means, it happened in a Pyrex tube. The bloom was allowed to unfold for only eight days, then the tiny almost-fetus was sexed, typed, classified, and dipped into the liquid nitrogen—until the sixth year of the flight.

Then they selected from the nearly two thousand stored embryos the twenty-eight that tests indicated would be strongest, most agile and adaptable. Four were male. Twenty-four were female; and, with some ceremony, each of the twenty-eight female crew members retired, one after another, to place her feet in the familiar stirrups. This time nothing was taken from her. Something was added.

Nine months later, twenty-five of the twenty-eight delivered healthy babies. Thereafter the collection and the processing and the freezing resumed, and it was nest-building, diaper-changing, child-rearing time on the ark.

The result of this was that when *Intrepid* slowed in orbit around Van Maanen's star it carried, besides its original crew, more than twelve thousand frozen eight-day embryos and twenty-five robust young adults, and those were the ones the erks greeted.

Erks and Yankees met ... and talked ... and each found in the other something badly needed.

What the Yanks found was an unexpected ally.

What the erks found was a cause to join.

And back on Earth, the survivors of the nuclear mutual suicide were trying to put together the scorched and shattered pieces of their world and knew nothing of what was being planned far out among the stars.

"Well," cried Big Polly, hoarse from so much uninterrupted oration, "have you had enough to eat? More java? A drop of berry wine?" The visitors looked at their almost untouched plates and faintly shook their heads. "Then we'd better get to the welcoming parade and reception!"

When the auditorium was at last ready, Jupiter's proud uniform was sweated limp and there were stains on the trouser legs. Jupe examined himself in one of the gold-glass frieze mirrors that decorated the entrance to the auditorium—the scene traced on the glass was Valley Forge, he thought, or maybe that other holy place called Okinawa. He swore angrily. But there was no time to do anything about cleaning himself up, for just then came erk squeals and human yells. "They're ready! The parade's going to start! Fall in, everybody, and pass in review!"

Hundreds of erks and scores of Yankees scurried around to find their places. Not all the human beings would be in the parade, of course. Someone had to watch it go by. So Senators and Congressones didn't march. Neither did the Governor and her staff; they were all up on the platform with the three new semidivinities that everyone craned a neck to see.

What's more, there hadn't been time for all the nests

to get representatives to Space City. While the State Congress had been in session almost uninterruptedly since the erk transporter ship had reached station in the solar system and the first signals began coming in.

So the reviewers outnumbered the reviewed—or would have, if it hadn't been for Space City's three companies of smart erk volunteer militia.

The human squads sandwiched the companies of erks. By the luck of the draw, Jupiter's squad led the parade.

If Jupe could have seen the review through Tsoong Delilah's eyes, he would have found a lot of comedy in the spectacle. (Up on the reviewing stage, Delilah morosely did.) World's light gravity was wrong for thirty-steps-a-minute march time. The feet did not naturally fall to earth that fast. Muscles had to kick them down. So on World the American army, for the first time in its history, had to do a sort of Prussian goose step. Even funnier were the erk militia. They didn't have the right sort of legs to march or the bodies to wear real uniforms. They had spray-painted their bodies in olive drab and black, and they bounced along to John Philip Sousa tempi. Jupe didn't think it funny. He thought it was grand. When he got the eyes-right command his heart thumped hugely as he first beheld his President.

So young!

And so tiny; and the two sisters with the President were tinier still, with skins so sallow and features so—well—strange that Jupiter wondered if they were ill. Even the President had a haunted, absent air as the colors trooped past and he returned the salute.

And then it was all past, and the Yankee military might, all two hundred and twenty of it, counting erks, column-righted around the edge of the reviewing stand, and halted by squads and were dismissed.

Ike scurried over, chirping with joy. "Oh, Jupiter, that was marvelous! What do we do now?"

Jupe looked at him in a superior way. "What you do," he said, "I don't know, but *I* have been invited to the reception."

"Oh, sure, the reception, we're all going," bubbled Ike, taking the wind out of Jupiter's sails. "Did you see him? Tell me, Jupe, isn't he small? Somebody told me Real-American males only ran a hundred seventy centimeters or so—is it something to do with the gravity?"

"Everybody knows that much," said Jupiter severely. "Are you just finding that out, Ike?" He observed that the dismissed squads were melting away and was galvanized. "Come on, if you're going to the reception and banquet—if we don't get a move on all the good places will be gone!"

The places weren't gone, because there weren't any places. Everybody milled around in a large room off the dining hall, and to Jupe's surprise there were tables and trays and buffets of inky-meat pâtés and tree-cheeses and crisp sour-pears and all sorts of good things. Yet tables were set in the hall behind the wide doors; were they going to have two meals?

That didn't matter. What mattered was that all three of the Real-Americans were lined up by the doorway, and one by one all the people at the reception were lining in their turn to pass by and shake their hands. Shake their hands! Jupiter grinned with joy; that was one of the Real-American customs he had learned as a child and never seen practiced on World.

He took his place in line, disappointingly far back, just after an erk whose name was Jutch. They had met before—Jutch was high up in erk council. Jutch was an old erk, with discolored skin and half his nails missing, but his chirp was as lively as Ike's.

Something occurred to Jupiter. "This handshaking," he said. "How are you going to do it?"

The erk's vibrissae wriggled. "Weren't you briefed? They gave us all instructions. We erks get up on our hind members like this"—he raised the first set of limbs off the floor—"and then they'll all stroke our foreknuckles. Then we say, 'Hello, welcome to World; we are all united in the cause of freedom.' Then they go on to the next one in line. Didn't you get these instructions?"

"I was very busy," Jupiter snarled.

"I see," said the erk politely. "Then maybe you don't know what humans are supposed to do—"

"I *am* a human! Of course I know!"

The erk's vibrissae drooped consideringly as he gazed at Jupiter. "Of course," he agreed, making an effort toward tact. "Then you know that you're supposed to bow before you hold your hand out."

"Certainly I do," said Jupiter, listening intently. "Were there any other instructions for humans?"

"I thought you said you knew what you were supposed to do."

"I do! I was only wondering if they got the instructions right—for people from nests that don't have the same advantages I do, you know."

"I see," said the erk, waving his vibrissae to stimulate thought. Then, "No, nothing about the ceremony, I think. There wasn't much explanation, either."

"What needs explaining?" demanded Jupiter. "Seems simple enough to me. The handshake is a Real-American custom when you greet somebody. Bowing is an expression of respect—of course, you bow to your President!"

"I didn't mean the ceremony itself," the erk explained. "I was thinking of how funny it is that we should be eating out here, and then in a little while we're going into the other hall and eat again."

"We are?" asked Jupiter, wondering. Then he recovered himself. "Of course we are," he said. "You mean you don't understand why we eat twice?"

"Not really," Jutch confessed.

"Then," Jupiter said kindly, "you should have asked me. You see, this is what they call the 'cocktail party.' It's an old Earth custom."

The erk said, "I see that, but why do we eat twice for the same meal?"

Jupiter said regretfully, "I wish I had time to explain that to you, but look, we're almost at the head of the line! Now, don't forget. Get up on your hind members and let them stroke your foreknuckles, all right?"

"Yes, thanks," said the erk with a grateful flick of whisker, and scuttled ahead to make his duty obeisance to the distinguished visitors. Jupiter watched him with a full heart. To touch the hand of the true and real and only President of the United States! A transcendental experience! The most fantastic dream of his childhood, incredibly come true!

Only, you know, once you'd done it it wasn't really all that transcendental. The President of the United States was—well, not a *letdown*, certainly. Your President couldn't be a disappointment! But it was true, all the same, that Jupiter had not expected President Pettyman to be hardly older than Jupe himself and hardly more practiced in the rites of protocol. All Jupiter could think of to say when he pressed the flesh of his President was

"Hello." The President didn't seem even to hear that, being preoccupied at peering down the length of the waiting line and frowning when he saw how long it still was. Nor were the two sisters with the President particularly grand. It was impressive that they were of Cabinet rank, but why did they look so peculiar? Why were their faces so flat and their eyes so black? Had there been something wrong with their implantation? Was it possible that all Real-American sisters were like these? (And if so, what was it like to copulate with them?) As he left the dais, having had a perfunctory handshake with the Governor and one or two other Yanks he hardly noticed, he almost tripped over the erk Jutch. "Oh, sorry," he said, flushing. It wasn't so much that he minded stepping on the erk— the erk should have got out of his way—but he didn't like being caught still staring at the President.

"Have you got a table reservation for dinner?" asked the erk.

"Reservation? No. What's a reservation?"

The erk said considerately, "I guess you got here too late for that. Anyway, you're welcome to sit at my table."

"Thanks," said Jupiter, thinking fast. "I, uh, I think I will use the excretion facilities now."

"Of course," said the erk, backing away. A well-mannered erk, thought Jupiter approvingly. Having invented the excuse, he decided in fact to excrete. He walked to the head of the waiting line without even thinking of the fact that he took it for granted that no one would be using the one stand-up urinal in the excretion chamber. Of course, no one was; everyone else on line was a sister. Struggling with the unfamiliar uniform fly made Jupiter rueful at his own clumsiness, and he bantered back and forth with the sisters waiting for the cubicles. At the very end of the line as he left he found his own Congressone,

Mary-May. "I'm surprised to see you have so much difficulty opening your pants," she called jokingly. "You never used to have that trouble in the nest!"

Jupe grinned at her fondly. As nest male the choice of the Congressone was his, as the choice of the nest's Senator was the Mother Sister's, so in a sense Mary-May was his protégée. "It depends on whether there's anything worth taking my pants off for," he explained. "Now, if one of those Real-American sisters were here—" There was a chorus of giggles and hisses from the waiting sisters.

"Ugly things," one young sister exclaimed. "Did you see how kind of spoiled their skins look? And neither one of them has a decent nose . . . Of course," she added lamely, belatedly remembering whose looks she was criticizing, "they do look very, uh, *dignified*, don't they?" She looked around for support. There wasn't much to be found. She made another effort. "I was quite close to them for nearly two hours," she said with pride. "I was an usher in the stands when the parade passed in review, so actually I was near enough to touch them. I could even hear what they said to each other, quite a lot of the time."

Well, that made a difference. The sister's gaffe was forgotten as the rest of the line closed in to hear what she had to say. Even Mary-May cocked an ear, for her place on the platform had been a good deal too far away to hear any exchanged confidences between the Earth sisters. Jupiter himself might normally have tarried to hear more, but he was beginning to worry about where he was going to sit in the dining room. Why had no one told him to make a "reservation"?

When he circled the dining hall he discovered that the failure was important. There was a head table, easily recognizable by the huge three-dimensional figure of a Living

God holoed on the wall behind it, and of course by the fact that the table was elevated a meter above all the others. There were plenty of tables set around it and nearby, in concentric half circles. But every one of those nearby tables was marked "Reserved." There were place cards (so they were called, the smart erk waiter Jupiter buttonholed patronizingly informed him), and the names on the cards were either important erks or high-ranking humans. For semi-important people like Jupiter, no places were set aside. The semi-important were left to take their chances in the unreserved tables. Furiously Jupiter boiled back to the excretion chamber and caught his Congress-one just as she reached the head of the line. "Mary-May, this is terrible!" he complained. "I can't sit way at the back of the room like that! Can you get me in at your table?"

"Oh, no, Jupe. There's no room."

He glared at her. "Have you forgotten whose Congress-one you are?"

"Of course not, Jupe," she soothed, giving him a peace-able smile. "You picked me, I know that. But I didn't make the seating arrangements—and really, Jupe dear, you're making me hold up this whole line, and they're going to start serving dinner very soon—"

He gave her a black look. At least he had the erk's invitation to fall back on. He started to turn away—then remembered the young sister who had been in the reviewing stand. He waited for her to come out of one of the cubicles, took her arm, led her away. "You can sit with me," he said generously; and when he found the table where the erk Jutch was sitting, far back against the distant wall, he said, "This is my friend. I've invited her to join us." If the erk had any objections, he kept them to himself.

Anyway, the occasion was exciting enough for anyone, even those condemned to sit practically against the far wall. Smart erk waiters were bringing little dishes of cut-up fruit soaked in wine. Dumb erks were trying to steal some of the dishes, amid laughter from all the guests. Gradually Jupiter's temper improved. After all, it was the greatest occasion of his life!

And the company was not bad. The erk Jutch turned out to be rather important in the hierarchy of erk affairs. Why he was not up in a reserved seat, Jupiter could not imagine, but there was much about the way the erks ran their lives that was still mysterious to the Yankees, even after two World-born generations.

Not only that, but the strange sister, whose name turned out to be Emilia, was full of interesting gossip about the Real-Americans. The President was quite shy, she said. He hardly ever spoke to either of his Cabinet members unless they spoke to him first.

But the most startling thing, said Emilia, was the *ignorance* of the Real-Americans. She gazed around the table. "Do you know," she asked solemnly, "that the Real-Americans never heard of the Living Gods?" All at the table, human and erk alike, automatically turned to gaze at the Living God figure behind the head table.

"How did they think we erks got smart?" asked Jutch in amazement.

"They didn't even know the difference between dumb erks and smart erks!" the sister chuckled. "Didn't you see that old sister, the one they call Delilah? In the receiving line? A couple of dumb erks sneaked in to steal some of the food, and she actually stroked the fore-knuckles of one of them!"

There was more that the sister knew, and that lasted Jupiter through the palm soup and the inkling fricassee, while smart erk waiters came through refilling java cups and reminding everybody to save their admission tickets and picking up the dirty dishes. The sister had a lot to say. She had overheard a lot. She had overheard the Real-American sister Delilah consulting with A-Belinka, the smart erk who was chief matter-transporter operator. Funnily Delilah hadn't seemed to want to talk about sending warships to Earth. (It had been very uncomfortable for Delilah, the sister giggled, because the erk had sat in her lap to talk to her.) The other Real-American sister, Miranda, had been constantly whispering to the Senators and Congressones, trying to find out just how the government of Yankee World worked. A Senator and a Congressone from each nest, yes, but what did they do? When they convened, did they pass laws? How were they elected? The Senator by selection of the Sister Mother alone, the Congressone by choice of the nest male? But didn't anybody *vote* on anything?

"What do we want 'laws' for?" Jupe demanded.

"She didn't say, Jupiter. And she didn't explain about 'voting.' There's a lot that's funny about the Real-Americans, and especially about the President! Let me just tell you—"

But she never did tell Jupiter the funny thing about the President, because the Governor stood up and tapped her java cup with her heavy glass spork for attention. "Ladies and gentlemen and honored erks," she said, "the President of the United States."

The hall became as still as it could be—no hall with dumb erks tumbling around under the tables could be wholly still. Perhaps it was the constant undermotif of happy or hurt erk squeals that made the President seem uncomfortable. Perhaps it was something else; Jupe noticed that President Castor Pettyman kept looking anxiously at Secretary of State Delilah Tsoong as he spoke.

And what he said was rather peculiar.

"On behalf of the peoples of the United States of America," he began, and stopped as the Governor leaned forward to adjust his lapel mike.

"Thank you," he said, licked his lips, glanced at Delilah Tsoong, and went on. "On behalf of the peoples of the United States of America, we thank you for having us here. This is a most important occasion. It will be written about in the history books for thousands of years to come."

"Why is he telling us that?" Jupe muttered to the room at large.

The erk Jutch said reprovingly, "This is a political speech, Jupiter. You weren't really briefed properly at all, were you? You're supposed to be quiet—except when it is time to cheer."

"When is it time to cheer?" Jupe demanded.

"You'll see. Please listen!"

Jupiter shrugged and paid attention to the speech. "—much time has passed," the President was saying. "Much history has taken place. Many things that were true one hundred years ago are true no longer, isn't that true?"

That seemed to be a time to cheer, because the Delilah sister leaned forward. "True!" she shouted. It was an obvious cue, and the eager erks and Yanks did not fail to seize it. All around the room, every Yank and every English-speaking erk shouted, *True, true!* Jupe was as loud as any. That was fun! He was in a real patriotic rally, with his real President! It was disconcerting that some of the things the President said were—well—strange. But still!

"So," the President went on, glancing again at the American sister with the strangely shaped face, "we must go cautiously. We must not make mistakes. We must confer and learn to understand each other's needs and problems, isn't that true?"

This time the shouts of *True!* were a little fainter, as though others in the audience had begun to wonder just what was being said—though this time even the dumb erks under the table yipped and chattered inarticulate somethings, too, enjoying the game.

Jupiter looked around the room. Every human face was showing some degree of puzzlement. Of course, with erk faces you couldn't tell. Still, Jutch leaned over to him. "Why doesn't he say something about the war?" he asked.

"Hush," said Jupiter severely, since it was the same question he had wanted to ask.

The President continued:

"So our first objective here is to learn what you have to tell us so that then we may tell you all we know. I have arranged with your Governor"—he turned and bowed courteously to the sister from Cherry Hill Nest—"to give us a week of briefings, including a tour of, ah, World. We will take ten of you with us, the names chosen at random. We will learn all we can. Then we will address the entire population of World, both human and—ah, uck?—erk— on television."

He paused and beamed around the room. Jupe had the idea that the President's smile was somewhat forced. Then he said, "Thank you," and sat down. The applause was considerable, but it frayed away into silence as everyone waited for something to happen up on the platform. Very little did, and what was happening was not very interesting. The Governor was whispering in the ear of the President, and the Secretary of State was saying something

175

nasty and punishing to the rebellious-looking younger Real-American sister Miranda. Jupiter could hear none of that.

The erk Jutch put his forepaws on Jupiter's shoulder and chirped, "Come on, Jupiter, tell me. Isn't there going to be a war?"

"Of course there's going to be a war," snapped Jupiter. He pushed the erk away and said severely, "Don't you know anything? You can't just have a war any time you want one!"

"We always did," the erk said sadly.

"You're erks! We're Americans! First there has to be a planning session. Then the military people have to make plans. Then there has to be, I don't know, like an exchange of diplomatic notes," he improvised, trying to remember his history lessons, "and then an ultimatum. *Then* we have the war."

"It sounds like a lot of extra trouble to me," said the erk.

"This is an *American* war. We'll do it the *American* way. Erks have nothing to say about it."

"Oh, now, really, Jupe," the erk objected. "Those are all our weapons and ships and things that we're giving you to fight this war with. We ought to have some rights. Not to mention a lot of us will be fighting right alongside you."

Jupe shook his head in irritation. "Erks always fight," he pointed out. "That's what erks are all about, isn't it? So pay attention and learn something. Our human rules of warfare are very sensible and simple—"

But he never got to the very simple rules, because from the tables all around them erks and people were shushing them and calling, "Shut up, you two. You're missing it!"

"Missing what?" Jupiter demanded belligerently and then saw that up at the center stage, where the Governor was standing patiently, the orchestra had just finished another rendition of "Hail to the Chief."

The Governor applauded politely and then called, "Fellow Americans! We are now ready to have the drawing. I hope every one of you has kept the stub of your admission ticket, which you will see is numbered. The numbers will now be drawn at random, and each number called will entitle the erk or Yankee who holds it to form part of the escort party for the President and his staff as they tour World."

The sixth number drawn was Jupiter's.

II

When the party was assembled there were twenty-five of them, the ten escorts who won the lottery, the three high officials from Real America, and about a dozen officials, erk and human, who appointed themselves to the group. Some had a reason to be there, like the Governor herself and the erk A-Belinka, head operator of the matter transporter, who would be an important part of any invasion of Earth—if any invasion of Earth was ever really going to happen. Most were simply just along for the fun. They were too many for carry-birds to deal with, so two hoverplanes were provided. That meant there was plenty of room to carry them all in comfort, but when the Real-American sister Miranda heard that Jupiter was trying to get permission to fly along with them in Flash, she fussed and complained and got on everybody's nerves until they gave Jupe his permission. Then she gave herself permission to fly with him in the carry-bird.

What a thrill that was for Jupe! Alone in a carry-bird pouch with one of the only two Real-American sisters on World!

What a thrill it was for Miranda, too. Nothing like it had ever happened in her life before. Nothing she saw was familiar. Even the farms were not the same as on Earth; Earth had nothing like erks to share a planet with. Everything she saw was exciting, even such silly and familiar things as herds of inklings pouring down a defile on their way to mate or released carry-birds preying on bird flocks. "Have you ever copulated in a carry-bird pouch?" asked Jupiter, generously. "No, of course not; you've never been in a carry-bird before. Here, let me show you what you have to do—"

And what a surprise that was! Because Miranda didn't want to copulate with him. She not only didn't want to do it in the pouch, which Jupiter could understand because although that was interesting it was also not really very comfortable, she didn't want to do it at all. Said she didn't, anyway. Said she was a "virgin," which caused Jupiter a whole incredulous shock of unbelief and almost revulsion; why would any sister want to be a *virgin*?

What she did want to do was talk. No. Not talk, really; she didn't offer much about Earth, although Jupiter's curiosity was immense. She acted as though she didn't enjoy the subject for some reason, almost as though there was something she didn't want to tell him, though he could not make out what it was. Annoyed, beginning to wish the flight were over, he resigned himself to answering her questions—"Because," she explained, "that's what the protocol is, right? First we all find out everything there is to know about you people and World. Then we confer, and then the President makes his address."

"You could tell me *something*," he complained.

"No, I couldn't. Won't, anyway. Now tell me: where did all you human beings come from?"

"From the interstellar probe, of course!"

"All of you? But there were only fifty or sixty people on the ship, they said."

"Ah, well," said Jupiter, marshaling his memories of the great story of the Original Landers, "that's true. But, you see, they collected all these fertilized ova and

179

sperm..." He began to cheer up. The opportunity to lecture was rewarding, after all, if not in the way he had more or less decided he would allow her to reward him, and it made a nice break in the boring, long carry-bird ride.

Miranda was full of questions. "And how many of you are there now?"

"Oh, hell, Miranda, who can keep count? Around eighty-five hundred, I think."

"And how many are men?"

He paused while, frowning, he urged Flash's teats a little higher; she had seen a covey of resting birds on the woods ahead and he didn't want her getting ideas. "Fifty or so. Adults, I mean—over fourteen. There's usually only one male to each nest, and that's how many nests we have."

"Fifty men," said Miranda thoughtfully. Fifty men and 8,450 busy wombs. "And all the women are pregnant all the time?"

"Well, no—once a year at most, usually. Sometimes they wait a whole year for a new implant. And there are some, like my Mother Sister, that just don't get pregnant at all. See, she's married, and she wants to be the father, not the mother—"

"Oh, my God," said Miranda, when Jupe had finished explaining to her how the Mother Sister took her own ova, fertilized them in vitro with anonymous sperm from the banks, and implanted them in her "wife."

But by that time they were almost at the first nest on their list.

Mining nests, farming nests, industrial nests, teaching nests—there were fifty nests to be seen, and all fifty

wanted their President and his colleagues to see them.
Wanted *urgently*. Damn well *demanded*. Would not be
refused. And of course it was impossible to accommodate
them all, and then people like Jupe kept getting messages
from friends in other nests, in his own for that matter,
begging and demanding and pleading: "Come on, Jupe,
you can talk them into it if you want to!" But he didn't
want to. He was getting tired, too.

Not as tired as the Real-Americans, of course, not by
far. After three days young Miranda was half-hysterical
with strain and fatigue and, mostly (to Jupe's permanent
astonishment), with fending off the courtesy copulations
every male offered her.

Now, why in World would she want to do that?

When away from her, Jupe spent endless hours discussing this oddity with the other males, with senior sisters, with erks, with anyone who would listen. Their
bafflement was as great as his: what woman (bar the
oddies like his own Mother Sister) wouldn't want a penis
inside her from time to time? As often as she could manage
it, in fact?

When with her, Jupe spent endless hours on the same
subject until, scarlet with rage, she forbade him to ask
even one more question on pain of being thrown out of
the escort party.

In school biology Jupe had studied the mating habits
of the sting-beetles, tiny warm-blooded creatures like
scorpions whose mating occurred only once in a lifetime,
after which the male crept into the female's womb and
lived on there, blind, limbless, brainless, for the rest of
his and her life.

The mating habits of the Real-Americans were as
strange, as repulsive, as incomprehensible to him. It took
him a long time to figure out the pattern, and then he

could hardly believe it. Miranda wanted to copulate Castor and nobody else. (Incredible!) Castor was in the habit of copulating Delilah, but was perfectly willing to copulate Miranda or any Yankee sister—or probably a tree-trunk, for that matter. However, Delilah wouldn't let him. Delilah copulated only Castor, and she got quite snappish at Miranda, or the Yankee sisters (or no doubt the tree-trunk) when Castor seemed to show an interest. She was going to lose that test of wills, Jupiter decided, but why bother in the first place?

How very strange it all was!

The strangeness did not end with their peculiar sexual practices—barely began there, to be sure, because what was of most interest to Jupiter was not how Real-Americans made love but how they lived. As to that there was only stubborn silence. The three Real-Americans differed on much, but on that they were united and resolute. They would tell all about what Earth was like—once they had learned what World was like, and not one minute before. The President's prepared statement had said nothing. They said nothing to add to that nothing.

But they asked—everything! Oh, what questions they asked! "Where did you Yankees get those dumb names?" demanded Miranda. How weird that she should not figure that out for herself! Were they not the names of the great male heroes of the past?—not only the Americans but the foreign, the real, and the mythical: Ulysses and Ajax, Robert E. Lee and Pickett, John Wayne, Thor, Brigham Young—and, of course, Jupiter. Why did they pick such names? Why, because they were heroes, for heaven's sake! All male Yanks were heroes! They lacked only the challenge to be heroic about!

And where did the erks get their names? Why, from the same source, naturally—except that the erks, not being really Yankees, were naturally even more patriotic than the native-born. They chose only the greatest of American statesmen. Abe Lincoln. George Washington. Franklin D. Roosevelt—"Damn it, Jupiter," complained Miranda, "why don't they say them right? They speak perfectly good English!"

"They do now," Jupiter agreed loftily, "because we've been teaching them for ages. But they didn't when we first arrived, you know. Didn't speak English at all. They spoke that crazy squeaky stuff they talk to each other, but of course they did want to take our names right away."

Miranda stamped her foot. "*Why?*" she demanded. "What kind of crazy people are they, that they want to name themselves after strangers like that?"

Jupiter sat back and looked at her thoughtfully. The question was in perfectly clear words and grammar, all right, but what a strange question! Didn't this sister know *anything*? Patiently he began at the beginning. "Because that is what they *do*," he explained.

"*What* is? *Why* do they?"

"They help the causes of righteousness and justice wherever there is a need, of course. And they do it because the Living Gods made them that way." Idly he gestured toward the figure of the Living God, gleaming in three-D color beyond the entrance to the nest they were visiting.

Miranda frowned uncomprehendingly at the figure. "I don't know what you're talking about," she said at last; and at last illumination came to Jupiter.

"Ah!" he cried, and then stood up and called to the other groups of erks and humans scattered around the nest grounds. "Listen, all of you! They don't understand! They don't know about the Living Gods!"

183

* * *

When two parties are arguing at cross-purposes and suddenly, revelatorily, the basic incomprehension becomes clear to one side, the other side usually reacts with irritation. "Don't be so damn smug!" Miranda raged. "Tell us! Then we'll understand!"

"I will, I will," smiled Jupiter, gesturing to the others to join them. "But let's do it in an orderly way, shall we? It'll save time in the long run." He patted her unresponsive hip, which did nothing to soften her mood. "Come on, all of you," he added, to Delilah and the President and the others. "Sit down. Here. Anywhere. We'll clear this up right away—oh, what's the matter?" he asked in annoyance, as the Mother Sister of the nest began shaking her head.

"We don't have time for this, Jupiter," she said severely. "You've given our nest only thirty-one hours, and now you're scheduled to inspect our district medical center, so the Real-Americans can see how the implants are stored and nurtured and transplanted and—"

"This is more important," Jupiter said boldly, looking to the Governor for support. She thought it over first, but then she gave in with a nod. So they all sprawled out on the mossy banks under the hot red sun. Erks came running up with wine and java and things to munch on, and Jupiter set himself happily to resolve the difficulty. "The erks," he said, enjoying himself, "were not the bosses of World. The Living Gods were."

The Real-American sister Delilah gave him a look of disdain. "Start at the beginning, Jupiter," she ordered. "What are the 'Living Gods'?"

But the Governor was having none of Delilah's disdain. She said authoritatively, "Jupiter will tell this his way or not at all." And then reversed herself by telling it herself: The erks had not been the dominant species on the planet. They were a sort of pet, which the dominant species— the "Living Gods"—kept around as livestock or for companionship.

Because the Living Gods were a technologically gifted race, in all the kinds of technology open to them, they did not leave their pets unchanged. For that matter, neither did humans. Human beings bred dogs into Chihuahuas and Malamutes. The Living Gods moved more swiftly and surely. They reached into the DNA itself and made the erks smart. Dumb erks were about as bright as chimpanzees and as childish. Smart erks were about as smart as humans—

But also still childish, in ways that appealed to the Living Gods, for they liked their pets to be amusing.

The Living Gods—the ostrichlike beings in the shrines—were rather like humans in another way, because they had not learned how to avoid war. Weaponry outraced wisdom.

And, in the long run, they killed themselves off. There was a Living God colony on another planet of the system that rebelled against their masters on World; the Living Gods on World annihilated that planet and all that were on it; but not in time to save themselves. Biological weaponry was another of the things the Living Gods were good at, and the viruses the rebels poured into the air and waters of World killed every Living God there was.

The erks survived.

"We don't breed true all the time," explained Jutch, climbing up in Castor's lap to peer into his eyes. "It's been a really long time, you know, and the gene alterations aren't as stable as that. So there are dumb erks as well as smart erks like me."

185

"All erks are dumb," grinned Jupiter. "Otherwise you wouldn't be trying to get into every war you can find, would you?"

The second day came and went, and the third, and the fourth.

They had covered nearly a quarter of the land area of World's one big continent and even a couple of nearby islands. They had shown the President's party the marvelous old Living God machines and cities that healed themselves when they wore and rebuilt themselves when they aged; they showed how the machines could be redirected to build new things and even new cities. Or nests.

Or weapons.

They were nearly at the end of the tour, and Jupiter saw with astonishment that the Real-Americans did not really seem all that clarified. They had learned a lot, but what they learned did not seem to make them wiser. It certainly did not make them easier to get along with. More and more they chose to wander off together, a closed group of three, to whisper and hiss and snarl at each other. They weren't getting along with each other any better than with their hosts, but what was the matter? Clearly they were troubled—

And then everyone was troubled; and the most troublesome thing yet happened at Ancient Nest.

They came to Ancient Nest on the sixth day of their tour, hot and tired and snappish with each other. The food at Rosy Nest had been poor, because the kitchen sisters had tried to please their visitors with a special Earthside treat of tamales and pizza, and the result had been horrid for everyone. The long flight had been through bumpy air, and half of the party were airsick. When Jupiter tried to cheer Miranda up by explaining the historic uniqueness of Ancient Nest she only said sulkily, "It's one more damn nest, and the hell with it."

Jupiter exchanged resigned looks with the erk Jutch. What a way to talk about Ancient Nest! It was the first colony the Yankees had ever had on World. It was nearly a shrine, and so was the erk city it was built beside—in fact, the city was even more of a shrine to the erks than Ancient Nest to the Yankees, because it was hardly an erk city at all. It had never been rebuilt for erk use. It remained exactly as the Living Gods had left it, millennia before; the erks visited it, for it was their Mecca and Lourdes and Independence Hall all in one, but no erk lived there. "Uh-huh," said Miranda as they stepped out of the hoverplane. She wasn't really listening to him. She was watching Delilah whisper angrily into Castor's ear as the two of them stood by the other plane, and her expression showed that she wasn't any happier than they.

"You haven't heard the most interesting part," said Jupiter.

"That's good, because honestly, Jupe, I haven't been all that thrilled with what you've told me so far." Miranda grinned sardonically as she observed Delilah carefully wiping Castor's sweaty brow with a fuzzy leaf as she scolded him—Castor had been more airsick than most on the flight—and turned her attention to Jupiter. "Well? So what's so interesting?"

"An Original Lander," said Jupiter proudly. "That's what's so interesting!"

At least this time he got her full attention—not only attention, but demands for explanation; not only that, but a quick consultation with the other Real-Americans. "Why didn't you tell us there were survivors?" demanded Delilah, and Jupiter only smiled.

"It was a surprise," he explained. "Besides—"

Besides, he thought, it was only sort of true that Major General Morton T. Marxman had survived. He didn't have to explain that. It was easier to show them; and as soon as Ancient Nest's Mother Sister Erica waddled out to welcome them they all went to take a peek at this last living survivor of Earth in the half-hospital, half-museum display where he lived. Or "lived," since what kept the old general alive was only the pipes and potions and plumbing of the erk biologists. Marxman was not really *incredibly* old—he was not much over a century, Jupiter explained, counting up for the Real-Americans—and of course other human beings had sometimes lived longer than that, hadn't they? But General Marxman had had a hard life. Especially since the stroke. After that he was really out of it, nearly all the time. The medics did, however, give him a trickle of stimulant now and then for special occasions.

"And this," smiled Mother Sister Erica proudly, "is certainly a special occasion! Do it, Lucille," she ordered, and one of the nursing sisters turned a valve and admitted a trickle of something extra into the constantly flowing liquids that had long since replaced most of the blood in Marxman's old veins.

The Real-Americans peered down at the shrunken old figure. "Nothing's happening," said Castor.

"It will take a while," said the Mother Sister and glanced at the nurse. "About half an hour? All right. Let me show you some of the interesting sights of Ancient Nest while we wait."

"Do we have to?" groaned Miranda, but the answer was yes, they did. Jupiter led the way proudly. He'd been to Ancient Nest before—well, just about every male Yank had, and a lot of the sisters, too, because visiting General Marxman was a pretty standard sort of class trip for the little ones. And when you were in Ancient Nest, naturally you visited the erk shrine. It was called the Hall of the Living Gods, and what was most interesting about it was that it wasn't just the Living Gods. "What are those damned things?" cried Miranda, her face wrinkled up in revulsion as she stared at the images ranked around the central stylized Living God.

Jupe smiled patronizingly. "Our predecessors," he said simply. "The erks have been sending out scout ships for many thousands of years, looking for survivors of the Living Gods."

"But those aren't Living Gods," Castor objected.

"No, of course not. Those are other clients. Just like us."

Castor looked indignant at that. He was staring at the niche with the tiny pale walruses, the next one with feathery-fronded sea anemones, the next one still with spiny squirrels the size of a horse, the next one still— "They're awful," said Castor. "What do you mean, our predecessors?"

"Just that they are the other races the erks have helped," Jupe explained. "That's what they do, you remember? The erks have never failed to give aid to the oppressed, in all their history. Of course, it hasn't always worked out the way you'd want it, but still—"

"But still," said the Mother Sister, getting a message from the door of the hospital, "we're ready for the general now! Oh, sisters, oh, Mr. President, what a noble experience you will have now!"

* * *

Well, it didn't seem that way. If the Real-Americans felt themselves honored, they didn't show it. They seemed if anything glummer than usual as they followed Jupe and the Governor back to the tidy green-decorated room where General Morton T. Marxman was being drawn back to the world of the living for their amusement. They didn't seem amused. "You know," Jupe whispered fiercely to the Governor, "these people aren't doing the right thing at all!"

The Governor gave him a bad look. Part of it was anger and part reprimand for daring to criticize his President ... but there was also a part that was agreement; for indeed things were not working out well. She said, "Be still for a while, Jupe. Let's get through this damned ceremonial anyway."

General Marxman had been taken out of his cocoon bed where monitors tested his blood and feces and urine and sweat and thoughtfully filtered out the bad parts from the blood and added the good parts he needed to keep what was left of his metabolism functioning, more or less. He had been reattached to the little shock-machine that reminded his heart when to beat and the gas-pipes that metered out what went into his lungs. He was reclining on his ceremonial couch, the one that propped him nearly half-sitting up and guarded him against falling.

He actually looked quite alive.

He could even talk, and he knew his lines. "Welcome," he rumbled. Some old men's voices get cracked and shrill— that's hardening collagen in their vocal cords. Some get deep and glottal, and that's better, so the medics in charge of General Marxman had selected for deep and impressive. His eyes were even open, though it was hard to tell what they were seeing, if anything. Taken all in all, he looked about as much as a living general should as any museum reconstruction of an extinct species.

He even impressed the President, thought Jupiter proudly. At least Castor was clearly fumbling about for some appropriate statement. He glanced at Delilah for help, got none, took a deep breath, and improvised:

"Ah, General Marxman," he said, "we, uh, have come here to pay our respects to a great American hero. You," he added, to clarify the matter.

He paused for a response. He got none. The general appeared to be thinking that over.

That was normal enough, of course. Stimulants or none, since his stroke, the general did not move very rapidly, but Jupe knew that the best medical opinion believed that inside that head a brain still frequently functioned. He wondered what it was like to be trapped and helpless in a dying old body. He looked on the recumbent figure with pity and contempt; how could anybody let himself get old? Was it really possible that the general had once been a boy, a youth, a second lieutenant desperate to be admired, an astronaut, a colonel? (The general's rank Marxman had finally bestowed on himself—reasonably enough, as the only commissioned member of the United States Armed Forces within nearly forty light-years.)

Belatedly Jupe heard a suppressed gasp from the Governor, and then he saw what she had seen.

There was a light in the general's eyes. He was looking as though he was seeing, and what he was looking at was not the President.

He was staring, with mounting emotion, at Tsoong Delilah and Feng Miranda, and the emotion was neither awe nor joy.

It was rage!

The nursing sisters saw what Castor saw. They understood as little as he, but they knew that something bad was happening inside the paralyzed head of General Morton Marxman. They came quickly forward to check pulse and breathing and vital signs, but the general squawked and croaked inarticulate sounds to warn them away. The eyes still glittered fiercely at Delilah and Miranda. He tried to move a wasted arm to pull the breathing tube out of the corner of his mouth; the arm would not move. He tried to push himself erect, but there were no muscles left in his wasted body that were capable of so Herculean a task. Indomitable, he did not surrender to the limitations of the corpse he lived in. He coughed. He gagged. He squawked and dribbled. And finally he spat the tube out, into the hands of the helplessly fluttering nursing sisters. "Treason!" he bawled, eyes flaming, glaring the sisters away. "Treachery! We've been betrayed! Arrest those two women at once—they're Chinks!"

III

So for the second time in a matter of days Jupiter's world turned upside down, but this one was no happy occasion. The hideous opposite of a happy one, it was an occasion for outrage and confusion. Chinks? The President had brought the *enemy* with him? How could such things be?

And nothing the President said helped to explain. Nothing the two women said was of any importance, of course: They were *enemy*. Enemies *lied*. They had to be arrested, just as the fierce old dying general had ordered— and that itself was a problem, because how did you arrest two members of the Cabinet of the real and true President of the United States?—especially when the President himself was petulantly demanding their release?

Something was terribly wrong!

It was not only wrong; it was just about incomprehensible. The rescue of the United States should not be complicated by this sort of madness! It made no sense— worse than that, the President only added to the confusion by trying to clear it up. Well, yes, he admitted, the Chink woman Delilah Tsoong was in fact Han Chinese—well, sort of Han Chinese. Well, she'd been born in the United States, all right, so she was legally American, too—if one could fit the words "legal" and "American" into the same sentence, when there had not

been any American government to make anything legal
or otherwise for a hundred years. And to make his
incomprehensible explanations less comprehensible still,
there was the woman Tsoong herself. She was uncom-
promising, even defiant. "All right," she sneered, "arrest
me if you like! But you are fools! There is no America!
It destroyed itself a century ago!" That was confusing,
yes, but it simplified things a little, too, for anyone who
could say such seditious things definitely needed to be
restrained. They bound her arms behind her back, kept
her quiet by threatening a gag if she didn't shut up, put
her in the custody of the Governor and three smart erks
with electric shock prods to see that she tried no tricks.
(Whatever tricks she possibly could try, almost alone on
a planet of beings who found her horrible.) She let them.
She sulked.

The President was another matter. How could you
arrest your own President? Even when he said such
shocking things? "I'm not a real President," he said and
"The election was a farce, really," he said and "We
haven't been altogether honest with you, you know," he
said, and then they simply wouldn't let him say any
more. Even General Marxman, the fading breaths rattling
in his throat, could only nod agreement when Big Polly
pointed out that farce or not, that Presidential election
was the only Presidential election they had and Castor
Pettyman therefore the only President. So Castor was
not arrested. He was put into the copilot's seat of his
own hoverplane for the trip back to Space City, staring
out in displeasure at the landscape of World fleeing by
beneath. The armed erks behind him were, in his case,
an honor guard.

And then there was Feng Miranda, altogether the
most confusing of all. "Of course I am genetically

Chinese," she cried furiously, "but what does that have to do with anything? My ancestors were *American*. For two hundred years they were *American*. They were patriots, and so am I! Loyal to *America*! You idiots, I'm the only American you've got! I'm far more of a true-blue American than that turncoat lackey Castor, who will lick the feet of the Han for a chance to ride in a spaceship every day of his life!"

What a puzzlement! Big Polly glanced around at the Real-Americans and the Yankees and the erks, looking for comprehension, for advice. There wasn't any. So they all bundled back into their hoverplanes for the trip back to Space City. The Congress might be able to decide what to do. It was beyond the capacities of even Big Polly.

As to Miranda, they compromised on her loyalty. They gave her only one armed guard, and that was Jupiter. The erk Jutch piloted their ship, and Jupiter left him to it as soon as they were at floating level.

There was a pallet at the back of the hoverplane. Miranda had thrown herself down on it, raging silently in anger and frustration. Jupe made his way back and stood over her for a moment, thinking. Then he touched her arm. "I believe you," he said, and added kindly, "If it would ease you any, we could copulate now."

She replied to him most unpleasantly, using a term for "copulate" that he had never heard before. It seemed almost obscene to him—imagine making copulation an obscenity!

Jupiter was a kindly person, for a male. Under normal circumstances he would have tried to jolly her out of it, perhaps even going to the trouble of stroking or patting her in spite of her nasty, hyperactive ways. This time, though, there seemed to be something going on up front. The erk pilot was chittering excitedly and twitching his vibrissae at Jupiter. Something was up, though Jupiter could not tell what. "I order you to stay right here," he warned the Chinese woman, who gave him a deadly look in return. Discomfitted, keeping one eye on her to make sure she was obeying (though what else, after all, could she do?), Jupe moved forward to the pilots' seats.

And even before he got there, as soon as the erk's reedy voice could reach him, he got the word: "Jupiter, Jupiter! You'll never believe it!" cried the erk.

"Believe what?" Jupe demanded, sliding into the seat next to him.

"They've launched another ship!" the erk babbled excitedly. "Look at the index screen! It's a big one, Jupe!"

Astonished, Jupiter leaned forward to activate his own screen. The right index was easy to find; the development was on a dozen theme channels at once, for it was big news in many ways. A new launch from Hainan Island! And, just as the erk had said, a big one!

The index screens in the hoverplane were not the same as those in the nest. It took Jupiter a moment to figure out how to do what he wanted to do. The erk tried to help him, but Jupe impatiently waved him off as he stabbed at the keyboard until he found the right setting. The blown-up still of the Han ship shivered and dissected itself into its parts. They weren't real; no erk or Yankee eye had seen inside the skin of the Han ship. What they were was the best erk specialist translation of the tracking data, optical scans, analogues with the Presidential yacht, and deductions from what was known of Han Chinese weaponry.

The ship was heavily armed. There was no doubt of that.

Its launching was, in fact, very nearly an act of war, and Jupiter's glands flowed in joyful torrents.

* * *

Miranda did not obey orders. She was hanging over Jupiter's shoulder all the way back to Space City. But Jupe did not reprimand, hardly even noticed, her flagrant disobedience, because she was by all appearances as thrilled as he. "They're going to attack!" she cried. "Oh, boy, Jupe, we're really going to fight them!"

"We're going to *beat* them," he corrected with the gruff kindness of a father whose child has responded in exactly the right way. "You'll see! The erks have been getting ready for this for a long time."

"Me, too!" she cried. "Oh, Jupe! You don't know how long my comrades and I have waited! You don't know what it's cost us—my own brother's life, a hundred years of slavery, all that hopeless time—and now—oh, *Jupe*," she repeated, flinging her arms around his neck. Well, thought Jupiter with some satisfaction, at last the sister was coming to her senses! Wrong again. To his surprise, when he reached back (somewhat awkwardly, twisting his arm to reach) to pat her bottom in response, she tightened up again. "God, is that all you think about?" she snapped, and drew away.

Jupiter gave up in exasperation. "Do you want to see what else is happening?" he asked coldly.

"Certainly I do. Just keep your hands to yourself."

He shrugged morosely and indexed the planning channels. It wasn't necessary. What needed to be seen was already in plain sight. They were coming into the Space City landing places, and just ahead of them, hovering over the city gates, there was a rainbow light-sign. It said:

Welcome
to the President
and the Plenipotentiary Congress

"What's a plenipotentiary congress?" Miranda demanded, staring over Jupiter's shoulder.

"It's what it says," he told her. "It's a congress of everybody important on World. It's just been called. As soon as they spotted the Chinese ship, Big Polly got on the communications channels. See, now we can do it!"

"Do what?"

"Why, declare war," Jupiter said gleefully, and was pleased, if a little astonished, to see that her breath came a little faster again. Her dour expression melted into almost a smile. He debated, then decided against, patting her again and instead said, "We're all going to be in session right away."

"Who's 'we all'?" she asked suspiciously.

"Oh, you too, I guess," he said. "Maybe even Tsoong Delilah. I don't know. Everybody!"

And everybody it turned out to be. Not merely the Congress. Most of them were already there, for every nest on World had been getting its Senators and Congressones there as rapidly as they could, ready for the return of the Real-American party and the President's expected address. That wasn't all, because the nests had also sent as many senior sisters as there was room for, and all the adult males. Nothing like it had ever happened on World before—at least not during the Yankee tenancy of World—and the mood was festive.

It was also serious, because there were serious decisions to be made. Big Polly had outlined the two main areas of decision making on the communications channels: to decide what to do about the surprising ethnicity of two of the President's party; and to prepare to meet and overmatch the threat from the Han Chinese on Earth. They were two quite different subjects, to be decided in quite different forums. The war plans would be made by

the joint Yank and erk military council; as a serving officer
Jupiter could attend that, his right beyond question. He
had no right to sit in on the sessions of the Congress of
the United States (in Exile), however, and was thrilled to
find out that as Miranda's jailer, with Miranda's presence
essential, he was allowed to go along. There were no erks
in Congress sessions, which were held in one of the old
city assembly rooms. The trouble with that was that dumb
erks didn't realize they were excluded, and so they were
underfoot and being shooed out all through the half hour
when Senators and Congressones drifted in to take their
places. At the last there was a small procession: Miranda
with her guard Jupiter; followed by Tsoong Delilah and
her two erk guards, to take their places in the front of the
room, but off to one side; then, walking together, Big
Polly and the President to mount the dais, sitting on paired
inkling-leather armchairs, to call the session to order. It
didn't take long. The verdict of the Congress was simple:
The President was the President. His executive authority,
however, would not come into force until Real America
was recaptured. Feng Miranda was a true and loyal American. Tsoong Delilah—

Well, Tsoong Delilah did not help her own cause a bit.
Yes, she said, she was the only legitimate Secretary of
State, but on the other hand the nation of "America"
didn't really exist; and she held to that in spite of ques-
tioning and pleading. The questions came from Feng Miranda, and they were pointed and cruel. The pleading
came from President Pettyman, who seemed to regard her
intransigence as one of those silly womanly notions that
were, most likely, associated with a premenstrual bio-
chemistry. She would not recant. The Congress decided,
after all, to leave that question open.

The Congress recessed itself, and all of its members

moved joyfully to the larger chamber where the erks of the War Council waited for them. Had not really waited, exactly. The erks tolerated Yankee political rituals, even found them quaintly endearing, but while the Congress was in session the erks had been taking the practical steps necessary to make war planning mean something.

The session lasted five minutes. The smart erk named A-Belinka reported that the Han ship was being tracked and soon would be captured. Big Polly proposed a state of war. It was passed unanimously, with one abstention. But as the abstention was only the sulking Secretary of State, chin on hand, staring angrily out the window, it was not even recorded.

A-Belinka and Big Polly between them quickly appointed a Committee for the Conduct of the War. Jupiter wasn't on it, but Feng Miranda was. And that, he told himself, was almost as good, because although Jupiter the cocky young male from a minor nest had no claim to such exalted rank, he had now risen above that station. He was now Jupe-the-Jailer. He was the keeper of the sworn (but possibly deceitful) ally Feng Miranda; and whither she went there would go Jupe.

It was almost as good as being on the committee in his own right, he told himself and tried to make himself believe it was so.

She still did not wish to copulate. She insisted on sleeping alone that night. She had been given a room actually inside the old erk city, and although Jupiter would normally have had no difficulty in inviting some sister or other to his bed, the layout of the rooms made it awkward. Annoyed, he slept that night rolled up in blankets just outside Miranda's door. Alone.

The next morning, though, he was all cheer and pleasure; they were to go to the vehicle-assembly sheds and discuss armaments and strategies. He hurried her through breakfast and commandeered a hoverplatform to carry them, spraying clouds of dust in all directions, to the hangar where the ship she had come in was housed. "What have they done?" Miranda demanded, staring around as they entered the huge shed. It was a rhetorical question. What they had done lay spread out before her. The ship she and the others had flown from Earth had been carefully, cautiously taken into its component parts. All the weapons that Tchai Howard and Manyface had concealed in its hull and drive systems and storage spaces had been dissected out. They stood alone now, a battery of murderous machines. Lasers of ionizing radiation. Missile projectors like the 75-millimeter cannon of bygone wars. Rocket launchers, both chemical and nuke. Even Miranda had not realized how lethal the spaceship had been. "They could have wiped you out!" she exclaimed, and the smart erk A-Belinka, scurrying over the spread-out pieces of a fire-control radar, wiggled his vibrissae at her in agreement.

"They could have destroyed our ships, yes," he chirped. "They could even have destroyed the spaceway—not by attacking the transportation field itself, of course, for that is not material, but by destroying the scout ship that generated it. But sooner or later, Miranda, our numbers would prevail. Once they were on this side of the spaceway they would have had no choice but to surrender—as they will have no choice again!"

Miranda looked at him doubtfully. "How can you be sure of that? What if they do shoot up the scout ship? Then you can't reach them at all, isn't that true? Not until you send another ship at slower-than-light speed with a new, what do you call it, spaceway?"

The erk's vibrissae flailed wildly. "They won't!" he shrilled. "They mustn't! What a terrible thing that would be! Jupiter, we must keep them from doing that!"

Miranda looked wonderingly from the little creature to her official guard. She shook her head incredulously. "I can't *believe* you people," she said. "God! Well, I see there's no help for it—I'm going to have to tell you how to run this war. Start by telling me all about this 'spaceway' thing, and we'll figure out how to handle the Chinese as we go along."

A-Belinka wasn't offended. He was entirely happy to explain whatever Miranda wanted to know. Communication by means of the spaceway, he told her, was circumscribed by the laws of physics and by the distances involved. Right, the spaceway could be generated only by material means—its generator was among the apparatus the scout ship carried. Right, in order to get a spaceway to any point in the Galaxy at all, it had to be carried there—and if there was no other spaceway already in place, it could be carried only by a conventionally propelled slower-than-light vessel. Right, if the scout ship was destroyed, all the erk and Yank plans would be set back by nearly half a century, because that was how long it had taken to get their spaceway-bearing ship into orbit around Earth's sun—and how long it would take to replace it if lost.

But, he said, vibrissae twitching happily, Jupiter nodding glad agreement beside him, they were not such fools as Miranda seemed to think! Having dissected her ship, they now had a good idea of what weapons the next one might carry. They could not prevent the Han from using those weapons—not, at least, until they were on the World side of the spaceway. But they could make sure they used them unprofitably.

A-Belinka turned to an index screen and called up pictures of what they had already done. Long since, they had supplemented the scout ship with small drone eyes. These were tiny, remote-controlled spacecraft that had been flashed through the spaceway toward Earth over the past weeks. The scout ship would hang back, out of range, and covered by a screen of drones. If the Chinese fired their weapons they would surely fire first at the nearer, more worrisome drones. They would be diverted, at least for a short time—and once the Han vessel was within range of the spaceway, a hundred thousand kilometers or so, it would take only moments to generate the field and swallow the ship up.

"And," finished the erk, twittering with excitement, "they are almost within range now, Secretary Miranda! Let us waste no more time. Our fleets are ready to deploy for the invasion—once we deal with this Chinese ship, which is already approaching the spaceway."

"And how do we do that?" demanded Miranda, bristling. "Are we going to do something or just sit around talking?"

A-Belinka said humbly, "We're going to do something, Secretary Miranda. Here. Let us look at what we have to deal with." He chirped quick commands to his erk assistants and then pointed with his vibrissae to an index screen.

The Han Chinese ship appeared before them, boosting itself out of low-Earth orbit toward the waiting scout ship. "We have fed into the data storage everything we know about your ship and its weaponry," said A-Belinka, "and also everything that any of you have told us or that we observed from our spy-eye drones."

"Yes, yes," said Miranda impatiently, studying the image on the screen. She listened with half an ear while the erk droned on about the biases that had been placed on the machines, the conjectures that had been fed in, the data from a score of other wars—other wars? Her ears pricked up, but A-Belinka was rattling on. The machines, he said, took all that in and appraised it. They considered the facts, the guesses, the theories. They studied the optical image of the Chinese ship, as well as what their other remote sensors could tell them about its radiations and its physical structure. Then Miranda saw something on the screen that had not been there before.

"Look at those ridges along the hull," she cut in. "They weren't there when they moved the ship to the gantry! And I think there are more antennae than there were—"

"Ah, very good, Secretary Miranda," said A-Belinka, chittering an aside to his helpers. The uncorrected optical blurred and was replaced by a stripped schematic. A-Belinka peered at the screen and said, "Missile weapons! And, oh, what big ones!"

"How did you do that?" Miranda demanded, staring at the index screen. Under the former bulges lay slim cylinders with bright tips.

"It is a most probable case, Miranda," the erk explained. "The machines have taken all the data and produced a best estimate. Usually they are quite reliable. Now the antennae—" And the smart erk assistants did something else with the controls, and the blisters that marred the smooth surface melted away. Underneath were parabolic dishes, great and small. "Why," said the erk with pleasure, "I think those are radiation weapons! You didn't tell us that the Chinese had radiation weapons."

"I don't know what you're talking about," snapped Miranda.

"Oh, it doesn't matter," said the erk dreamily, "but the machines have deduced that the Chinese understand that the spaceway is immaterial—energy, rather than matter—and so they intend to try to jam it. It will not work, of course—but how interesting, to find that the enemy is cleverer than we hoped!"

Miranda cast a doubtful look at Jupiter and a worried one at the erk. "'Hoped'?" she repeated. "That doesn't worry you?"

The erk bounced up and down happily. "It makes the game more fun!" he declared. "Where is the pleasure in shooting inklings on the nest? No, it is good that they should offer real opposition—for then, when we triumph, the satisfaction will be much greater!" He hopped off his perch and scuttled toward the door. "Come along, everyone," he sang. "Let's capture this dangerous enemy before he makes real trouble. The game is about to begin!"

And Miranda, tugged along by the firm, joyous hand of Jupe, followed slowly and thoughtfully. The liberation of America had been a hopeless dream for most of her life—only in the last few days a real and thrilling prospect. It had been something she was willing to die for, even to kill for.

She had never once considered it as a "game."

M A N Y F A C E

lay in his cocoon, watching the alien ship grow larger on the spaceship's screen. Manyface was not the only one in a cocoon. Every space traveler had a cocoon to cushion him against the shocks and drags of space travel, but Manyface's had to be more huge and more complex than most, since Manyface himself was. The part where his huge head rested, the part that cushioned the head against squeezing and the neck against snapping, was jelly-filled and twice the size of the others. It did not keep Manyface from seeing what was going on, although it reminded him that his survival was far more precarious than the rest of the crew.

But so was all of Manyface's life. Manyface had taken

on himself the burden of ten other minds in his own. Those ten other samples of brain tissue tucked inside his own imposed restraints on everything he did. If Manyface, high Party member, chose to overrule the restraints, that was the privilege of his position. It was also the risk of his choosing, for the launch directors had warned him that the flight might cost him his life. Or, more accurately, his lives. Some of the eleven lives that made up the committee called Manyface had opposed the plan.

Manyface twisted slightly in the cocoon. His head ached fiercely, and not just with the acceleration he had endured. For any human being, the venture of space required cosseting and armoring and training. Space was a sea where the sharks were swimming. One did not venture into it bare. For as peculiar a person as himself, thought Manyface—thought one of the personas of Manyface, and the rest of the committee concurred—the armor had to be twice as strong and all precautions doubled.

Lying supine in his cocoon, twitching uncomfortably at every slight change of thrust, Manyface decided that there was one other noteworthy thing about space travel. It was *boring*. He had been warned of dangers. He hadn't been warned that there would be so many long hours with nothing to do but lie there while the ship painfully lifted itself away from the Earth. Nor had anyone mentioned that other unpleasantness of space travel, that you smelled all your companions in all of their animal aroma. Like all Han, Manyface intensely disliked body odors. In the spaceship, they were part of the air he breathed, inescapably.

He drowsed off, thinking about the last few days. When the traitorous peasant woman Feng Miranda stole aboard the first ship, when that ship disappeared, suddenly and terrifyingly, there had been upheavals on Hainan-ko. All precautions were doubled at once. Tchai Howard had seen to that. He had been made to look a fool, and rage as well as prudence made him recheck every precaution. No treacherous young female would steal into a dressing room and stun an astronaut again! Nor would there be as easy a hijacking of this second ship as there had been of the President's yacht.

So for intensive days and sleepless nights the ship itself was refitted with the ultimate in weapons, and the crew reshuffled to use them best. The second ship was bigger than the first. It had to be; it had more to carry. Besides the new rocket launchers and the white-noise radio projectors that, some hoped, might damage that strange purple glow that had swallowed the President's ship, it had a crew of ten rather than three. There was Manyface himself, adamant on going no matter what the doctors or the administrators said. There was Tchai Howard, of course, cheated out of his first chance, urgent to punish and revenge. And there was a strike force, seven hard-trained, tough assault guerrillas just back from a little pacification mission in Botswanaland, along with their commander. All ten of them, those last days, slept in one huge room, relieved themselves in open toilets, were never out of sight of each other for any minute, all through their training, right up to the moment when the dressers fitted them all into their suits and the technicians handed them into the ship.

All the same, when the ship was ready to blast off, Manyface was frightened.

Nothing was easy or simple for Manyface, not even fear. He wasn't *all* frightened. Angorak Aglat wasn't frightened. Angorak had once been a security marshal in the Mexican protectorates, when courage was an occupational requirement. Neither were Shum Hengdzhou or

Tsai Mingwo, and Potter Alicia was too vague and cloudy in her perceptions to be really frightened. She spent her time asking to have the tape of her daughter's voice—a message they had coerced from Maria on promise of full citizenship and honors for her unborn child—played back to her. It didn't help when it was; she forgot it quickly again every time, for her connection with reality had always been tenuous. Those were the brave members of the committee. Corelli Anastasio, on the other hand, was scared blind. He had suffered all his life from agoraphobia, the fear of open spaces, and what space could be more open than space? Hsang Futsui and Dien Kaichung were edgy with the irritation of fear, and so the currents of emotion that flowed in the soupy sea that was the collective mind of Manyface were sour with tension. The orderly workings of the committee were troubled.

This was annoying to Manyface—to the original Fung Bohsien and to all his added selves—because, really, this couldn't have come at a worse time! Just when Dien Kaichung, the latest implant, was settling down! Just when the postoperative confusion and the psychic nausea had begun to pass, so that the committee could once again deliberate in orderly fashion and speak, most often, with a single voice!

So the takeoff was bad, really bad. The whole first battering thrust as the spacecraft pushed itself away from the surface of the Earth was tainted and sickened with the flood of panic from Corelli and Hsang and Dien; so was the recheck in low Earth orbit; so was the boost toward the alien ship. "Calm down! Calm down!" Manyface shouted inside his head. "We must keep control! Much depends on it!"

And as a matter of fact all the voices were saying much

the same thing, and all equally loudly; so that it was a pity they didn't hear each other.

When the voices of Manyface met in executive session—which was always, since they had no escape from each other but death—there were eleven of them.

There was Angorak Aglat, mountaineer from the southern provinces of the Chinese nation, former peace marshal and artillery officer. As a person with a body of his own, he had been slightly deaf from the explosion of cannon next to his ears. For that reason he often shouted. As a scrap of remnant gray matter tucked into someone else's skull he still shouted. Angorak was never wrong. He knew this to be true, though sometimes other people did not seem to believe it. Angorak was sardonic and greedy; Angorak was smart, but not smart enough to know that he was not necessarily smarter than every other human being he would ever encounter, even within the limited space of Manyface's swollen skull.

Potter Alicia was the sweet one, the one who hated to see her skullmates at odds. Potter would soothe one and plead with another, urging them all toward peace. Potter would arbitrate unendingly, even well past the point where arbitration and patience seemed reasonable. Even past the point where the disputants had begun to dislike her more than they disliked each other. Potter would accept any slight or insult or outburst of anger from any of those other minds she lived with, just for the purpose of bringing peace to their councils. Potter had been an agronomist, mother of two, and she was always sweet, except sometimes when the issue was something that Potter herself wanted.

Su Wonmu had been a high Party member, though not

one who mattered much to the other high Party members. Su had been a soccer player. Su had always been thoroughly reliable in a political sense; he grasped new Party lines as soon as they were formed. He managed quickly and easily to live within them, to defend them, to explain them—even when they were hardly explicable. So when the high Party officials decided it was an investment worth making to humanize their image and looked around for a popular, safe candidate to join the Presidium, Su was an easy choice. Inside Manyface's skull he was still easy. He just was not of much use. He was the person in every committee who seconds motions other people make.

Corelli Anastasio—ah, he was a weird one. Pure indigene. Ancestors American for two centuries. He was the scientist. He was also a wimp. He was as politically reliable as Su Wonmu, which is to say he lacked any conviction of his own as wholly; this made him trustworthy. What made him weird was that he was glad to be dead. He had left behind him grown children and a bitter divorced wife. He didn't mind being in Manyface's skull. It was safer there.

The other one that mattered, really, was Shum Hengdzhou. In his life as an autonomous human being he had not been anything much. He had been the father of two middle-sized girls and a section leader in a steel mill when the ladle of molten metal splashed over his body. No political background. Unknown outside his mill and home. All that had given him salvation, or as much salvation as anyone could find in somebody else's head, was that he had been the first totally destroyed, biologically compatible human being available with a salvageable brain when Manyface proposed to continue the implants as an experiment. He was also rather a decent person. The other implants, vainglorious about their more illustrious past histories, tended to look down on him. Shum accepted that. He was second only to Potter Alicia in anxiety to smooth out stress and less likely than Potter to make demands of his own. For Shum had little of his own to demand and no right to demand it.

Of most of the others, not much trace remained of "personality," for their implants had been taken from far more fundamental regions of the brain. Yet every one of them contributed his own special flavor to the soup. To Manyface himself, as chairman of the board, each voice was uniquely distinctive. He could not have told how he recognized them. There was no sound to carry clues. A choice of words, an intensity of will, a tremor of self-doubt—those were the characteristics he could recognize.

And he could hear them all, all the time—and sometimes the voices were maddening.

Manyface was nearly stable within his own head when he got into the rocket. It had been long enough since the implant of Dien Kaichung for Dien to settle down. His terrified screams and convulsions at finding himself dead, trapped, imprisoned within the skull of Manyface had dwindled to an occasional sob—the soundless equivalent of a sob. The rest of the inhabitants of Manyface's now healed skull had moved around to accommodate him. ("But no more, please," said Corelli pettishly. "It's getting really crowded!")

But then there was the stress of the flight . . .

"Old fool, wake up!"

It was Tchai Howard bellowing in his ear. "I was not asleep," Manyface said instinctively, in the honest lie that every drowser tells when caught. But he had been. Behind him the assault team was muttering among themselves while their captain methodically went through the checklist of his weaponry; on the screen before him was a confusing pattern of bright spots.

"What are they?" demanded Tchai, waving a free arm toward the screen.

Manyface could not answer. Whatever they were, there were a lot of them—a dozen solid blips at least, maybe a hundred if you counted the fainter ones. The radar could not reach far enough to see details. But his inner voices could see enough to scare some of them and anger the others. Said the voice of Angorak-the-warrior, glumly, "It looks like a fleet!"

"A fleet is impossible!" cried Tchai, glowering; Manyface realized that Angorak's voice had spoken aloud, through his lips. Well, a fleet *was* impossible. But the blips were real enough. Manyface peered at the radar, trying to make sense of what he saw, trying even harder to quiet the shouting within his brain. All the voices were talking at once. He could not make them stop. Worse, they couldn't stop themselves, so that all ten of them were yammering at once, and sometimes the words leaked through Fung's own lips. "Stop it!" roared Tchai, wriggling to thrust his face into the swollen face of Fung. "Old man, you endanger the mission if you cannot get a grip on yourself!"

Well, that was what Fung most desired! At least there was unanimity in that respect. All the concern and fear and anger of his implants found a new direction, and together, in half a dozen voices, they cursed Tchai Howard, so that the assault team lifted their heads from their rests to admire. When the committee's anger was spent, reason returned. A whisper from one of Manyface's implants, a consequence drawn from another; Manyface, speaking again with a single voice, said coldly, "They are not a fleet, Tchai. They are simply drones. A great many of them, but none is the alien ship itself. Study the ranging data! They are too small to be dangerous."

Tchai Howard glared at the old man, then turned his attention to the screen. "You are right," he said reluctantly. "But where is the big ship?"

Manyface said with disdain, "It is you who are supposed to be the pilot and navigator. Find it, Tchai!"

"And when I do?" Tchai demanded. "Will you be able to carry out your task?"

Manyface said cuttingly, "My task is to communicate with them. I cannot do that until you establish a communications link."

"The question is," Tchai snarled, "whether you can do it at all. Was it a mistake to bring you, after all? Is that freak's brain of yours really under control?"

"Oh, Tchai," said Manyface sorrowfully, "you speak of endangering the mission, but what else are you doing now?" It was taking all of his effort to keep the parts of his mind focused on the same task. Rage made them hard to control; rage was what Tchai Howard produced so easily.

For Manyface, even to answer a simple question was sometimes not simple at all. No question was simple when eleven complicated persons—or scraps of persons—each heard it and invested it with the overlay of attitudes and habits of thought that modify every received message in the mind of everyone. The committee gabbled back and forth, in the quick communication that was possible within a single skull. It took no time at all, really, for communication took the form of a kind of shorthand—sometimes, really, only a sort of feeling. In this present confrontation, for example, Potter, Shum, and Dien responded only with a general outpouring of consent and support. Sometimes, though, the communications were articulate, explicit, even furious: "Do it, damn it!" ordered Corelli in a rage. "I'll speak if you don't want to," offered Su. And, "Tell that ass Tchai that we, after all, are in charge of this vessel," commanded Angorak; and what came out of the single mouth held in joint tenancy by the fragmented minds of Manyface was "Shut up, Tchai. Of course I'll speak to the alien."

He loosened his retaining straps and glanced around the cabin. The assault team lay still, but their straps were loose, too. Tchai Howard had freed himself completely of his cocoon, all but a single belt to keep him from flying away; their vessel was without acceleration now, and therefore they were all without weight. Manyface leaned forward and turned on the communications mike to say, "Unidentified alien vessel, please respond. What have you done with the president of the United States?"

Then they waited for an answer.

It was a long wait, and out of the corner of his eye, Manyface saw Tchai Howard's fingers busy on the armaments board. "Stop that, Tchai!" he commanded. "First we must find out what has happened and what their intentions are—remember, we may want their help against the Indians!"

Tchai opened his mouth to reply, but the radio preempted him. A familiar voice: "This is the President. What do you want?"

Puzzlement. Consternation. Even the assault team lost discipline enough to mutter among itself. "How can that be the boy," demanded Tchai, "when his ship was destroyed by their energy weapon?" Manyface did not answer at once. He could not, because the dialogue in the ship was echoed by the debate in his own head. "We will ask," he said at last. And, to the microphone: "Where are you, Mr. President?"

Pause. Then the voice of the jumped-up houseboy: "I am safe, Manyface." Manyface! The voices inside Manyface's head gasped in shock and anger; no one dared call Manyface by that name in his hearing! Even the assault team giggled.

Then, "Keep them talking," ordered Tchai Howard, his hands busy on the armaments board again, and Manyface was angry enough, this time, not to order him to stop. And, all in all, the parley went well, thought Manyface in all eleven of his parts—

Until he heard Tchai Howard groan and a moment later gasps and cries from the assault team—

And until he felt, more than saw, a curtain of violet fire rush toward him, and envelop him, and pass beyond him—

And until he looked out the window before him and saw that the Sun that had been to the right of the window, striking fiery reflections off the sharp angles of the alien ship, had been replaced by a smaller, redder sun on the left—

And then the panic currents poured forth again, and Manyface, all eleven of Manyface, screamed at once in the certain knowledge that they had been overwhelmed by something they could neither comprehend nor control.

Manyface was not surprised that they were captured. He had warned against it in the first place. Had told the Generalissimo of Missilery and the Deputy Chief of the People's Militia, his equals in those last days of briefing before the takeoff from Hainan-ko, that these aliens were far better prepared than anyone in China could

possibly be—had had fifty years to get ready and plan
surprises. They could not catch up in a matter of months.
He told Tchai Howard the same, and the assault team. It
was true that in the excitement of the takeoff, he had
forgotten his own warnings, but he had even told his own
brainmates the same, when they were not telling him.
"But don't hurt my son-in-law," said Potter Alicia, and
Manyface sighed—all the other parts of Manyface
sighed—and said,

"He is not your son-in-law. He has divorced your
daughter. But anyway," he added, in that quick internal
flash between tissues, "we are not likely to hurt anyone.
The big problem is to keep anyone from hurting us, very
badly." And when they were in fact captured, ripped out
of this new orbit around this new planet and dragged by
force down to its surface, even in the violent jerks and
fears of the reentry Manyface shouted to Tchai Howard,
"I told you this would happen! Now be still! Do nothing!
Let me plan for all of us, and I will issue orders!"

Whether Tchai accepted the command was hard to tell.
It did not matter, either, because as soon as their vessel
had been irrevocably grounded they were surrounded by
troops and weaponry. What troops! Even Tchai and the
assault team were too stupefied to resist. Resistance would
have meant little against the overwhelming odds, ten men
against an entire planet, and in any case nothing had prepared them for Amazons with rifles and queer little floppy
beetles that chirped and chattered and, to show that they
were to be taken seriously, every now and then discharged
some sort of projectile weapon in great bursts of explosive
power into the air.

No, they could not resist. And the final blow was when
a great, ungainly hovercraft machine came sliding toward
them across the broad, barren spaceport. It bore one per-

son, looking incongruously majestic. When it stopped the person hopped off and strutted toward them.

It was Pettyman Castor.

"I welcome you to World," he said gravely—as though he had a right to welcome them anywhere, as though anything he might say could be important to anyone! "Although you do not come in peace, we welcome you here to see our resolute purpose and our overwhelming might. The liberation of America is ready to begin!"

It was fortunate that the assault team had long been disarmed. The Amazon guards behind them saw them stir and tense and lifted their weapons warningly. Even Manyface could hardly believe what he heard. "What have we done?" moaned many of his voices, whispering together inside his head. "Is this amusing game we were playing suddenly going to be *serious*?"

II

What Manyface saw in space, what he saw on landing, what he saw in the queer, crystalline city that became his jail—they were all scary. The game had indeed become serious. Astonishingly serious. The "spaceway"—that terrifying, immaterial purple veil through which they passed from one space to another in the twinkling of an eye—that was serious, all right! That meant a technology no Han Chinese had ever dreamed existed. And it was not the only thing. Their ship had been captured by a shuttle and dragged down to the planet's surface just as some misbehaving weather satellite might have been brought home for repair by human beings in the great days of the space age. But that was only because the Chinese technology was so inept, so primitive, that primitive means had to be used against it. As they landed Manyface saw off toward the skyline a huge skeletal structure like a mad roller coaster and learned it was called a "launch loop"—a better, faster, cheaper, more *deadly* way of launching ships than anything on Hainan-ko. And it was launching them! New ships every day! Already dozens, maybe scores of ships were in orbit, waiting for the time to attack. It was an armada! And if one single ship had been able to destroy an island, what hope was there that the Han Chinese could resist scores or hundreds of them?

The Yanks were serious enough, all right. No, "serious" was not the word—"fanatic" was a better one, for they seemed to think of nothing but warfare and revenge against the Han Chinese. How Tchai Howard and the assault team felt about this Manyface could not know, for the party was broken up at once. Even the erks, queer little beasts though they were, were obviously able to deploy great force for whatever campaign they planned. They were not funny to him, after the first moments. They were real. The Yanks and "erks"—what strange names these strange creatures had!—had had half a century to make their plans. Han China would have no defense at all.

The future was hopelessly black, Manyface's internal committee concluded somberly. And yet—

And yet, the experience was interesting in itself. Manyface had started out as a scientist, was still a scientist in several of his parts, retained the curiosity and interest of a scientist in strange phenomena.

There were plenty of strange phenomena on World!

The erks themselves were fascinating. If they did not speak Chinese—none of them did—at least many spoke English, and one in particular became a guide, almost a friend—at least, a being with as much curiosity and interest as Manyface himself. His name, he said, was Jutch— "Jutch Vashng'nun," he explained, "since I have taken the name of your great first President!"

"He was not *my* President," said Manyface frostily, but then relented. "Haven't you got any heroes of your own to name yourself after?"

"Many, many," Jutch assured him, "but it is a courtesy to our allies to take some of their names. We have always done this so. Now," he said, dropping off the stool he had been perched on and scuttling through a doorway, "if you will follow me, we will have a nice dinner together and talk."

The talk was delightful, Manyface found. The erk had so much to tell, all of it so new and wonderful! There were some minor embarrassments, as when a naked erk climbed up on the table and began to feed itself from the platter that held their dinner, but Jutch shooed the little creature away. "It's a dumb erk," he apologized. "Please don't let it disturb you. They mean no harm."

Manyface laid down the two-pronged fork he was eating with. "Dumb erk?" he asked. "You mean, ah, of inferior intelligence, perhaps?"

"Oh, very inferior," agreed Jutch. "Let me see. Where shall I begin? Do you know anything about us erks? No, of course not. Well, to begin with, we were domestic animals..."

And Manyface listened, his eyes popping, as he heard how the erks had once been only pets; that they had somehow—it was not clear how—been caused to mutate so that they became quite intelligent; how the creatures who had been their masters had, somehow, destroyed themselves; how, as the ages passed, the artificial mutations had begun to backslide, as the genetic material reverted to type. The dumb erks were what all erks once had been...

The astonishing revelations went on forever, and Manyface was enjoying himself. From time to time he remembered to think of doomed China. It did not seem very real. Since Manyface, or at least a good deal of Manyface, was very old, he had learned some hard lessons. One was that there are events that cannot be controlled, and this, it seemed, was one such... And, meanwhile, how fascinating and strange it all was! How many questions to ask! How many thousand new questions each answered question created! Once he had begun to understand the erks themselves, there were all these other things to ask about—these long-legged, fish-looking creatures who did not exist anywhere alive, apparently, but whose effigies were all over—"Living Gods"? What were "Living Gods," then? And once that was explained, so many others that needed explaining: why the erks made a religion of warfare, how diligently they had sought places to wage it and issues to wage it on—

The questions did not end.

There was also the great question of what had happened to Castor, and Tsoong Delilah, and Feng Miranda, for none of them were quite as Manyface remembered them from just a few short weeks ago.

Apart from Potter Alicia's deluded love for the boy, the parts of Manyface could not see much good in Castor. It was true that he seemed more mature now. He was still quite arrogant and self-centered . . . and entirely too sure of himself with women. (So thought the man who had rarely had a woman love him since the first tumor was taken from his brain.)

And Delilah! How easy it was to destroy a valuable public official with calf love! Anyone could diagnose her failing from the way she spat jealousy at the Feng girl. Anyone could see that in the long run Castor would certainly choose the younger woman over her—or a dozen younger women before he was through, because the other thing that was evident was that there was hardly a sister on World who would not enjoy making love with the boy. Anyone could see that but Delilah.

As to Feng Miranda, Manyface had no opinions worth mentioning. She was too silly and childish to require much thought, he decided. That was rather a big mistake.

* * *

Miranda was no longer a prisoner. The conceptual bar that had kept the Yanks from understanding that a genetic Han Chinese could still be a patriotic U.S. American had dissolved in the war room. Yes, Miranda was clearly as loyal as Jupe himself or even the Governor.

Delilah was no longer a prisoner, either, though the reasons were not at all the same. It was not that she was trusted. It was simply that there was obviously nothing in her power to do that could do the Yanks any harm. She was not allowed near the war room or the Space Center, and if she had gone violently ragingly hostile in some nest or farm settlement, what difference would it have made?

Castor, of course, had never been a prisoner. That, thought Manyface, was perhaps an error on the part of the erks and the Yanks, for the boy simply was not mature enough to have solid political opinions. It pumped up his ego to be called President, of course. But it pumped up his ego almost as much to have the bitches in heat sniff after him, and he got very much of that every day—to Delilah's conspicuous disgust.

The really surprising thing (thought Manyface) was that he himself was not imprisoned. No one was. The assault team had been politely dispersed to five other cities for "debriefing and discussion"—not that those trigger-happy hit men had anything to discuss with anyone! Once there, they roamed as freely as any . . . and they, too, were having a truly fine time with World's sisters. Even Tchai Howard was not behind bars—though, as was the case with Manyface himself, he was followed everywhere by erks at least, often by sisters with multiple motives for curiosity.

But those erks and Yanks were not actually guards. Manyface was sure of that. They didn't consider Manyface an enemy. He knew what the smart erks thought of him: they thought him a truly fascinating laboratory preparation . . . as indeed he had been on Earth, for that matter.

As on Earth, even more on World. The Living Gods had taken a great interest in biological matters—the development of the erks themselves proved that—but the concept of transplanting parts of one brain into another, it seemed, had never occurred to them.

It took some time for Manyface to understand what it meant to the erks to be in the presence of a kind of technology the Living Gods had never thought of. It almost made Manyface himself honorarily divine.

If the erks were fascinated by Manyface, Manyface was fascinated in turn by the erks . . . and their Living Gods . . . and their world . . . and their history . . . and especially by their planetary houseguests, the Yankees. For a time the sheer intellectual joy of discovery was enough for Manyface. Was almost enough for Manyface. Learning was a special experience for Manyface, because what he learned he learned eleven times over. Each of his subbrains had his own special interests and his own expertise. Potter-the-agronomist was fascinated by erk farm practices. Corelli-the-anthropologist delighted in erk and Yank social customs. Angorak-the-soldier thrilled to erk and Yank weaponry and drill. Dien-the-engineer thrilled to the marvelous Living God construction. And Hsang-the-psychologist—

Ah, Hsang-the-psychologist! For him the Yanks were not merely a puzzle. They were a threat to his most basic beliefs.

It happened that those beliefs were illicit, but that did not make them less strongly felt. As in most Socialist countries, the Han Chinese had early on repudiated the foul-smelling and antipeople ravings of that degenerate toady to the bosses, Sigmund Freud. The sexual interpretation of dreams was not merely heretical in China. It was punishable by law.

As in most Socialist countries, however, the psychologists of Han China found ways of making eclectic use of forbidden therapies. Now and then, into their behavior-modification therapy they managed to sneak a Freudian diagnosis. Did the patient have a fascination with eating bananas, carrots, and juicy red sausages? Ah, to be sure, Comrade, to your work and study regimen we will recommend adding some cold showers.

And when Hsang-the-psychologist saw how the Yankees lived, he saw, too, that—for the first time in two centuries—the work of Sigmund Freud was not merely heretical. It was irrelevant.

There were no vast, punitive father figures in the minds of the Yankees on World.

There were no fathers.

So Hsang babbled endlessly to his skullmates. What nonsense this made of Freud's theories!—no, not nonsense, they were known to be a bourgeois illusion. Still, on Earth they had—ah, that was, they had been thought to have—some limited, tenuous reality—The others shut him up, because they had their own babbling to do; but then Hsang burst forth again. He was more secure now, having reflected that there was, after all, no way the Han Chinese state could effectively discipline heterodox psychology under the very special circumstances now existing. The father was gone! He did not exist! The son need not wither under the larger shadow! And as to penis envy, why, with women outnumbering men by, what was it, some 180 to 1, there were not enough penises around to make a good fantasy-envy!

And then Su Wonmu, the nonspecialist, the humble soul—Su said gently, "It is interesting, Hsang, that you are interested in the shape of their psyches and interesting, Dien, that you admire their grasp of structural techniques . . . but is it not time that we, all eleven of us, devote our collective minds to making a plan? A plan, let us say, to keep these erks and Yankees from wiping out everything we cherish in our beloved Home?"

III

"I vouch for this old man," said Pettyman Castor, President of the United States. He put his hand patronizingly on the sloped shoulder that supported Manyface's huge head. "He is peculiar," Castor conceded tolerantly, "but he can't do any real harm. You see, he's all mixed up inside himself."

Just beside him, seated on her Governor's chair, Big Polly pursed her lips. She gazed out over the Congress of the United States (in Exile), looking for signs of agreement or rejection, but all the Senators and Congressones were as noncommittal as herself. "So you want us to let him go anywhere he wants to go, Mr. President?" she asked. "I mean, just as if he were loyal?"

"Absolutely," Castor said grandly, giving Manyface's shoulder a friendly thump. "Like I say. He's harmless. Besides, he's a friend of mine, kind of."

Big Polly sighed. "It is so ordered," she said, gazing around for objections and finding, as she expected, none. "So now we might as well adjourn this special session, right? And get on with the war?"

Well, there were no objections to that, for sure, and Manyface allowed himself to shake Castor's hand. "That was nice of you," he said as they walked out together.

"Any time," said Castor carelessly, smiling at a couple of barely pubescent sisters waving amorously from the steps. "It's all over, you know. Once these people get their fleet through the spaceway China's finished."

"So it seems," said Manyface. "Well. I see you've got friends waiting for you, Castor. Don't worry about me. I'll find my way wherever I want to go all right."

He walked away as briskly as an elderly man supporting an extra fifteen kilograms of head on a weary neck could do. It was a good thing the gravity of World was light, compared to Earth's. It was a bad thing that the climate was so muzzy-clammy-*hot* because the old man tired quickly. That couldn't be helped, he decided—his internal committee decided, nearly unanimously; he had things to do, and no choice about doing them.

The first thing to do was to convince himself that what Castor said was true. That was easy. Manyface managed to catch a ride on a hoverplatform skittering across the field to what the erks proudly called Mission Control. Jutch was on duty there and had no objections at all to satisfying Manyface's curiosity. Yes, there were thirty-one vessels already in orbit, fully armed and ready to go. (He obligingly called up images of them on the index screen.) Yes, there were plenty more in reserve, still on the ground—not all of them operational, to be sure, but then any dozen of them would surely be adequate to the job of knocking out China's pitiful combat forces. Manyface stood on the open platform of Mission Control, with the soft, warm rain of World falling on him, and felt very cold. Off on the horizon the great open tracework of the launch loop was getting ready to throw another ship into orbit. On the ground erks were bustling around the tractor that would pull the next vessel to the loop.

Yes. World's forces were surely adequate.

He shivered in the slow, sloppy raindrops. The drops splashed over the instruments and controls on the roof, too, but they were built for it—everything on World was built, or evolved, to stand chronic wetness and warmth. Everything but Manyface, anyway. "I think I'll get out of the rain," he excused himself, and the smart erk reared himself up on his hind legs to touch vibrissae to fingers as a handshake in farewell.

It was just as Castor had said. The forces of Yanks and erks were unbeatable.

Manyface entered the city, toweling himself to get the rain off his body—not that that was much use, since a film of sweat sprang out at once to replace it. He gazed around benignly at smart erks and dumb, at the Yank sisters and occasional males who stared at him and whispered to each other. There was no sign on the little face in the front of the pumpkin of the great debate going on inside.

Not all of Manyface's committee was quite united. Corelli, Potter, Angorak, and Dien were, after all, not genetically Han Chinese. They did not have the same inbred devotion to Home as Fung himself or the rest of the implants. But all did have an aversion to racial suicide and even to unnecessary murders. All had seen what happaned to the island the erk ship had wiped sterile in a single pass. All agreed that something had to be done.

When the committee was in agreement it could act with great speed and precision. Manyface did not need to retire to ponder and regroup. He had eleven concurrent data processors going inside that pumpkin that so wearied the muscles of his neck. Each datum of information that came in went straight to the mind (or minds) that could make best use of it, and integrate it into knowledge already stored, and be ready to patch it into the general pattern when needed.

So Manyface did not change his ways. He continued

229

to rubberneck and sightsee and question. The only difference was that now the questions were more pointed, and the points of interest on the tour more pointedly chosen.

The Yanks and the erks did not seem to notice.

The same gaggle of soft-skinned beetles followed him around in fascination. Most of them were dumb erks, tumbling over each other in excitement to see what this weirdest of biped creatures was up to. But smart erks were always somewhere around, too, equally curious. Even the Yankees—almost all of them female, of course— also took an interest—when they were not taking an interest in Castor, of course.

Manyface covered the erk city—no, he corrected himself (or Dien-the-engineer corrected all of them), it was not really an erk city, but a Living God city. It was not hopelessly wrong for human beings. But for erks it was grotesquely out of scale. The erks had made patchy attempts to adjust it to their tininess. Soft-surfaced ramps lay over staircases that would have been a trifle steep for even one of World's tall Yankees; the erks, smart and dumb alike, scuttled up and down them and did not seem even to wonder why they had not reprogrammed the Living Gods' machines to rebuild in their own scale. There was hardly a window in the city that an erk could look out of. The kitchens—they were more like chemical laboratories—were all two-tiered. An elevated platform had been built in to run along the sides of tables and stoves and benches of mixing devices. The erks who chose to create their own cuisine, instead of letting the automatics do it, climbed to the upper level for their work. The lower was not used at all—except by the exploring Manyface. It was the same in the public rooms and the libraries and

230

even the living quarters, where erks had to hop up a bench to get into the tall, wide beds.

Manyface explored them all . . . especially the libraries.

It was too bad that the language the erks spoke among themselves, which was the language the Living Gods had spoken long ago, was not Chinese. Or even English. But the problem was not fatal, because much of the data in the library stores was pictorial, and there were English language summaries, prepared for the use of the Yankees, for the most important parts.

Corelli-the-anthropologist was busy there, learning what he could about the Yankees. He learned a great deal. He learned, for example, that when the original interstellar ship reached Alpha Eridani and was transported direct to World, the first thing the erks did was construct another transporter ship and send it back through the same portal to begin the long, slower-than-light trip to Earth. That trip had taken forty-two years. That was a very significant datum to Manyface; the Alpha Eridani outpost was the closest the erks had come to Earth. He learned, too, that the Yankee population amounted to just under 8,500, 8,450 of them female. He snickered to the rest of Manyface, "If they had just waited two more generations they could have outnumbered us!" And he learned a great deal more that did not as yet fit into a pattern.

The Yankee records themselves were wondrous. Not only were they in English (of course), but they were automatically kept current. The journal of the Yankees on World was updated every day. The most interesting files Corelli-the-anthropologist found were the files that covered the Earth visitors themselves.

Manyface had not realized those files existed. It was a surprise to him to deduce that among the erks and Yanks who flocked after them, there must have been some with cameras. And not just those who followed Manyface; and sometimes the camera must have been hidden in the walls—how else to account for the shot of Tsoong Delilah, naked as a skinned cat, furiously haranguing a naked and sullen Pettyman Castor over his attentions to the Feng girl? Or—this was a surprise—the zealot Tchai Howard observed in the act of vigorously seducing one of those huge, healthy Yank sisters?

Nothing was left out, it seemed. And nothing was hidden from the casual curiosity-seeker. The erks had never had any reason to mark any data "classified." What one erk knew, they could all know. The Yanks had never questioned the customs of the erks, and so it was all there.

All of it. Even the parts that made sweat pop out on the great forehead of Manyface and drove his component parts to panicky debate.

Even the parts that told how the erks had helped the cause of freedom all over the galaxy for thousands of years. The library was very productive for Manyface, and not only of risqué entertainment.

"Those poor little pink things," sobbed Potter Alicia, and Angorak thundered, "To hell with those animals, Potter! What about our homeland?"

To that there was no easy answer. To that there was only silence in response, until Shum said diffidently, "Comrades? I think we have failed to understand the complexities of this situation."

"Indeed," said Angorak heavily. "Please enlighten us all, Comrade Shum!"

"Thank you, Comrade Angorak, I will. I propose that we consider the possibility that we have underestimated

232

these erks. They are quite comic little creatures, to be sure. But they are not entirely ludicrous."

"Of course they're ludicrous, Shum," Potter said crossly. "They're not even *human*."

"I think that is an incorrect view, Comrade Alicia. They are all too human. Let me explain," he added hastily. "Are they silly clowns, so foolish and inept that no one can take them seriously? No. They are far too powerful for that. Are they so wicked that anyone would recoil from them? No. To speak of helping the oppressed become free is not wicked. Comrade Mao endorsed just that principle many times. No one would recoil from such a sentiment."

"Shum, you fool, are you taking their side?" Angorak's cry was more incredulous than angry.

"Not at all, Comrade Angorak, only pointing out that they are not so unlike human beings as one might suspect. The erks are very like certain world powers of a hundred years ago. They have elevated slogans to the point of dogma. In doing so, they have lost sight of the principles that made the slogans valid in the first place."

"Speak plainly, you fool!"

"I will, Comrade Angorak. Do we not see just such behavior in history? Was it not just so with the great powers that destroyed each other in nuclear war?—that they spoke, the one of 'freedom' and the other of 'equality,' so loudly that neither could hear the rightness in what the other said?"

"Our ancestors, Shum," thundered Angorak, "were well aware of these contradictions! It was for that reason that China decided to have nothing to do with either of those hegemonistic, imperialist, war-mongering, power-hungry tyrannies!"

"Our ancestors," sighed Shum, "had that choice, yes.

But we do not, do we? We can't decide to have nothing to do with the Yanks and the erks. We can only hope that we can find a way to prevent them from 'helping' our planet in the way they have helped so many others."

"Like those poor little pink things," sobbed Potter Alicia.

"And what is that way?" demanded Angorak.

"I do not know," said Shum respectfully. "But we have the knowledge. The question is, how can we use it?"

No knowledge is of much value unless it is used. To use knowledge means to share it with someone; and who could Manyface share with?

His first thought was a right thought, saving the unfortunate fact that it was impossible. As a high Party official his first duty was to find Tchai Howard or the assault-team commander and tell them what the library held. The erks had made that out of the question. The erks were trusting, but not entirely crazy, and so Howard and the soldiers were well out of Manyface's reach.

What about Castor?

Yes, thought Manyface to himself (or, yes, concurred the committee within Manyface's skull by majority vote), Castor was a good choice. (A strong minority within the skull opposed the choice on the grounds that Castor might get hurt. The minority was only one, and anyway she was not being rational most of the time.) So Manyface acted. There was something in his possession that would lure Castor to him; it was time to use it. He composed a letter to Castor and found a smart erk who was willing to promise to deliver it.

The letter said:

Honored Mr. President:
  I am glad to say that your wife, Maria, is
alive and well in Saskatchewan. Before we
left, she prepared a taped message to deliver
to you. I have it. Would you like to meet me
to view the tape?

Fung Bohsien

It was a simple and straightforward bait, right? So the
committee viewed it. But Castor shook their confidence.
He didn't take the bait. The smart erk toiled back to
Manyface with the doleful report that the President said
he couldn't care less about messages from ex-wives who
had run out on him when he was poor and unknown and
certainly shouldn't be given any special consideration now
that he was the President of the United States.

Manyface swore at the erk. That did not help anything,
except to entertain the erk. When Manyface stopped
shouting and went back into executive session inside his
head, the erk went disappointedly away and the minds of
Manyface accepted the fact that it was not going to be so
easy.

If Castor would not come to Manyface, then Manyface
would have to go to Castor.

But where was the foolish boy? Manyface asked Tsoong
Delilah, who replied only with a furious, "How should I
know, you old fool?" He asked among the smart erks and
got, in essence, the same answer, although more politely
phrased. He retired that night without sleep coming easily,
for the parts of his brain were snapping at each other. It
was after sunrise that he woke with a start, for one of the
voices inside him woke to cry, "The library!"

Of course, the library! Manyface should have figured
that out at once. The erks didn't know where Castor was;
but then, the one who had volunteered to be a messenger

could not have known either. Manyface had simply asked them the wrong question: Not "Do you know where Castor is?" but "Where is Castor?" Obviously the erks had a way of finding out such things—so obvious that none of them thought to mention it.

So Manyface made his way through the sweaty morning to the library. The index screen disclosed Castor's current whereabouts at once—the city nest, in the sleeping quarters—and what it disclosed him doing made Manyface blush.

He had to hurry out of the city, over to the nest, up to the sleeping levels—it was bright morning now, in the short day of World, and most of its inhabitants were long since aroused from sleep. If Castor's main interest had been sleep he, too, would no doubt have been long gone; but he was in the nuptial chambers. Manyface had to wait for him to come out. When at last he appeared it was with a young sister on each arm, the women looking very contented, Castor himself looking mostly tired. "I don't care about the damn tape, Manyface," he said at once. Manyface shrugged.

"Then perhaps you will just take a walk with me?" he urged politely.

Castor looked at him with dignity. "For what? I'm not your houseboy anymore."

"No," agreed Manyface, "but my friend, I hope. I would like to take a friendly stroll, is all."

Castor gave him a puzzled look, for they both knew that that was a preposterous suggestion. Walking in the sultry air of World was work, even though they weighed less, with the air so hot and steamy. But only by walking, Manyface believed, could he even hope to avoid those all-watching lenses. They crossed the strip of purple-blue moss that the erks (or the Living Gods) had fancied in

236

the way that human beings liked lawns. They walked in the opposite direction from the spacecraft tarmac, for fewer people were there. Of course, a gaggle of erks followed them, but Manyface looked them over carefully and decided they were all dumb erks. They wore no clothes; they did not speak intelligibly—above all, they seemed happy and carefree, and not even smart erks were those things all the time.

They reached an irrigation ditch. Manyface joyfully removed his sandals and rolled up his culottes. He stood in the ditch, squeezing the thick mud of World between his toes, and gazed up at Castor, watching and frowning from the bank. He said, "You know that these people will destroy China completely."

Castor shrugged.

"I understand," Manyface said. "China is not your homeland. It does not matter to you that the Great Wall will be lava and the Forbidden City a cinder, since you have never seen them. But tell me, Mr. President of the United States, do you think North America will escape the same destruction?"

Castor pushed a dumb erk off his lap as he sat on the bank. Wading in the mud was not interesting to him, since he had had enough of that at the Heavenly Grain Collective. He shook his head and said tenderly, "Foolish old man, these people are my allies. Why would they hurt my country?"

"Ah," said Manyface, nodding the giant head. "You don't know then, do you? You have not been in the library."

Castor's expression changed, now interested and a little resentful.

Manyface chuckled. "I know that your studies here have been mostly anatomical. I can't blame you for that.

If I were young and good-looking, I would certainly do the same. Still, Castor, I wonder."

"What do you wonder, old man?"

"I wonder what happened to the boy who spent all his time with the teaching screens and the young man who was so thrilled to be admitted to the university."

"I don't know what you're talking about!"

"I am talking about the acquisition of knowledge, Castor. The library has knowledge for you, and knowledge is the thing that makes the difference between you and that dumb erk who is trying to get something out of your pocket—do you have food there, Castor?" The President impatiently shoved the creature away. "I thought I saw in you a person who wished to know everything there was to know, Castor, a true scholar, a person who knows that knowledge gives guidance and is worth having for its own sake." And inside his head Potter Alicia was whispering, *He does, he does*, and Hsang-the-psychologist warned, *You're laying it on too thick!* But Manyface was in charge of the committee. He climbed regretfully out of the blood-warm water, wiping his feet on the mossy bank. As he slipped the sandals back on, one hand on Castor's shoulder for support, he said, "Knowledge is power, Castor."

"Oh," said Castor, lost in his thoughts, "I guess so."

They started back toward the crystalline and colorful city in silence. Even the dumb erks were almost silent as they followed.

As they reached the first outbuilding Castor said, "Where is this library?"

"Ask any erk, Castor," Manyface said cheerfully. "Ask them to show you the war records of the past eight thousand years."

CASTOR

sat in the open shed with the damp World air soaking the part out of his hair. Pieces of erk weaponry were in his hands, and along the long trestle table next to him were Jupiter and Miranda and five gunnery sisters. They were all learning the field-stripping and reassembly of erk hand weapons. The erks didn't specially want them to do that; it was a notion of the Yankees; the Original Landers had mostly been through military training and, as they had had to field-strip weapons, felt that all those who followed should do the same. Castor thought it was silly. "You don't have enough experience to judge," judged Miranda. "If you don't know how the parts go together, how can you know what may go wrong?

239

Or what allowances to make if the guidance systems can't reach a solution? Or if they're confused by countermeasures from the enemy?"

"I can't," said Castor, "so I'll just throw the gun away. I'm never going to be in hand-to-hand combat anyway."

"You don't know that," Miranda said. "At most you just hope that. And anyway, pay attention to what you're doing!"

Castor shrugged. This should have been a fun session for him, who had never been allowed weapons before.

The library had spoiled that.

It was really too annoying of that old freak Manyface to have given him that hint. Manyface had been right. Any erk was glad to show him where to find the library. Manyface was right again; what it held was scary.

If only Manyface had kept his mouth shut, thought Castor, he could have been really enjoying this arms lesson. He fumbled with the springs and catches of one of the projectile weapons, aware of Miranda's eyes disapprovingly on him. He offered her a tentative grin. "I think there have been too many wars," he said, and a spring slipped out of his fingers and spanged halfway across the room.

"Oh, Castor," she said furiously, "are you *trying* to make us late for the War Council?"

"Of course not, Miranda, only—"

"Then *please* try to keep your mind on what you're doing! Now, what was that about wars?"

"I was just thinking," he said, accepting the spring from a dumb erk who had leaped from under the bench to retrieve it.

"You said there had been so many wars."

He nodded.

"So what does that mean?" she demanded. "Some wars are *necessary*, you know."

"Oh, of course," he agreed. But were they? Was war ever a good thing, really? He thought back over Earth history; so many centuries, so many bloodbaths of battle. So many millions who had died horribly, in trench or airplane or nuked city or sunk ship. Of course, that was all a long time ago, and every one of those people, of course, would have been dead by now anyway. He tried to take comfort in that thought. There wasn't much comfort to be had. Their terror and pain had been real, and time did not change that. Wars *killed* people.

And was there anything, really, that made it worthwhile to start all that terror and pain over again? "You know," he said, leaning conversationally across to Miranda at the next bench, "there's a lot of erk history that's really interesting. You ought to take a look in the library sometime."

She said forcefully, "And you, Castor, ought to pay attention to what you're doing! If you ever tried to fire that rifle with the escapement in that way you'd blow your silly head off—and damn well deserve it."

"I was only saying—" he began, but she cut him off.

"I give up. You'll never make a soldier, Castor, and you make a damn poor excuse for a President right now. Come on, put it back together right—then we've got a meeting of the War Council. Try to pay attention there, will you?"

"I always pay attention," he protested.

"Then," she said grimly, "heaven help us all." She raised her own rifle to the sky, aimed, snapped off an imaginary round, and set it down. "Oh, hell," she said, "give me your weapon and I'll fix it for you. I certainly hope you never have to fire it in actual combat!"

Castor handed it over. "So do I," he said.

The War Council was chaired either by Big Polly or by one of the leading erks, A-Belinka or Jutch. There was no particular rotation order; it mostly depended on which one got to the meeting first and took the chair, or perch, at the head of the big oval table. It had never occurred to any of them to let Castor assume the chair, but then it had never occurred to Castor, either.

If you made allowance for the fact that erks were intrinsically comic rather than dignified, then it was in some ways an impressive scene. The table was huge and gleaming. There were carafes of honeyberry wine, none of your cheap everyday stuff, at every place. Over the head of the table was an immense new portrait of Pettyman Castor. The erk artist had put him in robes of office like a Supreme Court judge, but that was all right; that was artistic license, and besides it gave dignity to the twenty-two-year-old face. The erk artist had also made him subtly older, so the face was not twenty-two anymore; it was, actually, the face Castor might have a couple of dozen years in the future, if he led quite a dissolute and troubled life in between.

The erk artist had done one more thing for his art, and that was to subtly elongate the neck and to broaden and shorten the arms. It was Castor's picture, all right, but it was the picture of Castor as he might have been if he had been part Living God.

As a matter of fact, the likeness did not please Castor at all. He stared up at it from his place at the foot of the table (he had decided not to point out that he belonged at the head, since of course the erks couldn't be expected to get everything right). He thought that if he was going to grow into the person he saw there, he'd rather not grow at all.

But he couldn't help growing.

No one can. No one is ever ready to grow up. No one is ever ready for anything, but the time comes when the anythings become real and then they have to be dealt with, ready or not.

Castor's realities were coming up on him now.

Because Jutch had managed to beat out the other two candidates, he was in the chair—or on it, crouched on his rear legs while the frontmost limbs rested on the oval table. Big Polly and A-Belinka flanked him, one on each side, and straggling down through the other places were Jupiter and Miranda and half a dozen technical-specialist smart erks, ready to fill in any needed details. Manyface could have been there, but wasn't; heaven knew where the old man was wandering. None of the other recent arrivals could have been, either because they didn't have permission, like Tsoong Delilah, or because they were safely scattered all over World, in singles and groups too small for critical mass.

The first order of business was readiness reports. Castor watched them absently as they were projected on the index screen. They had not changed much from day to day, except that at each day's briefing there were a few more attack and support vessels that had been hurled into orbit by the launch loops, and a few more standbys still on the ground. All the council watched attentively, erk and human, but this wasn't the fun part. The fun part was the plans. The index machines had been busy, assimilating data and preparing strategies based on Jutch's synoptic

version of the council's deliberations. Now they were
ready.

Jutch snapped his fingers, and one of the minor erks
rose to the index controls. In a moment he projected a
picture on the screen beside Castor's portrait. The picture
showed the erk scout ship, floating in orbit around the
Earth.

"This," said Jutch earnestly, "we must protect at all
costs. If we let the Chinks hurt the scout ship we would
not be able to deploy another for forty-two years."

Snap of the fingers again. Now the scout ship was
hidden in the rings of Saturn, and its violet spaceway was
flickering into life. Another vessel was coming through.

"So we will hide the scout ship where the Chinks can't
find it," said Jutch, "and send our forces through at a
considerable distance from the Earth. There will be a loss
of transit time, of course. But the scout ship will be safe.

"Here," he said, picking up a pointer with his teeth
and indicating the vessel emerging through the spaceway,
"is our first advance party. As you see, it is the President's
own spacecraft, just as it arrived here—or so it will seem.
It will display the recognition signals. President Pettyman
will be aboard it to talk when there are any challenges.
It will approach the Earth, soothing any fears the Chinks
may have. And then, following it a few hours later"—
snap of the fingers; new picture on the screen, this time
of one war vessel after another pouring through the spaceway—"a whole fleet of transports and warcraft.

"The President's ship"—*snap*: a schematic of the vessel—"will be fully armed.

"The other ships"—*snap*—"will contain full continent-
blaster weaponry on the attack vessels, and the transports
will contain eighteen hundred crack troops, Yank and erk,
with portable nukes. Of course, once we have landed we

will recruit additional combat personnel from the Real-Americans themselves, and in the third wave there will be cargo vessels to provide them with weapons, materiél, and some of the nicest blue-and-white uniforms you ever saw." He looked irritably at Castor. "What is it?"

Castor said, "Those aren't the right colors. The Americans wore khaki or olive drab. It was the sailors that wore blue and white."

"Oh, Castor," said Jutch impatiently, "what tiny details you worry about! *I* picked the colors of the uniforms. They are the same ones the Living Gods wore. Now, are there any *serious* questions?"

There were none. Jutch waved his vibrissae in satisfaction. "Then," he declared, "there are only two things left to do: choose the crew of the President's yacht and set a time for the invasion to begin."

Big Polly had been silent longer than she liked. "*I* think," she said, "that we can wait to select the crew until the last minute."

"That makes sense," said A-Belinka approvingly from the other side of the chair—meaning, as did Big Polly, that he wanted all the time he could get to think of good reasons why he should be part of the party.

"Then," said Jutch, "what about the date? I suggest it be eight days from now, exactly."

Big Polly frowned. "Why eight days, exactly?" she demanded.

"Why not?" said the erk sweetly. "Let's put it to the vote." And when the votes were in and almost unanimous—Big Polly had abstained out of annoyance, Castor because he was lost in thought—Jutch said in triumph, "Then we liberate America in one hundred and ninety-two hours from—now!"

And another smart erk darted from his place at the

table to the index screen controls, and in a moment a digital readout spread itself across the screen:

COUNTDOWN H191 M59 S30

and, flick, flick, the 30 changed to 29, to 28, to 27 as the last hours of America's occupation by the Chinese began to pass.

No one spoke to the President of the United States as he got up from the oval table and wandered out into the sultry, misty outside air. There really were serious questions, he knew. He had a lot of them himself.

But where could he ask them? He couldn't ask them of Jutch, or any of the erks. He could not ask them of Manyface, because Manyface was clearly committed to the Chinese side in the war of the Yanks and the Chinks. He could not ask them of Delilah for the same reason or of Miranda because she was so clearly on the Yank side. There seemed to be no living thing on World not committed to one side or the other of the war that he wished need not be fought, so where could a neutral go to ask questions?

The library was the only neutral source.

It was not really neutral, of course. It was erk-programmed and erk-compiled, and it reflected erk pride in battle plans and weaponry. They were not all erk designs, of course. In fact, the erks themselves had contributed rather little. It was the Living Gods who had first started the military sections of the indices; what the erks had added was less their own contribution than what they had gleaned from the strategies and technologies of the enemies they had joyously elected to fight.

And how many of them there were!

In his first visit to the library Castor had got only an impression of many wars. He did not stop to count them. Horrified, he jumped away from the viewer seeking the clean outside air. (But all there was was the damp and sticky breeze of World.) The room that housed the library was not only damp and sticky. It stank. Dumb erks slept in it when they chose and relieved themselves in it when no one was looking, which was usually. The smart erks had other libraries, better adjusted to their physical needs. In the old library that Castor used the viewers were binocular, but set for two eyes not very much like a human beings (though even less like an erk's). They would have fit just perfectly against the eyes of the Living Gods, set birdlike on the sides of the head rather than in front. For Castor to use those eyepieces for any length of time gave him a most amazing headache.

What he saw was more painful still.

There had been, he counted, no fewer than nine wars! Nine external ones, not counting when the Living Gods had wiped themselves out. Every war all but total! To be an enemy of the erks was clearly suicide. To be an ally was not much better. There were the winged creatures whose worlds had all been incinerated because the erks had not understood in time that to attack the world of one side in the dispute would bring prompt and over-whelming retribution against the other. There was the single planetary system of wormlike beings, two species, one huge and horny-skinned, the other tiny, soft, sharp-fanged. They wriggled and snuggled among each other's coils—and fought—and killed each other and devoured each other. When the erks joyously chose sides and entered the lists against the "enemy" they discovered too late that the races were symbiotic ...

For the erks had never found an undivided civilization. There were always differences of opinion or policy or religion or habits of thought . . . and to the erks a difference meant a struggle.

And a struggle meant a war.

Castor forced himself to stay at the index screen for hours, well into the time when he should have been asleep. When he walked out he almost tripped over a pair of drowsing dumb erks curled up in the doorway while they waited to see what fascinating thing the human would do. He looked at them with horror. They weren't comic, capering little monsters anymore. They, and their smart kin, were deadly.

If there were a war between Yanks and Chinks, would anyone win at all?

Or would the assistance of the erks mean that both sides lost, eternally?

Tsoong Delilah slept fitfully in the hot and stuffy room the erks had given her. There were no guards at night and no need for them. If she ever stirred outside her chamber there would soon be a gaggle of dumb erks following her, making enough noise to alert a few smart ones. And anyway, where did she have to go?

Delilah's days on World passed in a sort of angry fog. The fact that her loins lusted for Castor confused her. The fact that this planet of armed lunatics was planning, as one might elect to shoot a passing duck, to destroy her Han Home terrified her. The fact that she could find no solution to either problem frustrated her . . .

And when she woke, dreaming that Castor had invited himself to her bed without warning, and discovered it was no dream, she exploded in resentment.

"Now, then, boy!" she snapped, scuttling over to the far side of the bed as he slid in on the near, "what are you doing? Have all the Yank sisters got their periods at once? Are you trying to change your luck? Have you taken pity on an old woman?"

"Delilah," he said persuasively, a hand coming to cup her shoulder and a moment later the other reaching over to cup a breast, "don't you remember how much we like to make love to each other? So what is wrong with our doing it, simply to give each other pleasure?"

"You call it pleasure!" she began, sneering. But in fact she also called it pleasure, and angry though Delilah might be, insane she was not. When Castor tugged her toward him she did not resist. When Castor kissed her lips she returned the kiss; and, all in all, she did in fact remember how much they liked to make love to each other and discovered all over again how true that memory was. It was only when they had finished and Castor was lying on top of her, his slight frame molded into hers, slowly and reminiscently moving in her with no urgency, that the anger began slowly to seep back...

And then he put his mouth down to her neck and nibbled gently and whispered something.

"What?" said Delilah aloud.

"I said sssh," he whispered. "The erks watch us everywhere. Don't say anything."

Delilah felt herself tense up. Her mouth formed a question, but his left hand moved up from her breast to gently cover her lips. "Delilah," he whispered, "pretend you are a real Yank. Convince them. Convince the erks, too. Convince everybody, even Manyface."

She turned her head, looking about the room to see if indeed there was an erk somewhere watching him. The ornate wall paneling could, she realized, conceal any number of panels. A microphone could be anywhere. Why? She could not guess why. She rubbed her cheek against Castor's—how good it felt!—and whispered, "Why?"

"Because," he breathed, "otherwise they will wreck our world. Go to the library. See for yourself." And then the nibbling at the neck got serious and the hand on her breast more urgent; and when at last he left for his own bed, Delilah lay back spent and content and wondering what he meant.

The wondering continued. The delightful lassitude began to go when she began to wonder if, indeed, he had come to her bed for no other purpose than to whisper in her ear.

II

When Delilah had seen the library records she retired to her room, among the queer-smelling flowers that
the erks decorated guests' rooms with, and retired further
to her bed and would, if she could, have retired to the
womb or out of life forever; because for the first time in
Tsoong Delilah's life she was scared. The situation did
not involve merely a criminal who might outwit the re-
sources of her Renmin police and do violent, terrible things.
It was not anything so trivial and personal as the unfaith-
fulness of her innately faithless young lover that she feared.
It was so large and terrifying an event that she could not
contemplate it at all.

If the library was trustworthy, the erks were very likely
to annihilate everything Delilah had ever sworn loyalty
to. And she could see no way of stopping them.

After a long time of hugging herself in the bed, eyes
closed, awake, unseeing, trying to be unfeeling, she began
to think. That first terrible paralysis of fear seeped away.

There had to be something she could do. She acknowl-
edged that the odds were immense against her, but that
did not excuse Inspector Tsoong Delilah from trying! As
she lay there, eyes open, staring at the ceiling that probably was staring back at her, she began to scheme.

Her first step, of course, had to be merely to do what
Castor had demanded of her. She had to pretend to be

more Yank than the Yankees. She had to acquire trust, and she had very little time to do it in.

It was an unfortunate necessity that the best way to be trusted was to do something personally obnoxious to her.

So, as soon as she could, Tsoong Delilah went to the shed where the warriors were rehearsing their arts, marched up to Feng Miranda, and said, "You are right. We must fight for America's freedom. I am a trained pilot and commander. Use me, Miranda. Let me help."

She saw at once, of course, the way Miranda glanced quickly to Castor; and saw, too, the faintly patronizing look Miranda gave her. She had made up her mind in advance that these would not matter to her, and although that did not turn out to be true, she accepted them. Let Miranda think what she liked. The advantage was all Delilah's. She knew what Miranda was thinking, although the knowledge displeased her. Miranda did not, however, know what Delilah was thinking—would not be allowed to—least of all to know that "We must fight for America's freedom" was only a specific and particular excerpt from a larger and more important statement: "We must fight for America's, and the rest of the Earth's, freedom, from the erks."

If Castor could come to her bed to whisper secrets, Delilah could employ the same stratagems. What she decided to do next was so grotesque that she smiled all the way to Manyface's room. "Old man," she said roughly and tenderly as soon as she got there, "I am horny. Are you still capable of sex?"

The battered face that dwelt in the middle of the huge head peered at her. "Of course I am!" he said testily.

"Don't you know anything of medicine? I can be physically capable of whatever I wish, only—"

"Only," she finished for him—surprised to discover that now she was more tender than rough—"you are a freak, and so it embarrasses you to have a woman make love to you. Well. It is a different world here, Manyface. There are very few men. Marginal cases are upgraded greatly. You are very attractive to me now, my dear old pumpkin-head, and I would like it if you and I were to retire to some pleasant place in the countryside and enjoy each other as best we can."

And, to her surprise, Manyface was quite a tender and ardent lover; and, when they had explained to the following erks that human beings from Earth really required privacy for their copulation and the indulgent smart erks had herded the dumb ones away, she found that sex in the performance of one's duty could be almost as satisfying as sex for hygienic purposes and a lot more so than sex with an offhanded, reluctant, and untrustworthy lover.

And then, under the great orange vines that parasitized the grove they lay in, she whispered in Manyface's ear, "I've seen the history index material in the library. I know what will happen if the war begins."

Manyface was lying beside her, face-to-face, his eyes closed. They opened slowly, and he looked into hers. He did not speak for a moment, and then there was faint disappointment in his tone. "Ah, I see. I wondered why you were doing this." She started to speak—to lie, out of embarrassment and apology, but he wouldn't let her. "Please, whisper as softly as you can. No, it doesn't matter about why." The eyes, soft under the bulging forehead, were understanding. Then they hardened. "What we must do," he said, "is make these people believe we have taken their side. Cause them to trust us."

"Yes," agreed Delilah, moving slightly. The motion made Manyface remove the hand that had remained resting lightly on her hip, and she wished it were still there. "And then? After we've won their trust, if we can?"

Manyface said soberly, "Then there is still almost no hope that we can prevent the war, but what choice do we have but to try?"

The good thing about their impossible task was that the erk experience of war, though vast, was incomplete. To them "war" meant actual combat. It meant the destruction of cities, the killing of enemies, even the annihilation of planets. It meant nothing else. Espionage and dirty tricks were not in their repertory. If the Living Gods had also known the arts of espionage and betrayal of trust, they had failed to teach them to the erks. And so there was no problem for Tsoong Delilah or Manyface in doing what they wished to do. Jutch accepted Manyface unquestioningly into the planning section, and A-Belinka welcomed Delilah to weapons training. Gladly, in fact, for she became at once his star pupil.

There was much to learn! The erks had weaponry Delilah had not imagined. Not merely missiles, lasers, heavy-particle beams, artillery, hand weapons—it was more than any individual weapon, it was the system in which each weapon played a part. Over the stretch of eight thousand years the erks had acquired the military technology of nine separate civilizations. Of course, much of it was not applicable to the task of liberating the U. S. of A. from its oppressors: the sonic grenades that wrought such havoc among the arachnids who had invented them would only give human beings headaches.

But nearly all the rest of the armorarium was terrible.

Delilah did not let herself feel terror. Weapons were weapons. She had craftsman's pride in her skills. She took great satisfaction from the fact that starting from nowhere, she quickly excelled every erk, every Yank, and every Real-American but Miranda in gunnery. She was a natural. It was not simply a matter of calculating deflections for targets. It was a more primitive and deadly thing. Even on the erks' range—even where the targets were sometimes Han Chinese rockets and sometimes the ruffed needles that the Living Gods had flown and sometimes the spheres or teardrops or polygons of the other races the erks had "helped"—even with ion-beams or EMP grenades or slashing, shrapneling rockets that punctured shells—even there, what made the difference between the talented gunlayer and the champion was the will to destroy.

That Delilah had.

It was an annoyance to Delilah that she could not quite surpass Miranda even at destruction, but she took glum pleasure in noticing that Castor was unable to match either of the women in gunnery. His special skill was something else. To Delilah's surprise, the boy was a natural pilot. He did not have much to pilot, only drones at first, airborne ones in World's soggy atmosphere to begin with, then orbiting minimini spacecraft, no more really than a telemetry system on top of a fuel tank. But he had the gift. His long hours at the teaching screens had supplied what natural talents could not provide, and he was able to read a navigation signal, verify a proposed course-change solution, and execute a maneuver as smoothly and surely as Delilah, with all her long years of experience. And then they gave him an Eye! A real, Earth-system spy drone, launched through the gate and sent down to near-Earth orbit to keep an eye on the Han Chinese and all their works. It was the culmination of all his dreams! He had a spaceship of his own! He could make it go where he liked! It thrilled him so that Delilah found herself thrilling for him, and one afternoon when pilotage training was over she followed him out the door of the shed and across the tarmac. "Come back here, boy," she called good-naturedly. "I won't hurt you."

He turned and saw her, flushing. "Oh, Delilah," he said. "I thought—I was thinking—"

"Yes? You were thinking what? That I planned to tear off your clothes here, in front of our little friends?" For, of course, they were as usual followed by a posse of dumb erks.

"I was thinking I might see you later," he finished.

"Oh, yes, if the old woman wants to make love you will accommodate her," said Delilah and listened to herself and did not like what she heard. It was that cursed Miranda, she thought. Miranda made her jealous. She did not want to be jealous, she only wanted to have a quite reasonable sexual relationship with the young man and prevent him from wasting himself on foolish young women or the hungry harpies of the Yankees . . . She listened to herself think and did not like what she thought, either. "Castor," she said, humbly, or as close to humbly as Tsoong Delilah knew how to get, "I just wanted to talk to you."

He looked at her appraisingly. What he saw in her face she could not tell, but he said, "Sure, Delilah." Then he grinned. "I was just going to watch the kids play. Do you want to come along?"

"Come along where?" she demanded, looking about. The only place on this side of the tarmac was the Yankee nest, and she had already seen that many times. Too many times; the hostility these Amazon warriors had shown her was not pleasant.

"You'll see," he said; and she did.

It was the nest. It was the school outside the nest. It was the children, the girls from tiny three-year-olds to young teens, the trainee conquerors. They walked into the schoolroom, and the teaching sisters beamed welcome at Castor, gave guarded looks of suspicion to Delilah, raised warning fingers to their mouths for both. The children were rapt before a prismed screen where war games were being played. On the screen, models—Delilah thought at first they were models, then realized with a heart-stopping shock that they were films of reality—ships were in battle, huge ships, planet-busters, crushers. A fleet of them slid across the screen toward a violet-and-brown planet, and although an intervening screen of defensive vessels attacked them and destroyed some and committed suicide by hurling themselves into some, the defenders were outgunned and outmassed. The planet-busters got through.

And the planet was destroyed.

Delilah fled outside, for in that long-ago, now-gone planet what she saw was the Earth.

In a while Castor joined her, followed by the chattering children and, of course, the squeaking, excited dumb erks; but this time some of the dumb erks were there for a purpose. "What now?" Delilah demanded, and Castor looked fond and indulgent.

"They play their game," he said. "Just watch."

The girls knew the game. So did the erks. They needed very little instruction from the teaching sisters as they descended on a rank of toy carts at the side of a mossy lawn. Each cart had a dumb erk driver; and when the erks had hopped into their seats and the carts had drawn themselves up in orderly squadrons, the game began. For each girl in the school a cart and an erk to man it; the erks were trained (as Earthly dogs are trained) to carry out voice commands from their mistresses ... And the game began. They attacked each other in fleets and single-cart sallies, bashing into each other with gleeful yips and squeals. The girls shouted orders; the erks carried them out. Smash! Bash! The kids were having fun.

Castor, too, was having fun, Delilah saw. The erks ran the brightly colored toy tanks and self-propelled cannon; the girls controlled the erks; but Castor appointed himself general of them all. Both sides! "Bring up your right wing," he ordered. "Watch that attack in the center! Go on, smash through, smash through!" *Pop* went one of the cannon, and a dumb erk leaped out of his tank, chittering and squealing as he ran off the battlefield. A trickle of purplish dye from the toy cannon shell stained the ground behind him. Castor turned to grin at Delilah. "Isn't this a good game?" he demanded. "We never had games like this in my school."

"Neither did we," said Delilah, scowling. The game did not please her, any more than the video-game war inside.

The Amazon warriors, six and ten years old, got carried away and began hitting each other with flower stalks until the older sisters, laughing, restored order and the battle went on to its conclusion. The erk team won the war, of course. The erk team always did. And on the way back Castor glanced around casually, stopped, put his arms around Tsoong Delilah, and kissed her. In her ear he whispered, "I do not want to play this game with real guns. Do you understand?"

"I understand," she said, wishing he would kiss her again.

He did. Then he whispered, "We may not be able to prevent it, but we have to try." Delilah shivered, not from the kiss. It was almost what Manyface had said to her. And all too likely true.

III

"I don't trust them," snapped Feng Miranda, peevishly pushing Jupiter's hand off her arm. He sighed. How incredibly obstinate this Earth sister was! It was curious that this strange and unpleasant disinterest in copulation she displayed seemed to make her more attractive, not less.

"What harm can they do?" he asked reasonably.

"Who knows what harm?" She was glowering toward the front of the War Council room, where Castor, Tsoong Delilah, and a couple of the erks were chattering animatedly. "Do you trust them?"

Jupiter looked scandalized. "Trust my *President*?"

"That's a farce, Jupiter! And it's not him so much, it's that old bitch Tsoong. She's Han Chinese all the way through!"

He put his hand absentmindedly, and very lightly, on the small of her back. She didn't seem to notice. "You're the one who told us she offered her services," he pointed out.

"So I made a mistake!"

"I don't know why you think that. After all, why would she lie?"

"Oh, you fool!" she snapped, and twisted vigorously away from the hand that she had, after all, noticed. Then she scowled blackly at Castor, who had, also absentmindedly, put his arm around Tsoong Delilah's waist. "Oh, well," she sighed. "You're probably right about one thing, anyway. There's not much harm they can do. Come on," she said, taking his hand and tugging him toward the table. "We might as well sit down and get on with it."

Feeling much more cheerful, Jupiter let her lead him to seats halfway up the table. He didn't take his hand from hers, nor did she. What a strange woman, he thought; but, on the whole, one worth a little indulgence. That peculiar sallow complexion was not really unattractive; in fact, after a while it became quite nice-looking, as did the tiny nose and the jet eyes. And the size of her! Jupiter had almost never experienced copulation with a female shorter than 180 centimeters. Miranda was tiny, 150 at the most; how interesting it would be to have a bed partner whom he could pick up with ease, who would be featherlight on his belly if they should happen to turn in that direction and almost lost beneath him if—He heard Miranda giggle next to him, looked down, and realized that his thoughts were displayed by his body. But the giggle wasn't unfriendly. He grinned at her, then turned to the proceedings of the War Council, feeling indulgent and pleasurably anticipatory.

For this final meeting, Big Polly and the erks had ceded the chair to the rightful President. Castor stood up, tapped gently on the table with the closest thing they had found to a gavel—it was a sort of mixing spoon from one of the kitchens—and said, "As you all know, our invasion is ready to begin. I want to start by expressing my thanks to Governor Polly and her able legislature, to the males, Mother Sisters, and seniors of all varieties from all the nests, and above all to our hosts, the erks, without all of whom this happy day could never have come about." The council happily applauded itself as Castor beamed at them.

261

"It only remains to make the final decisions as to personnel. Who will be in the first party to go through the spaceway, along with me, in my yacht? I have given this a great deal of thought. I have discussed it privately with the Governor and many of you, one on one. I think the basis for our decision is clear." The council nodded—the human members of it did, at least—while waiting to hear what that clear basis was. Castor did not keep them waiting. "Our first priority must naturally be to avoid arousing the suspicions of the Han Chinese, do you not agree?" The Council agreed. All around the table human nods and smart erk twitches registered that fact.

"The way to do that," he explained, "is to provide my yacht with a crew they will recognize and trust. Myself, of course. Miranda, to be sure—we have no more dedicated patriot than Miranda, and she looks Chinese. Also, she has earned the right to be in the first ship."

"Of course" followed "of course" among the council.

"Then that is settled," said Castor, "but who else? I suppose," he went on meditatively, "that Manyface should be present. I for one accept his declaration of support. In any case, he is too old and feeble to do us any harm." Delilah caught the black look the old man threw at Castor and grinned internally; Castor was putting on a first-rate performance. "I thought of adding Tchai Howard, or perhaps some members of the assault team. But they are trained fighters. That would be dangerous. They might try to take over the ship somehow, and they might succeed. So I think that would be too risky—but, of course, it is not what I think that is important, but the will of the council. Speak up, please? All of you?" And one by one they spoke, all around the great oval wooden table. Each one decisively pointed out the advisability of including

Manyface but not Tchai or the assault team in the first wave. The motion passed unanimously.

Castor leaned back. "May I say," he inquired gratefully, "how much I appreciate your solution to this problem? Now I think we have only one decision left to make." He nodded ruefully toward Tsoong Delilah. She stared back, avoiding the looks of the rest of the council. She could feel her face flushing olive. "Inspector Tsoong," he went on, "would obviously be an asset on the ship from the point of view of deception. As a Renmin police inspector, she would certainly be trusted by the Han Chinese. But for that same reason we cannot ourselves trust her. It is a real dilemma." He shrugged humorously to indicate the hopelessness of the situation. "So," he concluded, "I suppose that we should take the more prudent course. Leave her here on World. She can do us no possible harm here. It is true that this might jeopardize the success of our mission. Still, there is no way out—" He paused, struck by a puzzling thought. "Unless"—he hesitated— "unless in some way we could manage to bring her along, but prevent her from doing harm—"

And the council table was aboil. First to get the floor was A-Belinka. "Tie her up!" he cried, and all around the oval human voices and erk chimed in agreement.

Castor smiled admiringly. "What a perfect solution!" he proclaimed. "We will do just that! And now we are ready—let the war begin!"

All of the council clapped and exclaimed. Even Tsoong Delilah—a cynic, yes, but moved by a great performance. Even, she saw, the figure lurking at the doorway and looking annoyed—that young Yank, Jupiter? Yes, that was his name. He was not a member of the council, of course. In fact, Delilah realized, his only reason for being present, ever, was that he was the guard for Feng Miranda. It had been many days since anyone among the Yanks or erks thought Miranda needed a guard, so his continued presence was simply another example of the foolishness and sloppiness with which these creatures pursued their activities—

Their *deadly* activities. In spite of herself, Delilah shivered. It was so easy, watching buffoons, to forget that these buffoons could be lethal!

She turned to rescue Castor from a prolonged discussion with Big Polly, who had made it clear, these last few days, that even a Second Generation senior sister did not consider herself too old to take an interest in a strange new male, particularly her President. She wondered just what it was that Jupiter was discussing so glumly with Miranda. Sex, no doubt. She thought virtuously that that was about all these weird rebels ever cared about. Well, he was a poor young fool to take an interest in that young hoyden, thought Delilah, but his problems were none of hers. In a matter of a few days at most he would be gone from her life, with all this planet and its capricious, stupid, ludicrous, dangerous inhabitants.

So thought Tsoong Delilah then.

IV

Said Feng Miranda scaldingly to Jupiter, "You're a fool! You don't see that he's planning to betray the mission!"

Jupe groaned. "Ah, you're not going to start that again, are you? Come on, Miranda, let's go watch the last pre-invasion launch. There's a grove of trees just off the field with some very pretty flowers—" Pretty to look at and soft to lie on, he happened to know; but she was too angry to be seduced, it seemed. He said reasonably, "Castor didn't do anything wrong, did he? He put the whole thing to a vote, didn't he? Even Big Polly and the erks voted with him, didn't they?"

"You're a fool!" she blazed.

"You're repeating yourself," he said glumly. "If you're serious about this, why didn't you speak up in the meeting?"

"And let them know I was suspicious?"

He looked puzzled; these refinements of intrigue were beyond him. "Well, at least, uh—at least tell *somebody*."

"I'm telling you! And you're not listening!"

"I'm missing the launch," he protested, stung—for that was manifestly unfair; certainly he'd been listening, silly though what she said was.

The tiny woman glared up at him, so furious that Jupiter involuntarily backed up a step. Then she said one of those curious words for copulating that the Real-Americans seemed to use in a derogatory way. "Go watch your launch," she snapped and actually pushed him away.

Jupe was getting angry now. "Very well," he said with dignity. "If you're sure—"

"I'm sure."

"All right, only—"

"Oh, *go*," she cried. "I might as well talk to the erks as you! In fact—" She hesitated, then glanced toward the front of the room, where Big Polly was stuffing papers in her shoulderbag while Jutch and A-Belinka chattered at her. She turned back to Jupiter. "Go watch the launch," she ordered, and although her tone this time was not at all angry, it was also not at all friendly and even less amorous.

So Jupiter whistled for his carry-bird and mounted it, as much confused as annoyed. (But quite annoyed, all the same.) What a strange woman! He caught a glimpse of a couple of working sisters lounging along the mossy bank of one of the drainage streams and almost diverted Flash toward them—why not? One needed copulation now and then, didn't one?—but the mood had left him. He flew the short distance to the edge of the space center, peering out to make sure the launch had not yet gone off.

It had not. That was at least some satisfaction. Jupiter was very nearly as avid a space buff as his President, and besides, he had a special interest in technology. The launch loop, he knew, had an interesting history. It was not a legacy from the Living Gods. The Gods had known no better than to throw their spacecraft into low-World orbit in the same thundering, blunderbuss way as human beings, all fountains of fire and shattering blasts of violent noise.

That was the obvious way to break gravity's grip, so that real space voyages could begin.

It was not, however, the best way. In that case, and a few others, the erks had learned better than their gods ever knew. The war among the hopping crustaceans of the system surrounding an F4 star eighty-five light-years away had not worked out well for the crustaceans. It had, however, left the erks with, among other kinds of booty, a magnetic launch system for spacecraft, one that used every bit of its mechanical energy for the task at hand. The magnetic loop launch was hardly noisy at all. ("Noise" is energy wasted on shaking the air.) The crustaceans had done that task far better than the Living Gods—though the fact that their technology was in other respects not as good was made clear by the fact that none of the crustaceans still survived.

Jupe dismounted, one hand on the carry-bird, to see the launch. The ship to be launched was not truly a dummy, because it carried fuel and supplies to the waiting fleet parked in orbit; but it was matched to size and mass and shape with the Presidential yacht. It was a dry run, to insure that nothing would go wrong in the launch of Castor and his crew. From his post under a peacewood tree, Flash incuriously sampling fresh shoots to pass the time, Jupiter had a good view. The control porch for the launch system was outside the fabrication building, a kilometer and a half away from Jupiter's tree. At that distance the erk and Yank technicians swarming over their instruments seemed tiny and irrelevant. But they were the ones who were making it all happen. All the way across the field the entry end of the launcher loomed gigantic, but what happened there was determined by those tiny figures on the porch. Punch one set of commands, and the grapples picked up the launch vehicle and lifted it to its ready

267

position, just above the smoothly streaming cables of magnetic alloy. Punch out another, and the grapples gently released themselves as they set the vehicle onto the cable itself. The vehicle never quite touched the cable. Magnets held it close to the spinning loop and just above. The cable raced away under the squat, lumpy launch vehicle, but the cable felt the vehicle's presence, and the vehicle felt the cable's tug; strain gauges on the operations platform showed that the cable was pulling three percent more kiloamps because of the new load; accelerometers inside the vehicle reported that it was beginning to move.

Jupiter did not need the telemetry to see that the vehicle was moving. Heartsick as he watched the real launch of a real (if not very important) attack vessel for a real war, he felt like one of the kids with their erk-driven toy bash-'em-up war tanks. True, he had his own command and his own assignment, fifty erks with blasters to come down in the Kweilung area in the third wave. Third wave! By then the action would be over!

So his eyes were fogged with angry tears as he watched the launch vehicle slip away from the hovering grapples, pick up speed, flash down along the long spinning track. From Jupiter's tree it looked like a child's birchbark boat tossed into a stream. It rode the cable to the boost-off incline at the end—

Then it was free.

All instruments on the operations porch reported *launch completed*. The capsule tore through the sky, its stubby maneuvering fins turning it up and out. In a moment it was gone. Moments later the *craaack*-boom of its passing the speed of World's sound made all the erks and Yanks giggle and swear and turn to each other in congratulation.

Jupiter had no one to congratulate. He had no special desire to do it, either. How much of his mood was due to the infuriating obstinacy of the Real-American woman Miranda and how much to jealousy of those who would ride the first waves of invasion, he could not have said. He had plenty of both irritations. One hand resting on the wing-root of his carry-bird, he looked on, sick with envy. Flash grunted plaintively, anxious to get back to feeding, if not to the breeding that was her ever-increasing preoccupation. Jupe gave the mount a look of anger. What was the use of a damn carry-bird? These Real-Americans had actual spacecraft! He should have the same, or at least—

He felt Flash's muscles tighten under his hand, just as he heard his name called from above. "Jupe?" The voice was female and elderly; he looked up and saw that it was the Governor, peering out at him from the pouch of her own silver-gray bird. The mount settled down near him, careful to avoid collision with the trees. It rubbed beaks with Flash—only a friendly gesture, since both were female—and the Governor wriggled herself free. "Why did you not report what Miranda Feng told you?" she demanded.

Jupiter automatically extended a hand to help her get out of the pouch. "What was there to report?" he asked, honestly confused.

"Her report that she suspected some of the Real-Americans of treason," said the Governor firmly. "You should have told me before the vote, Jupiter."

"I didn't know before the vote!"

Big Polly said regally, "That is of no importance. Do you realize that our entire mission is now endangered?"

"Is it? Oh, Polly!" he cried, struck to the heart. "Don't let it be!"

She shook her head. "It has passed the point where I can prevent it, Jupiter. Someone else must take action. I have decided that it must be you."

"Me?" What a dazzling thought! Jupiter, the savior of Real America? It was every dream he had ever had— "How do I do that, Polly?" he begged.

"You will go along in the Presidential yacht, and—oh, damn, won't the fool erk ever give up?" She had turned to gaze upward as the squawk of another approaching carry-bird told them they were expecting company. The head that peered out of the pouch was not human this time, it was the old erk Jutch.

"Wait," he cried. "Polly, don't send him! Send me! You owe us that much!" He was still talking as his carry-bird dropped to the ground between Flash and Big Polly's mount. He wriggled out of the pouch and scuttled to them, raising himself on his hind legs to beg. "Without the erks all this would be impossible. An erk must go along!"

"Oh, what a fool you are," said the Governor in disgust. "What will the Chinese think if they see you in the ship?"

"I'll hide! We won't allow vision! I'll pretend I'm a prisoner! Anything! But," cried the erk, "you *humans* don't have the battle experience we do."

Polly's glare cut him off. She actually stamped her foot. "That's nonsense! Human beings have fought many more wars than you erks ever have! Why, for thousands of years there have been wars almost every year. And, in any case, you may have battle experience, but you don't know anything about deception and guile. In that," she said proudly, "the human race is *superb*. I have decided. It must be Jupiter."

Jupiter, standing there with his mouth hanging open, cut in. "What must be Jupiter?" he demanded.

"Why," explained Polly, "the most important assignment of the war. You will go along on the Presidential yacht. You will be secretly armed. If it is indeed as Miranda says and the rest of the Real-Americans are actually false, then you will take command of the ship, shoot any who resist, explain our demands to the Chinese—"

"*Me*?" cried Jupiter, intoxicated with joy.

"You," said the Governor firmly. "Now come back to the city. I will prepare your orders in a fashion that cannot be denied. We will say nothing until just before the launch. Remember, you can trust no one but Miranda, not even the President—"

"It would be better with an erk in charge," chittered Jutch sadly.

"It will be a human! And the human will be Jupiter. And there will be no more discussion at all," said Big Polly. "You will arm him, Jutch. We will do the rest!"

So as the crew was gathering to board the yacht, Jupiter came to the launch loop in style. What style! He was a marvel to all who saw him. He had a hovercart for his own. He had more than that, because tucked inside his breechclout was a rapid-fire automatic pistol; around his neck was a concussion grenade hastily reshaped to look like an amulet; in his hand a small bag that might have contained clean clothing but in fact held a pair of stun-weapons. They were what he fully expected to use, if needed; the other things were as dangerous to him as to any foe in the closed quarters of the spacecraft. He stood on the hovercart, holding to the safety rail, staring grandly about. Yanks and erks cheered him as he passed. He was not alone on the cart. He had a guard of honor to display his rank, for four paint-uniformed erk troopers crouched at the corners, armed and ceremonially alert. A smart erk colonel of Marines guided the cart across the tarmac. Jupiter stood negligently holding the rail of his perch, with the look of eagles on his face. He stumbled a bit as the cart sped toward the first-wave crew, but held tight against the sudden jolt as the erk colonel threw down the ground brakes. Jupiter gazed sternly down on Castor and the rest as he proclaimed,

"I have new orders. I will join your ship for the first attack, Mr. President."

The faces that stared up at him showed all the expressions he anticipated—surprise, worry, annoyance; most of all surprise. Gratified, he added, "It is no use arguing, because my orders have been countersigned by Jutch, A-Belinka, my Senator, and my Senior Sister, and by the Governor herself. Come. Let us get ready to take off."

The faces did not change expression. The persons who owned them did not move, nor even speak. Delilah did not speak to Castor nor Castor to Manyface; but within the head of Manyface there was speaking enough, oh, yes! "They suspect something!" moaned the scrap that once had been Corelli Anastasio, and "Don't let him come!" begged the fragment formerly Su Wonmu. "Don't be foolish," cried Angorak Aglat, "how can we stop him? But we must be alert!" And Potter Alicia said soothingly to all of them, and mostly to herself, "But he's only a boy like my Castor. He won't do us any harm . . . I think." It made no difference what any of them said, in the secret voices within Manyface's skull or out loud; the orders were real, and there was no time to try to change them.

"Get on board, then," chittered the erk A-Belinka grumpily. "Start now, please. Before there are any more complications!"

And so the spacefarers entered into the ship, one by one, each attended by technician erks to strap them in and check their fit and make sure no one looked like being spacesick or hysterical.

"What a mess," said Castor out loud, not looking at Jupiter.

"Shut up, Castor," said Tsoong Delilah, not looking at anyone.

"They're lifting us!" cried Jupiter, and his voice at least was filled with certain joy.

He didn't have to say that, of course, because they all knew it—all felt the jarring lift as the grapples caught their ship and then the pause for recheck and window verification—

And the sudden, loosely sprung shove against all their backs, as the launch loop caught them and tugged them away—a terrible, urgent, belly-squeezing, breathstopping pressure that mounted swiftly and then held and crushed them—

And then was gone.

They floated free. They were on their way out of World's soupy atmosphere that screamed outside their ship as they split it open on their way.

They were on their way to Earth.

The initial launch carried them well into World's stratosphere and beyond. There was no need for rockets in that first thrust; the speed given them by the racing loop was enough for escape velocity and to spare. They would not burn a rocket until more than ninety-nine percent of World's air was below them, with only enough left for their external guidance surfaces to lever themselves against for positioning for the suborbital thrust.

It was only a matter of minutes, but minutes were long enough for all of them to realize how final the parting was. Even with no additional burn, their ship was now free of World forever; it would enter an orbit by itself now if no hand ever touched a control. They were not wholly weightless. There was a small but definite negative thrust, each of them pressing against the restraining straps, as the slight deceleration caused by friction with the air slowed the exterior of the ship while its contents wished to keep going. "Our neck hurts!" complained Su Wonmu. "I hurt very much," agreed Potter Alicia, "and I wish it would stop." But they did not speak aloud. All of Manyface was hurting, and the committee's decision was that it was best to lie as still as possible, hoping to feel better soon.

Feng Miranda was feeling very badly indeed, for a less urgent (but far more humiliating) reason. She had wet her pants. She muttered angrily to herself (but all the others heard, too), "Baby! Fool! What is the matter with you, Miranda, peeing your panties like a silly child when the cause demands heroism and strength!"

And Tsoong Delilah, forcing herself to hyperventilate to pump oxygen back into her starved blood, heard the American girl's bitter self-reproaches over the harsh rasping of her own breathing passages. Her first thought was contempt for Feng. Her second thought was also contempt, but this time it was directed at herself. "Baby?" "Fool?" Those were apt words also for a Renmin police inspector who wasted time gloating over the humiliation of a rival in love. A *rival*. In *love*! And love, at that, for a foolish, selfish, unripe boy! And all this when duty had never called more urgently! Delilah grimly reached out to the navigation board. Her fingers were shaking, she observed with chagrin, but they also unerringly touched the proper studs. The course solution flashed on the screen before her. It had a validity score in the high nineties; the error bar was tiny; there was no indication of malfunction. "Stand by," Delilah called to the others in the cabin and pressed the *Execute* stud.

The spacecraft's control fins reached out to the muggy air of World and spun the vessel to its boost attitude. The main boosters fired a twelve-second burst. The navigation board confirmed the correctness of the new delta-V; the maneuver was complete. The spacecraft was ballistic.

Now it was just waiting.

"You can unstrap," Delilah advised her crew. She saw with sardonic pleasure that the first one out of the straps was Feng Miranda, awkward and uncomfortable as she gingerly stretched her legs in the tight suit. "Don't worry, Feng," Delilah called maliciously, "it's only fifty-eight hours until we land on Earth!" And was gratified by the glare she got from the girl.

Swiftly she checked the rest of her charges. Manyface seemed quite relaxed, eyes still closed. The Yankee Jupiter was methodically releasing himself in the next couch, warily watching all the others from the corners of his eyes. Castor—ah, Castor! His face glowed like the sun. There was some of the mother in the rending complexity of feeling Delilah had for Castor, and the mother feeling was warmly rewarded by the joy in his eyes. "Delilah?" he begged. "May I take the controls for a while? Please?"

Indulgently she said, "But there's nothing to do now, Castor. We have two hours of coasting before we make course corrections to rendezvous with the spaceway." But, of course, it was not the actual piloting that Castor wanted. What he wanted was the illusion of power. He wanted to form a picture of himself—captain of a great spacecraft on an urgent and perilous mission—that he could take out and look at, in his mind's eye, for the rest of his life. "Well, why not?" Delilah said. "First call in to Mission Control for a report, though."

"Of course!" cried Castor, complying eagerly. The surface control responded at once; they had been waiting for the call. Big Polly herself spoke to the ship:

"Your course and speed are fine," she said. "Congratulations on a successful launch." The funny thing, thought Castor, was that she didn't particularly look congratulatory. She looked as though she were harboring some secret resentment, her plump jaw set, her words controlled. Sour grapes because she wasn't along, maybe, Castor decided, and said considerately,

"We're the ones who should be congratulating you, Polly. Please extend my thanks to the entire launch-loop crew, and of course to all the others who are taking part in this historic occasion."

"Sure," said the Governor shortly, and leaned down to the erk Jutch, raising himself on his hind legs to chitter in her ear. "Oh, all right," she said, straightening. "I guess you'd like a situation report?"

"Certainly we would," called Delilah from her own position, frowning at the screen.

"Well," said Big Polly, leaning again to listen to the erk, "Jutch says you've got nine hours and about twenty minutes before you get in range of the spaceway; then transition; then you'll come out two days from low-Earth orbit."

"We've already calculated that," called Delilah.

"Well, that's a confirmation," said the Governor. "Then, let's see, then the first assault wave will follow you through the spaceway ten hours later. Those are long-range attack heavies—"

"We know," snapped Delilah. "We've been all over this plan a hundred times." The frown on her face had deepened. She glanced questioningly at Castor, then addressed the screen again. "We can watch the fleet assemble on

276

our own screens, you know. Do you have anything we don't know to tell us?"

"Ah, yes," said the Governor. "There's a transmission from the Earthside scout ship. It seems the Chinese are launching ships again. Wait a minute—" She nodded to the erk, and her image disappeared from the screen, replaced by visuals of space. Some space or other—no, Delilah saw, definitely Earth space, because there was the continent of Africa on the planet in the distance. The Governor's voice said: "We've calculated rendezvous times, and they won't get anywhere near the scout for at least fifty hours. However, just in case they have some new weapons we're redirecting the scout away from the Earth. Also, of course, there are the drones, which may confuse them again—"

"Drones won't fool Han Chinese twice," Delilah sneered, studying the screen. Yes. There were three blips on it, crawling up out of low-Earth orbit. She cast back in her mind: what ships did the Chinese have ready for launch? Not much. Nothing big enough to carry significant armament, at least nothing more dangerous than Tchai Howard had had. She said reluctantly, "I agree they don't represent much of a threat, but keep on displaying them for us."

"All right," said the Governor wearily. "Is, ah, is everything all right on board? How's Jupiter?"

"He's fine," said Castor, surprised. "We're going to quit talking for a while now, all right?"

"All right," said the Governor, and the voice stopped.

Delilah twisted in her cocoon to look at the others. "She sounds funny," she said. "What do you suppose is wrong with her?" But Castor could not tell her, and neither could Manyface; and of course neither Jupe nor Miranda would.

277

* * *

Jupiter would not tell Delilah anything, no, but what he was telling himself was *glorious*. The fate of America rested on him! He returned Delilah's look boldly, trying to keep expression off his face; but he could not keep his fingers from patting the bag of stun weapons that lay beside him. In the launch they had stabbed into him most cruelly. He could feel the bruises still—welcome bruises, badges of heroism! He turned to smile at Miranda, who winked back conspiratorially. Perhaps, he thought, he should give her one of the weapons? There had been talk about arming her, too, but she was clearly not in the confidence of the others. One wild card was all that could safely be slipped into the deck. She turned to check on Manyface, still silent beside her, and Jupiter gazed placidly at Delilah and Castor, now handing themselves over the tricky stretch between his couch and hers. As they were in coasting mode there was no gravity to hinder, but also no firm support to orient to. Jupiter chuckled to himself as he saw Castor lose his hold on a strap and begin to flail wildly, Delilah grabbing for him—

"Jupiter! All of you!" It was Miranda's voice. "What's the matter with the old man?"

And then they all dragged themselves hastily to Manyface's couch, Delilah grabbing at his wrist to check pulse, Castor pulling down an eyelid set into the great pumpkinhead to peer at the pupil.

The pulse was faint but regular, the breathing shallow but steady. When Castor released the eyelid it closed and stayed closed.

Manyface was certainly alive. From all external signs he was merely, and contentedly, asleep. But they could not wake him up.

V

Within the patchwork brain of Manyface some voices called out in panic; others were ominously silent. Said Potter Alicia nervously, "What happened? Are we all right? Why do we have pain?" Said Angorak Aglat, as always shouting angrily, "The old fool has had a stroke or something. What a useless creature he is! Now we're all in for it!" Said Su Wonmu, "Comrades, comrades, let us be at peace among ourselves! We gain nothing by squabbling. Something has happened to our body, yes, that is clear. But let's not blame anyone—not, at any rate, until we learn what stupid thing Fung Bohsien did to land us in this mess!" And Fung himself said wearily, "Oh, shut up, all of us. Can't you see there is an embolism somewhere, or perhaps an aneurism?"

Silent shrieks and yells of rage: Embolism! Stroke! It was no use telling the voices to shut up. They couldn't be coerced, and they saw no reason to cooperate. A couple did not speak at all. "Corelli?" called Fung, as loudly as he could. "Hsang?" But they did not answer. The committee had lost some of its members, it seemed. The quorum still present yelled even louder, if silence can ever be loud—drowned each other out, in as wild a display of confusion as ever accompanied any implant. It was not merely fear that gripped them, it was actual pain. The skull they held in joint tenancy seemed to throb with

279

explosions of agony, and each time the voices screamed louder. "Please, quiet," Fung begged his colleagues. "It doesn't help anything to go crazy!"

"But what are they doing to us?" wailed Potter, trying to make sense of the skewed sensory impressions that filtered through the disturbed perceptual systems.

Surprisingly, it was Shum Hengdzhou who answered. The whilom ironworker had listened bashfully while everyone else shouted and ranted, but now he ventured, "Alicia? I think they are only trying to help us."

"Help!" several voices sneered, but Shum was steadfast.

"Yes, I think help," he said mildly. "I think they are attempting first aid. Of course, it is true that this vessel has no complete life-support system, and so perhaps they cannot do much, but still . . . Comrades? Is there a point in shouting at each other, since there is nothing we can do while we are acting this way?"

"What a fool you are, Shum," said Su Wonmu in spiteful disgust. "However we act, what can we do?"

"Well, Comrade Su," said Shum, "I do recall that the first advice to any stroke patient is to relax. We could do that much, anyway, while our shipmates attempt to do what they can."

For a wonder, there was a moment's silence. Then Fung spoke heavily. "That's good advice, Shum. It is not likely to save our lives—not all of us, anyway, since it seems we have already lost one or two. But it is the best we can do, only—"

Pause of a microsecond or two, while the surviving members of the committee waited to hear what came next. "Only?" prompted Potter Alicia worriedly.

"Only what I am thinking is that our lives are not really that important. By all rights we should all have been dead long ago anyway. What is important is to keep the erks from wiping out everybody on Earth...and about that we can do nothing at all."

They had long since set up a patch to the diagnostic machines on World, and it was the pilot, Delilah, who was assigned to watch the readouts. "He's alive all right," she reported. "But there's something wrong with his brain."

"There's a great deal wrong with his brain," Jupiter agreed. He was trying to hold the medical sensors to arm, chest, head, and throat; the sticky pastes were not strong enough to withstand Manyface's erratic movements. "Tell them they mustn't let him die!" he ordered. Delilah gave him a surprised and ironic look. "I mean," he explained, "have you thought about what it *means* if we're stuck with a corpse for the next couple of days? He'll begin to *smell*." He looked surprised at the expressions on the faces of his shipmates. "But it is only sensible to think of such things," he protested indignantly.

Miranda said, "Just shut up and hold those electrodes on, will you?" She was cradling the old man's huge, queer head in her arms. It weighed nothing, of course, but when he had a spasm he seemed likely to bash himself or even snap the overstrained old neck. "Can't they tell us anything to do?" she demanded fiercely.

"They've been telling us," sighed Delilah. "Only we don't have any of the things to do it with."

"It's the wrong ship," said Castor sadly. "The other one had life-support systems for Manyface."

"Then we should have taken the other ship!" snapped Feng Miranda. It was only when she, too, noticed the expressions on the faces looking at her that it occurred to her that her concern was odd. Manyface was an enemy, after all! Jupiter might easily have to shoot him if there was any nonsense aboard the ship—she herself had made sure that could happen. And yet, looking down on the face beneath the great domed forehead, Miranda's thoughts were all of saving life, not taking it. "Shouldn't we give him more anticoagulants?" she asked fretfully.

"Tchai Howard says no," said Delilah.

"Tchai Howard is no doctor!"

"But the Yank medical sisters agree with him, Miranda. Please try to control yourself. We're doing the best we can."

"It's been hours! How long can he survive like this?"

"However long it is," said Delilah steadily, "that is how long he has to do it. Wait. They are complaining about a degraded signal. Are the electrodes in place?"

Guiltily Jupiter looked back at his charge and readjusted his holds. The currents that flowed through them measured resistances and temperatures, mapped the alpha and beta waves of the brain, told all that could be told of the invisible struggle going on inside the huge head. Thousands of kilometers below them, the erks and humans gathered at Mission Control knew more about what was happening within that structure of bone and metal and plastic than they could see. Miranda sobbed, "He really was not a bad old man."

And realized she had spoken in the past tense.

And within the skull of Manyface the committee was beginning to think of itself in the same way. "I wish I could have seen my grandchild," sighed Potter Alicia.

"We all have regrets," said Angorak, for once not shouting.

They were all silent, thinking of regrets, until Shum

spoke up. "Our biggest regret, I think, should be that we are doing nothing to keep the Earth from being destroyed," he said mildly.

"We do regret that, you foolish person," said Angorak at once. Then, repenting, "I am sorry, Shum. I spoke out of anger. I am angry because I am helpless. There is nothing we can do."

"Yes," agreed Shum, "if we are helpless we can do nothing. If we cannot speak or act, we are helpless. If we are imprisoned here among ourselves with no contact, then everything is in vain for us; but is that true? Are we completely without contact?"

Silence for a moment. Then Potter Alicia, diffidently, "Shum? I did think I saw just a flicker of light a moment ago. Is that what you mean?"

Quick, hopeful hubbub; then Fung Bohsien himself heavily, "One of my eyes perhaps opened just a bit. Probably someone lifted the lid; it is nothing."

"I do not altogether agree, Comrade Fung," said Shum diffidently. "It is very much, I think. It implies that our perceptual systems are not destroyed. That has implications, I believe."

"Say what those implications are!" barked Angorak.

"Why, that we are paralyzed, yes, but not in coma."

"Of course we are not in coma! We are speaking to each other, are we not? Oh, Shum, what a fool you are! You see hope in what is the worst truth of all—that we are not dead, nor even in terminal coma, but condemned to be awake in this prison forever!"

"Shut up, Angorak," said Fung roughly. "Shum is right. Listen! Everyone! If we can do nothing but think, at least let us think logically." He paused the microsecond that amounted to a meaningful delay in their lightning exchanges to see if there was any dispute. There was none.

"Very well, then. Let us see what we know. First, we have suffered a cerebrovascular incident. Does anyone doubt this?" There was no doubt, only murmurs. Dejected murmurs. "Second, it is not overwhelmingly serious, for as Shum has said, we are at least able to communicate with one another—many of us are, at least," he qualified. Again there was no dispute. "Third, it is true, I believe, that we saw a flicker of light some full seconds, perhaps minutes, ago." Concurrence to that. "The question then," finished Manyface, "is whether we can exercise any motor control over any part of our body. Has anyone felt kinesthesia?" Doubtful denials, except for Potter Alicia's even more doubtful possible yes. "Shall we try to effect some muscular movements?" More confident yes—not confident, exactly, perhaps, but certainly more affirmative. "Then the eye," instructed Fung to his cohort. "Let us see if without bickering among ourselves or wasting energy in panic we can perhaps open one eye. Shall we do that? All right then; let us try!"

"I can't," whimpered Su Wonmu, but was at once drowned out by all the surviving fragments: *You can! You really can. No, probably you can't, you pompous fool, but at least be still so the rest of us can try!* And try they did—over and over—endlessly, repeatedly, in that faster-than-life time that they shared inside Manyface's great skull.

They did not succeed.

"Try something else," suggested Shum, almost panting with effort—if a fragment of brain tissue could pant. "Try speaking, please. Try to warn the others—"

And try that they did, with no more success. With certainly far less success, in fact, for the warring scraps of tissue could not agree on what it was they should say; and the eons that were hours wore on, until—

"What was that?" gasped Potter Alicia. "Oh, Fung! Have we died?"

It was not Fung who answered but Angorak, roughly. He had felt the same queer thrill in the tired sensors of Fung Bohsien's old body, but recognized it faster. "We haven't died, foolish woman!" he bellowed. "We would not be speaking if we had! We have gone through the spaceway, that is all—and, oh, comrades, are we too late? Is the issue already decided while we are trapped here?"

Was the issue decided? It was not only the clumps of cells in Manyface's brain that wondered. Tsoong Delilah wondered, too, and so did Castor, and even Miranda and Jupiter were nervous and irritable under unidentified strains of feeling. The spaceway had caught them all as unaware as Manyface. Delilah's first impulse was to slide as inconspicuously as she could back to the pilot's place. Miranda had been bending over the old man's unresponding head, staring hard as she pillowed the great mass in her lap. "I could have sworn I saw his eyelid move," she offered, "but then there was nothing—"

And then she had frozen, as the strange, slipping feeling came over them all. "We're through!" she gasped. From the controls Delilah confirmed,

"Yes, a successful transit. Look—" And the screen that had flickered to static now lit itself again with a picture of Earth and the Moon peeping bright from behind it.

Jupiter said joyfully, "Then the plan is working! And I don't have to bother with this old man anymore." He let go of the electrodes, flexing his fingers. Surprised again at the looks he got, he said defensively, "Well, after all, we've lost direct contact, haven't we?"

"What a sod you are," said Miranda in disgust, but then she forgot about Jupiter. The eyes opened again. "He's awake!" she cried. "I—I think he's trying to talk."

"That's good," said Jupiter eagerly, generosity sparked by the promise that they wouldn't have to live with spoiling meat for the next days.

"Shut up!" she ordered, bending her head close to Manyface's lips. "What?" she whispered, and the faint breath of voice tried again:

"Don't..." it said—was that what it said?—and stopped.

"Yes, yes?" Miranda encouraged. "Don't what, Fung?"

"Don't...let...the...erks...destroy...the...Earth."

"What?" she asked, incredulous. It was a pointless thing to say; the old man hardly had the strength to go through that again. "He said, 'Don't let the erks destroy the Earth,'" she repeated for the others, then bent back to Manyface. Worriedly she said, "Oh, but they won't, Fung. I mean, I know you're a patriotic Han and all that, and maybe there'll be some damage to China—but all they want to do really is free America."

The eyes stared at her mournfully. The lips moved again, but no sound came out.

She said sorrowfully, "You're wearing yourself out for nothing, Fung. Don't try to talk. I promise it will be all right—"

The tongue reached out to lick the dry lips. Then, faint as breath itself, one more word: "Please."

She shook her head, then looked up, startled, as she felt a sidewise thrust. She called to Delilah: "What are you doing?"

"Course correction," said Delilah briefly, eyes locked to the controls, fingers busy. There was something strange about the way she held herself. It was strange, too, that

Castor, who had been intent on listening to Manyface, began idly to move between Jupiter and Delilah, his eyes fixed on the other man as though expecting something—

"What is going on?" Miranda demanded; and, belatedly, Jupiter came to, dived for his bag, came up with a stun weapon pointed at Delilah.

"Treason!" he shouted. "Stop there, Tsoong! Don't touch anything else!" Delilah froze. Stun weapons didn't kill, but no one wanted the vicious pins-and-needles agony of recovering from a shot—not to mention that while stunned she could hope to do nothing to save her world. Castor froze, too, for the same reasons, multiplied by the fact that he was closer. Even Miranda froze, mouth open in an uncomprehending gape, and that drove Jupiter to fury. "Why are you sisters so *stupid*?" he demanded. "Can't you see what they were doing? You were right; they are out to betray us!"

"But, Jupiter," she began reasonably, a beginning for a sentence for which she had no clear ending in mind.

"Don't argue! Let go of that stupid old man! Take Delilah's place at the controls." She could not move. "Now!" he shouted angrily. "She was going to destroy the spaceway ship! Push her away! Save America!"

VI

Save America. Well, there was a clear-cut directive.
The words moved Miranda out of the reflexes of all her
life. She felt nothing, understood nothing; she was numb,
but she heard the call to action. She gently lowered old
Manyface's head to its cocoon and moved toward the
control couches, always careful not to get between Jupiter's gun and Tsoong Delilah. "Excuse me, please," she
said absently to the older woman, and didn't even notice
Delilah's look of surprise. Miranda wasn't looking at her.
She was looking over the pilot board, where the display
screen was showing the blue-white marble with its soiled
aspirin-tablet companion. "Jupiter? What did he mean
about the erks destroying the Earth?" she asked, gazing
at the planet.

"What a stupid question!" he snapped. "Pay attention
to what you are doing! Great matters are being decided
here and now!"

"Yes," she said reasonably, nodding, "but I would like
to know what he was talking about. Can you tell me?"

Delilah paused, holding on to the restraining straps of
the copilot's cocoon. "He could, but he won't, Miranda,"
she said.

"Shut up, you! No talking!" ordered Jupiter, but Miranda warded him off with an upraised hand.

"Why won't he?" she asked.

288

"Because he does not understand what is happening," said Delilah tautly. "Any more than you do. Ask him about the other erk 'allies.' Ask him how many of them survive."

"What 'allies'?" Miranda asked, frowning as she tried to pursue the subject.

"All of them! And all dead—just as we will all be if this lunatic gets his way!"

"Oh, now, *really!*" howled Jupiter, waving his gun. "How dare you say that? I am no lunatic! You think I am a lunatic simply because I am no traitor to my country!"

"Only to your species," Delilah snarled, but Jupiter was having none of that.

"Now be quiet *really*," he commanded, "or I will make you so! Go ahead, you! Get over there next to Castor. Miranda! Take the controls. Make sure neither of them gets near them!" His face was tight with rage—what impudence of them! And yet the rage could not long persist in this very best and most exalted moment of his life. He waved the weapons, one now in each hand, to force Castor and Delilah against the far bulkhead of the spacecraft. "Don't try anything!" he warned and, again, "And don't talk!"

It was annoying that they obeyed only the orders they chose. Castor said steadily, "I am the President of the United States. I order you to give me those weapons."

Jupiter frowned. "That's not a proper order," he objected.

"The President is Commander in Chief of all the military forces," Castor said. "Any order I give you must be obeyed."

"Then you're not a proper President!" Jupe decided. "Anyway, I won't. We're going to go through with the plan. We're going to talk to those Chinese ships and tell them to hold their fire, draw them down close to Earth

289

orbit, give the fleet a chance to follow us—and you can't stop it!"

Castor shook his head. "And then what, Jupiter?" he asked.

"Why—then we liberate America, of course!"

"But who is 'we,' Jupiter? Do you mean the erks? Do you know what will happen once the erks get into the fight?"

Jupiter frowned. "Mr. President," he said formally, "I would like to continue treating you as a real President, but I must warn you that to talk treason against the erks is wrong!"

Castor hesitated. Miranda could see that he was sweating. His face was pale and his hands shook, but he said, "You owe no loyalty to the erks, Jupiter. They are not Americans."

"They are our allies!"

"The erks are nobody's allies! Have you ever looked at the histories? Have you seen what the erks have done?"

Jupiter shrugged angrily. "Oh, everyone knows that stuff," he said. "Now be still! Look at the screen—the drones are all around us, and we are nearly within range of the Chinese ships!" As Castor started to open his mouth again, Jupiter shouted, "I said be still. I might not kill you, but I'll surely knock you out!" Delilah touched Castor with a warning hand; the President hesitated irresolutely.

Miranda said suddenly, "Why won't you let him talk, Jupiter? What's he trying to say about history?"

"It is nothing!" snapped Jupiter. "There have been some bad incidents."

"There have been no good ones!" Delilah said, her face almost as strained as Castor's as she stared into Jupiter's guns. "Every time they've intervened in a war, they've destroyed both sides! Is that what you want, Jupiter? The human race wiped out entirely?"

"It won't happen!" he cried, furious at the attack on everything he believed in. "They've had some bad luck."

"Bad luck!" Delilah began, but Miranda stopped her.

"Tell me about this bad luck," she ordered.

Jupiter looked at her sulkily. "It is true that none of the races the erks assisted survived," he said, shrugging. "But we know better. We've had years with them to plan. The whole thing is very clear. First we destroy China from space—what's wrong with that? Perhaps India will want to take over, but they will be even easier to knock out than China. Then we land ground forces for mopping up. True, we can't land more than a few thousand troops, and the erks aren't much good at hand-to-hand combat. But there's always the fleet in space! If the locals don't surrender, we'll just knock out a few cities—"

"Jupiter! What are you saying?" Miranda demanded.

He said mulishly, "They've got it coming." Then he looked surprised as he saw Delilah moving toward the controls. "Don't do that!" he warned.

Tardily Miranda realized that their ship had been slowly swinging around, was now pointed almost directly back at the scout ship, where the pale purple gleam still lingered. Instinctively she reached to stop the swing; and, as she was doing so, Castor leaped toward Jupiter. There was a crackle of high-voltage charge as Jupiter fired. The stun-gun knocked Castor back against the bulkhead, his face a sudden mask of astonishment. Angrily Jupiter swung the gun toward Delilah...

Miranda looked down at what her fingers were doing on the controls and sighed.

"Jupiter," she said absently, "don't shoot anybody else. It doesn't matter anymore."

He turned an amazed face to her. "What?"

"I said it doesn't matter," she repeated, watching her fingers tap out an instruction. As she pressed the *Execute* key she added, "The erks aren't coming now, you see."

His expression was now as much scared as angry. "What are you talking about, you stupid little sister? Of course they're coming! It's all planned!"

She shook her head and gazed up at the display screen. "Not for a while, Jupe. What is it, forty-two light-years to here? So they can't get here for forty-two years at least without the spaceway." On the screen a tiny white spark of fire was climbing away from them toward the scout ship. "Without the ship there's no spaceway. Without the spaceway, no erks for half a century or so. And," she added simply, watching the spark connect with the blip of the erk scout ship, "I'm a real good shot. So now there's no more ship."

Jupiter gazed pop-eyed at the screen. They all did, even Castor (whose only mobility was in his eyes), even, almost, Manyface, whose bleary old eyes seemed to be straining to focus. What they saw was the same for all.

The erk ship flared bright, actinic white.

When the glare died away, there was no ship there at all. A haze of particulate matter was swelling and dissipating. Nothing else.

"Oh, my God," whispered Jupiter, "you've really done it, haven't you?"

Miranda nodded. It was the simple truth. She had. "I hope I did the right thing," she said meditatively, and Tsoong Delilah, bursting free of the numbed paralysis that had gripped them all, shoved herself toward Miranda and caught her in an unexpected and powerful hug.

"Oh, you did," she said, almost sobbing. "You really did!"

"Traitor!" grated Jupiter. He waved the gun helplessly at the two women, stared at it, then hurled it across the chamber. It barely missed Miranda, who retrieved it and handed it to Tsoong Delilah. "I hope you do better," she said. Then, thoughtfully, to the Chinese woman, but also to the whole of humanity, "I hope you do better than anyone ever did before."

"And if they don't?" demanded Jupiter. "If they just keep on having wars?"

Miranda leaned forward to call the distant Chinese vessels. Over her shoulder she said, "Why, then we deserve what we get, don't we?"

About the Author

Frederik Pohl has been everything one man can be in the world of science fiction: fan (a founder of the fabled Futurians), book and magazine editor, agent, and, above all, writer. As editor of *Galaxy* in the 1950s, he helped set the tone for a decade of SF—including his own memorable stories such as *The Space Merchants* (in collaboration with Cyril Kornbluth). His latest novel is *Heechee Rendezvous*. He has also written *The Way the Future Was*, a memoir of his first forty-five years in science fiction. Frederik Pohl was born in Brooklyn, New York, in 1919, and now lives in Palatine, Illinois.

THE HEECHEE SAGA

an epic galactic trilogy
by
FREDERICK POHL

There's an epidemic with 27 million victims. And no visible symptoms.

It's an epidemic of people who can't read.

Believe it or not, 27 million Americans are functionally illiterate, about one adult in five.

The solution to this problem is you... when you join the fight against illiteracy. So call the Coalition for Literacy at toll-free **1-800-228-8813** and volunteer.

Volunteer Against Illiteracy. The only degree you need is a degree of caring.

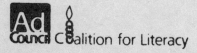

Ad Council Coalition for Literacy

LV-1